MW00606644

The Girl Everyone Wants

ENDORSEMENTS

An unwillingly gifted young woman. A pair of deranged psychopaths who covet her unique spiritual ability. A twisting plot, lots of fast-paced action, a colorful cast of characters, and a sparkling writing style. Mix them all together and voila! A story that rivets your attention from first to last page. *The Girl Everyone Wants* is a powerful and highly entertaining tale of self-preservation, selfless heroics, and personal discovery, and a true work of art.
—**Elizabeth Noyes**, author, the *Imperfect* series

Dena Netherton knocks it out of the park with her novel, *The Girl Everyone Wants*. A gifted young woman kidnapped. Her ability to heal is causing a problem for her and everyone around her, until she finds that being granted a gift is not what she thinks. A taut suspense which unravels a woman's beliefs about being chosen. I held my breath wondering who would survive in this thriller!
—**Claire O'Sullivan**, author, *Romance Under Wraps*.

The Girl Everyone Wants

Dena Netherton

PUBLISHING THE POSITIVE
Plymouth, Massachusetts

COPYRIGHT NOTICE

The Girl Everyone Wants

First edition. Copyright © 2021 by Dena Netherton. The information contained in this book is the intellectual property of Dena Netherton and is governed by United States and International copyright laws. All rights reserved. No part of this publication, either text or image, may be used for any purpose other than personal use. Therefore, reproduction, modification, storage in a retrieval system, or retransmission, in any form or by any means, electronic, mechanical, or otherwise, for reasons other than personal use, except for brief quotations for reviews or articles and promotions, is strictly prohibited without prior written permission by the publisher.

This is a work of fiction. Names, characters, businesses, places, events, locales, and incidents are either the products of the author's imagination or used in a fictitious manner. Any resemblance to actual persons, living or dead, or actual events is purely coincidental.

Cover and Interior Design: Cheryl Lynn Childers, Derinda Babcock

Editor(s): Cristel Phelps, Deb Haggerty

PUBLISHED BY: Elk Lake Publishing, Inc., 35 Dogwood Drive, Plymouth, MA 02360, 2021

Library Cataloging Data

Names: Netherton, Dena (Dena Netherton)

The Girl Everyone Wants / Dena Netherton

290 p. 23cm × 15cm (9in × 6 in.)

ISBN-13: 978-1-64949-422-1 (paperback) | 978-1-64949-423-8 (trade paperback) | 978-1-64949-424-5 (e-book)

Key Words: faith healers; miracles; personal growth; spiritual growth; healing of illnesses; God's actions on earth; publicity

Library of Congress Control Number: 2021950263 Fiction

DEDICATION

For my Lord Jehovah Rapha, the ultimate healer, and my husband, Bruce, who has cheered on my own healing process.

ACKNOWLEDGMENTS

Thank you, Kim and Bruce for carefully listening to and reading my chapters. I appreciate how you gently offer wonderful suggestions to help give my words extra punch.

And thank you, lovely Dori Harrell for doing such a great job editing my manuscript.

Many thanks, also, to Cristel Phelps for following up with additional great edits and helping me grow in my understanding of formatting.

Thanks, Deb Haggerty, for believing in this story and for investing your time and energy to make *The Girl Everyone Wants* a novel everyone wants.

Praise also goes to Cheryl Lynn Childers for her excellent artwork on the cover.

Every good and perfect gift is from above, coming down from the Father of the heavenly lights, who does not change like shifting shadows.—James 1:17

CHAPTER ONE

I was five years old the first time I wished I'd been born normal. It was August, and Janey and Jenna, my twin friends who lived on the farm next to ours, told me how they couldn't wait to go to kindergarten because it would be so much fun.

I had picked out my favorite dress, my favorite hair clip, and my favorite pink-and-lavender shoes for my first day of kindergarten. I cried when Mom told me I couldn't go because then the teachers and the other kids would know I was different. Almost twenty years later, being normal is still the first thing I ask Abba for each morning and each night before I go to sleep.

"Please, Abba, make me normal. Please, Abba."

Like today, for example. Dad and Mom and I are driving to the hospital to see my older sister, Abby, and her new baby, Cora. Mom's all worried about how I'll behave when we get inside. She looks in the rearview window to check that there are no gaps between my sleeves and my flesh-toned gloves.

"Zara, you gotta not touch anybody when we go inside the hospital."

I want to roll my eyes, but instead, I say, "Yes, Mom, I'll be careful." It's not like I don't know the drill. After all, I'm twenty-four. I've lived with my abnormality all my life. I've just graduated from college with a master's degree in

English, and everyone says I possess a rather formidable brain. I've had lots of practice not touching people. I keep my gloves on for any foray into the public. Without them, my bare fingers sometimes zap people, that is, if there's anything wrong with them.

But Mom is worried I'll slip up and something will happen—my secret will get out. "Remember Aunt Evelyn," Mom always says. She was my mom's older sister. But she died way before I could form concrete memories. I only remember bits and pieces of Aunt Evelyn and how she shed the gray and gray-green colors of depression.

We park the car and start toward the hospital entrance.

I remember the stories about Aunt Evelyn, though. I don't know how much of my family's lore is true or if it has expanded into legendary dimensions in the span of twenty years since her untimely death. That's the one thing I don't know—how she died.

I'm trying not to show my mom and dad how beyond excited I feel to go to the hospital—not only to see my niece, little six-pound, two-ounce Cora, but to be around people. Their energy attracts me. I am like a bee drawn to clover. People have auras surrounding them. Not like I can see an aura with my eyes. But I can see in my head and then feel with my heart. All the colors of the rainbow and some I'm guessing no one's ever seen. It's why I like to be around some people and why I want to run away from the ones who shed ugly colors, like turd brown or bile yellow. But the people with lovely colors remind me of how it feels to stand at the base of a mountain waterfall on a sunny day and thank my Abba for the rainbows.

In the hospital lobby, we take the elevator to the second floor. Just now, my mom's colors lean toward the greens of anxiety, and I want to give her whatever comfort I can. I take her hand, and she smiles at me and squeezes as if to say thanks. A nurse at the birthing center gives us nametags and presses a buzzer that lets us go through a heavy door to the maternity ward. I step through, and it hits me, like the first wonderful *whomp* of a kid's pillow fight. This is what I've been anticipating all morning. I want to laugh and dance around because I'm feeling like a new mother, and I'm tired from childbirth but elated. Folding my arms across my heart, love cradles and rocks me, caresses my being. Mothers' lullabies fill my soul and float me down the hallway. In my head, the echo of baby giggles lifts me onto my toes. If I could fly, this would be the hallway that sends me heavenward.

"Zara, Zara." My mom hisses my name through tight lips.

But I ignore her. The maternity ward may be as close to motherhood as I'll ever get, and I want to savor it.

We reach room 208. My older sister, Abby, looks tired but beautiful. Her hair is strewn about the pillow like a tangle of gold ribbons, and a hint of roses colors her cheeks. *Abba, why couldn't I have been more like Abby?*

When Abby looks up, she reaches for me. I go to her and wrap my arms around both her and the baby. "Ya done good, Sis," I say. Then I whisper, "I love you."

"Love you, too," Abby replies and gives me one last squeeze. I straighten and get my first look at the new family member. Snuggled in Abby's arms, Cora is beautiful, and I "ahhh" because her fingernails are so tiny and perfect, like she just came out of a nail salon.

Abby hands Cora to me, and I cradle her tenderly, nuzzling her downy hair. I can hardly believe it. I'm an aunt. My heart is dancing, and I want to sing, but Abby wouldn't appreciate that nor would the nurses.

"Mom, look how thick and dark her hair is." Which I hadn't expected because both Abby and her husband, Rolf, are blonde.

Mom gently strokes Cora's hair. "Zara, your hair was just like this when you were born. All thick and black and shiny. Aunt Evelyn had dark hair, and she was tall too. I guess you and Cora both inherited her hair. I wonder if Cora will be tall like you."

I inherited other things from Aunt Evelyn, I've been told.

Mom looks up, and I read in her blue eyes the memory of a much younger woman holding a tiny baby with dark hair.

"She's just like you," Mom murmurs. Her chin trembles, and I feel her heart expand to welcome and love this new life.

I want to hold Cora forever, but I know Mom is dying to cradle her first grandchild. I expertly slide Cora into Mom's arms. Holding and handling babies—wearing my gloves though—comes naturally to me, as I've volunteered in the church nursery since I was a kid.

Dad is hanging back. He loves children but never got the hang of little babies. Mom goes over to him and lets him have a good look at his granddaughter.

"She's mighty pretty," he says, barely stroking one calloused farmer's finger along the top of Cora's head. "We'll have to beat the boys off when she gets older." Then, he looks embarrassed by his words, and he moves over to the window to check the view.

"Hey, where's Rolf?" I feel stupid that I didn't even notice his absence.

"He went down to the cafeteria," Abby answers with a sleepy tone. "He didn't get too much sleep last night. Or food."

"Abby," Dad says, "you must be tired. We should be letting you sleep. C'mon, Astrid."

Mom delivers Cora back into Abby's waiting arms, giving them both a kiss. Mom's trying hard not to display her emotions. But standing so close, I can feel her colors. She's relieved beyond words. Abby had a hard pregnancy, with blood pressure problems and rashes, and we were all praying she'd get through it okay. "We'll be back tomorrow, dear. Want me to bring you anything? A book, magazine, clothes?"

Abby looks like she's starting to fall asleep, so Mom gently lifts Baby Cora and settles her in the bassinet next to the bed. "I need to find the little girls' room," she says.

When we get to the elevator, Dad says, "I'm gonna find Rolf. You two meet me downstairs by the main reception, okay?"

Mom gives him a nod and steps into the nearby women's restroom.

"I'm taking the stairs," I say. "I'll get there before you do, Dad." Since childhood, Dad and I have had this little competition about getting some place first. And anyway, who has the patience to wait for the elevator when all the mommy joy I just took in makes me feel like leaping like a baby goat?

"Ha!" My dad grins because the elevator just made a ding sound to announce it's reached our floor.

I hurry to the stairwell door and fairly fly down the stairs, glad no one's in the stairwell to see a grown woman running and giggling like a child.

But when I get downstairs, I see that the elevator is still on the second floor, and I feel deflated because I'm all set up to laugh at Dad, and now I can't.

So, I walk through the sliding doors to the outside. The hospital has planted all sorts of spring flowers, and there's a water fountain and even a koi pond nearby. I've got a few minutes to spare to watch the goldfish.

An ambulance wails somewhere south of the hospital, probably coming up the same county road we'd driven on. The sound crescendos until the vehicle reaches the hospital drive then turns to proceed straight and silent toward the emergency entrance. When the ambulance stops, medical professionals come running out, and the paramedics pull the gurney out of the back of the ambulance. The body on the gurney is small, and I'm close enough to see the tubes attached to the child and a mask over his or her face.

I stand and stare while thunder pounds at my head, and I can't tear my eyes from the scene fifty yards away.

A feeling comes over me, small but growing, and I try to resist it because it always gets me in trouble. My family has always warned me not to let the feeling come, to deny it and get it under control. But they don't understand that it's like a mother's labor pains, and there's no way to stop it from rolling forward.

Now it crests just like a wave and swallows me. It retreats, pulling me away from land and into the deep like a riptide, and I'm riding the wave up, up, up. I'm impossibly high, and way below me on the shore I see this speck. It's the gurney with the little kid.

Just when I think my wave can't rise any higher, it bends and folds and sends me plummeting at ninety miles an hour. "Abba, no!" rips from my lips.

Numbness and darkness crash over me in that instant when I transfer from my body to the little boy's. My heart is fluttering, and I'm gasping for air. I open my eyes but see nothing.

There's something on my face, over my nose, and I want to pull it off. I want my mama. "Mama, Mama," I cry, but Mama doesn't answer.

I'm floating, and I want to keep floating. Up here, I don't hurt. I look down and see me. I have blond hair, but it doesn't look blond now. There's a lot of blood on my face and all over my hair. I'm on a funny bed with wheels, and I'm following me. They push me down a hall and into a little room with curtains around it, and all kinds of people come in and stand around me. They stick needles into me. It's funny that I can see myself. It's like watching TV. A man is pushing on my chest.

I hear Mama and Papa talking, but not in this room, so I float down the hall till I find them. Mama is sitting on a chair, bent over, crying. She keeps calling my name.

"Timmy, Timmy, Timmy, oh, Timmy!"

"I'm here, Mama. I'm right next to you. Don't be sad, Mama. Mama, don't cry." Papa is crying too. I've never seen him cry before. I put my hand on Mama's arm, but she doesn't notice.

A man comes into the room and says, "Mr. and Mrs. Horton, I'm Dr. Wellsley, one of the emergency doctors."

My mama jumps up and grabs the doctor's hand. "How's Timmy?" Her voice sounds funny.

"We're working on him. Doing everything possible. He's a very sick little boy. I think it would be best for you and Mr. Horton to come with me."

"He's not ... oh, please, Doctor, is he going to ... to ..." My mama almost falls down, and Papa grabs ahold of her.

"We don't know," the doctor says. "We're getting him ready for surgery."

I follow my mama and papa as they crowd the doctor, hurrying down the hall. They go into the little room where I'm lying on a bed. Mama cries some more when she looks at me. She leans over and takes my hand.

My eyes go black again. "Mama, mama, ma ... maaaa ..."

Wind rushes around me and sucks at me harder and harder until the pressure makes me want to die. Just when I think I can't stand it anymore, a pop explodes in my brain, and I slingshot free of Timmy. Pins and needles prick at me like tiny electric shocks. Sunlight blinds my eyes, and I'm outside the hospital again. I've regained sensation, so I put my hands on my chest, feel its rise and fall, hear my heart pounding good and strong. Pain-free again. There is no sticky blood on my hair, no needles in my veins. I look down and see my sandals, my bare legs up to my skirt, my long-sleeved T-shirt with the logo of my favorite bookstore on the front, my flesh-toned gloves, and the long silver necklace glinting in the sunshine—the one Dad gave me for my sixteenth birthday. I'm not Timmy anymore. The fountain gurgles and splashes nearby, and goldfish zip back and forth in the pond.

I know I should hurry back into the hospital lobby to meet Mom and Dad, but I have to find out about Timmy. I have to comfort his parents. It's like my feet have a will of their own. A current of flower-scented air surrounds me and speeds me toward the emergency.

The emergency room sliding doors open, and I head straight past the nurses' station where they admit patients and do triage. The nurse is listening to someone else at the reception desk, so I slip past and hope she doesn't see me. Even if she did, I'd still barge through the door to where the patients are being treated by the ER docs and nurses. I pull off my gloves and drop them as I march down the corridor. I find Timmy right away even though the curtain is pulled. Mr. and Mrs. Horton are standing near the bed. I can hardly see Timmy because there are nurses surrounding his bed, and Dr. Wellsley is also leaning over him.

A nurse follows me and pokes her head through the curtain. "Doctor, OR two is ready."

I walk right up to the Hortons and touch Timmy's mom's arm. "He'll be okay."

Mrs. Horton gasps and whips her arm away like she's been burned, and stares. "Who are you? Are you a nurse?"

"I need to touch Timmy. Right now. It'll be okay." I slide past Mrs. Horton, who is standing close to the doctor.

Dr. Wellsley notices right away.

He turns to the Hortons, probably thinking I'm their daughter or some relative, and says, "Miss, you should wait out in the reception area."

I can't wait for them to figure out who I am. I need to touch Timmy right now, while the energy is in me. "Timmy, you're going to be okay."

"Miss, you need to move away from the bed," a nurse says. She puts her arms out to keep me away, but I zip underneath and put one of my hands on Timmy's little chest. I close my eyes, shutting out the movement of the startled nurses. With my other hand I grip the IV-line dripping into his arm so they can't seize me and drag me away.

I hear commotion around me, but I can't feel anything but Timmy's swelling brain, his little wounded chest, and his faltering heart.

Dr. Wellsley says "Call security" in an urgent voice.

Hands are placed on my back and shoulders, trying to yank me away. But I cannot be moved. I am cement that has cured. I am Timmy and Timmy is me.

I see nothing, and sound has faded to a denim blue. Rubber yellow ducks, toy fire engines, and Tonka trucks make little-boy "vroom-vrooms" along the road circling my brain. Liquid pours from my chest, vibrant red and pulsing, coursing through my fingertips, so hot I smell the iron of it, how it's scorched the sheets around Timmy's naked body. The energy bursting from my hands swells and spreads into fingers of reds, melting into oranges and yellows, then greens and blues. At first, they're swirling like smoke strands—curling, beckoning, dancing. Then they straighten and point outward, accelerating. The sheer g-force of the bands is pulling my skull apart. The energy swells my brain in its outward rush toward the atmosphere, expanding like the universe, until the separate waves of light all fuse. Nothing but white remains. A blinding, searing, consuming holy light. This is why no one can see God and live. My eyes are shut so I don't die.

When I wake, I'm lying on a bed in the hospital. My parents are standing above me, gazing down at me with a combination of worry, devotion, and utter disappointment.

CHAPTER TWO

In my hospital room the next morning, my mom tells me the police were going to arrest me and put me in jail for sneaking into the ER and practically assaulting Timmy Horton. But they didn't do it because Timmy didn't need surgery. Timmy sat up—so she told me—and called for his mama and papa. I don't remember any of this because I fell asleep after Abba's energy passed out of me. But Timmy's monitors had said everything was normal again. And Dr. Wellsley said so too. No shattered skull, no collapsed lung or failing heart. No cuts or abrasions. Timmy and his parents went home the same day.

Dr. Wellsley thought I might have a concussion from falling and banging my head on the tiled hospital floor, and he wanted to do a CT scan. They had taken blood from me, but I wasn't awake for that, which is good because I hate needles. He said my blood work showed my white cell count was high, and he insisted I stay the night for observation.

My parents begged the hospital staff not to talk to anyone about what happened. They didn't want any thanks from Timmy's parents, and they didn't want the media to find out about the incident. "Just let us go home and not be bothered," Mom had said to the doc.

Mom's sitting in a chair, her legs crossed, bouncing the top foot the way she does when she's antsy. And Dad's pacing the room, looking out the window every few seconds. Finally, Dr. Wellsley comes in with my release papers. He keeps shaking his head and throwing his arms out in giant shrugs. "I don't understand what happened yesterday. I've never seen anything like it in my fifteen years here. Scorched sheets on Timmy's bed. Your body so hot we couldn't even touch you." The doctor's eyes show white all around his irises. "We didn't even have a chance to do much more than basic life support. Zara, what was happening? What did you do to Timmy?"

I shrug too because my mom is standing behind the doctor, watching me.

When I don't answer, the doctor turns to my parents. "Your daughter is special."

Exactly the word I most hate to hear. My fists squeeze so tight, my nails dig into my palms. I've been hearing the word "special" from my mom and dad all my life. And attached to that word has always been a forbidding tone and a look on their faces that says being special must be kept a secret. *Please, God, make me normal. Please, God.*

"Amazing. The Horton boy probably would have died if … well …" Dr. Wellsley trails off as if he can't think how to finish his sentence and shakes his head again.

He taps the papers in his hand. "Zara, your numbers from this morning are totally back to normal, so I'm going to release you. But if you feel the least bit sick or dizzy or tired, you make sure to return to the ER. Okay?"

"Sure, Dr. Wellsley." I'm acting all nonchalant, like nothing big happened yesterday, and that probably makes him all the more confused and perturbed. I've already gotten dressed, and I'm anxious to get out of this sad place.

"Dr. Wellsley," Mom says, "it's essential you keep your staff downstairs from telling anybody about what happened yesterday."

"I'll do my best, Mrs. Nielsen, but we have to be very accurate in how we fill out our charts about Timmy's care while in the ER.

"Can't you just say that the boy recovered without needing special treatment?" my dad suggests.

The doctor shakes his head. "Why is it so important that no one hears about what Zara did? I would think you'd be proud of your daughter's act of healing."

"Oh, we're proud of our daughter, don't get me wrong, Doctor," my mom says.

I shoot her a look. It's the first time I've ever heard her say this about my healing ability.

"It's just that, with Zara's gift, if this gets out, there will be no peace for her or our family. Maybe even the whole town of Titusville."

The doctor purses his lips and nods slowly, as if he understands, but I'm not so sure he truly understands my parents' position or if this is just to soothe their fears.

"I'll do my best. But people talk anyway."

Dad shakes his head. "C'mon, Zara." He takes the release papers and fidgets with his keys while a nurse helps me sit in a wheelchair. They follow me and the nurse onto the elevator and down the hall to the front exit.

We climb into Dad's truck, and the nurse leaves us. But then Mom says, "Hey, as long as we're here, we may as well give Abby a quick visit."

Dad's lips tighten. "Isn't she due to check out later today?" Dad is trying to hold his impatience in check. He's glancing at his watch. When she doesn't answer, he says, "Okay, but let's not stay too long. I'm sure Zara wants to get home and out of sight."

We head back inside the hospital. The nurse at the maternity reception desk is nervous. I can feel it.

"Here are your name tags." She presses the buzzer, and the big door unlocks. At the door, I turn to say something to my mom, who's walking behind me, and spy the nurse staring at me. When she notices me noticing her, she drops her head to her paperwork. In the hallway this time, I don't feel the same elation I felt yesterday. I get the feeling from Mom and Dad that they wish I was wearing dark glasses and a wig.

We knock on Abby's door, and she says, "Come in." But when we go inside, she barely looks at us. She's staring at the TV. "Zar," she says in an accusing tone, "it's all over the news."

"What?" I hurry over and glance at the screen, and then my stomach goes taut. There's a news crew outside a house, and Mr. and Mrs. Horton are standing outside being interviewed. "No," Mrs. Horton says, "we'd never met the young woman before. She just barged into the ER and came and put her hands on our Timmy. Nobody could stop her. It was like she had some kind of a ... a ... white-hot force field around her."

The news lady says, "Are you saying this girl used a supernatural power to heal your son?"

Mr. Horton has a deer-in-the-headlights look on his face. "It was real weird," and then Mrs. Horton shoves her face back into the mic. "And I just have to say, we'd sure like to thank you, Miss whoever-you-are. We'll never be able to repay you for bringing Timmy back from almost dying."

The scene cuts away to the TV station, where the anchorman says, "Crews are standing by at the Titusville Community Hospital, where we're told the woman had been admitted overnight. A nurse has said she is not allowed to release the healer's name."

"Zar, what did you do?" Abby's face is red and blotchy. "Now the whole darned world is gonna pound on Mom and Dad's front door, and you'll have to live like some kind of Hollywood star, always ducking and hiding from the paparazzi. But maybe that's what you like."

"Abby, how could you say that?" My whole body is heating up. "I've always tried to hide my gift." *Some gift. Even my sister hates me now.* I hate it that I've made Abby upset. She's my big sister, and I've always tried to imitate her. But even so, I'll never be like her. She's so sweet and pretty ... and normal.

I kind of stammer, "There w-was this little boy, a-and a car had hit him, and they brought him in, and—"

"And you had to jump in and go all 'I'll save the day.'"

"No, it wasn't like that." Now I'm raising my voice too. "His chest was crushed, and ... and the doctor said he might not survive. What was I supposed to do?"

I can tell I haven't convinced her yet, so I say, "Well, what if this had happened to Cora?"

That thought does its work. Abby shudders, and a look of horror sweeps across her face.

Mom shuts the door, and my dad rushes over and puts his hands on my shoulders. "Shhh, they'll hear you in the hall. We can talk about this later."

"Jim," Mom says, "you heard the news. They know where Zara is, and they're waiting downstairs for her to come out. What are we going to say?"

"We don't say anything. We walk right through them and their cameras and mics and ignore them and get into our car and go home."

Mom's shaking her head. "We can't just say nothing. You know how people are. They'll build it up into a miracle and make her into some kind of saint, and the next thing you know, they'll do to her what they did to Evelyn. And on top of that, everybody at church will think we're weird. None of us will have a normal life anymore. Do you want that?"

"Mom's right," Abby says, her face has turned fiercely loving, and she's holding out her arms to me. I forgive her right away because I know she didn't mean to hurt me. I bend over her, and she hugs me and strokes me like I'm her baby. "It's gonna be okay, Zar," she whispers. Then she addresses Mom and Dad. "Let Zara say something. She's smart, and she'll know just what to say."

"Thanks, Abby." I whisper too. I straighten and look at Dad. He usually keeps his cool, but this family affair is shaking him. He's a private kind of man and has always prided himself on being a hard-working farmer who takes good care of his wife and daughters and employees. "The more we try to hide from the media, the more they're going to speculate. We need to arrange a meeting with the Hortons so we can let them thank us, and the media can film me hugging Timmy."

Dad looks doubtful. His lips are screwed up like he's going to say, "No way." But then he sighs while scraping his fingers over his bald head and nods.

A couple of days have gone by since we did the news interview with the Hortons. It was really nice hugging Timmy and seeing him all healthy and whole. He's adorable. A little towheaded six-year-old with enormous blue eyes and chubby cheeks. The cameras came in close when we hugged, and all the spectators cheered and clapped. I said the reason I crashed the ER was I saw Timmy get wheeled into the hospital and felt I needed to pray for him. Of course, the doctor and the hospital staff and his parents didn't know that, and they were just trying to protect him when I first came to his bedside. All I did was pray, and God did the healing.

That seems to have satisfied the media. I think they don't like to report on God stories. If I'd left out the part about prayer, they might have been able to spin the healing into more of a mutant-power story. Maybe Hollywood could cash in on my story by coming up with their next Marvel superhero character: Zara, the super-healer of humanity.

But by mentioning prayer, I hope I scared them off. So now, I'm upstairs in my bedroom, lounging on my bed and snuggling with one of Mom's quilts, with a mountain of purple and yellow decorative pillows stuffed around me, reading *The Complete Poems of Elizabeth Bishop*. My bedroom is smaller than Abby's old bedroom, but I like it because it's cozier, and it's cooler in the summer.

I'm saving tons of money by living with my folks while I save for more school. When I first moved back from school last year after I got my master's degree, I rented a little apartment in Titusville and worked at a clothing store. But I wasn't allowed to wear my gloves at work, which caused lots of trouble when it came to helping women in the changing room or receiving credit cards or cash at the check-out station. Invariably, a customer got zapped, so my manager moved me out of sales and into inventory. Next, the store cut my hours, which was a sure sign they were trying to get me to quit. So, I obliged. Without my job, I knew paying eight hundred a month for my studio apartment was going to rapidly deplete my financial resources.

That is why I'm back with Mom and Dad for the time being. They've been wonderful about having their grown daughter living with them. But there's always a tension floating around us. Mom, especially, is always worried about my interactions in public. And now the knowledge of my healing power is out, she's jumpy, always checking the windows, thinking twice about venturing out to meet friends for lunch or browse stores downtown.

I'm lying low, staying away from windows just in case the news media is still trying to get more photos of me. Which is silly since two of my bedroom windows look out on the acres of freshly plowed farmland, and there'd be nowhere for a cameraman to hide. Not to mention, he'd be trespassing.

The Hortons sent over a beautiful bouquet of flowers, which is sitting on my nightstand. I've been working on some of my own poems. Mom says my poems sing, and someday, I'll be published. I hope so. I've always loved words and the way they're put together. They have such power. I love literary words, poetic words, scientific words, big theological words, philosophical words. I love the way they feel on my tongue. When I was a kid, I used to read the dictionary out loud. Dad says it's fine to know lots of words, but to really use them well, you've got to experience the words in real life, not just in books. He always quotes

Benjamin Franklin's words: "Either write something worth reading or do something worth writing."

This summer I'm going to teach some classes on poetry to school kids at the Titusville library. I'm beyond excited to do this because it will be my first teaching gig. Yes, I actually get paid to teach six sessions about American poetry. And in July, I'm going to a poetry conference in Los Angeles, and I'll have some of my poems critiqued by professionally acclaimed poets. On top of that, being in LA will give me the opportunity to check out the University of Southern California and UCLA.

I hope I'll be able to return to school to work on my doctorate in another year. Without it, I won't be able to teach at a four-year college. My parents want me to go to a small college, but I want to go to a big university in a big city. I'd love to study at Oxford, but I'd settle for a good school in California. I had stellar grades in graduate school, so I hope I'll be able to get a sizable scholarship at one of my favorite schools. It would be my dream to find a teaching position in Southern California. I cherish this picture in my head—of me, living in a cute stucco-sided bungalow with a terracotta roof and arched doorways—which will probably cost a million dollars—in an artsy community. I'll plant an avocado tree and some citrus trees in my backyard, and jasmine and bougainvillea will trail over my fences. I'll sit under the shade of a pergola with my laptop, my books, a glass of iced tea, and listen to mockingbirds and parakeets call. Such a quiet, normal life. And no one will know that I'm "special."

I turn the page in my Elizabeth Bishop book, but the doorbell rings downstairs before I can even focus on the words. Mom's out running errands, and Dad is probably way out in the field or in the barn. They don't like me answering the door when they're gone. There's more ringing and some knocking, like somebody's desperate to have the door open. Scared, I jump off the bed and run downstairs. It could be some overzealous newsperson. But what if something happened to Mom or Dad and it's the police?

But when I open the door, it's Lester, one of Dad's oldest workers, and his face is pale.

"Pete had an accident. It's really bad, Zara. I called 911, but I don't think they're gonna be able to do anything for him."

I push past him because his truck is still running, and I know I'm supposed to come right away. Lester jumps into the driver's seat, I hop inside, and the truck lurches forward when he puts it in gear. We roar and bump down the dirt road amid clouds of dust, heading south to the hayfields.

When we get about a hundred yards away from the accident, I see right away what happened. The little tractor Pete and Lester use to help dig holes is standing about twenty yards behind the flatbed trailer. When Lester drove the tractor down the ramp and off the trailer, the trailer must've shot forward. I know this because it's the same mistake I made last summer when I was out helping Dad in another field. Without the parking brake, the trailer shot forward and slammed into Pete, who would have been standing somewhere around the front of it.

I jump out, even though Lester's truck is still rolling to a stop, and race over to Pete. I drop to my knees and scan him. His face is white, and his eyes are starting to roll back. His breaths are weak and erratic. I check his pulse and can hardly feel it, but it's going fast. Blood is bubbling and spurting from a horrible gash in one thigh, and his leg is bent at a weird angle. There's blood all over the place.

Now I hear sirens—911 responded quickly, but I know Pete's not going to make it, not with this amount of blood loss. I wrap my hands around the gash. The blood is almost hot, and I can feel it pulsing against my fingers.

I hear motors crest the rise that hides the state highway and roll down toward us. But my sight fades. Tromping and men's voices are getting close, talking to each other and into radios. They're telling me to step aside. But it's too late. Farm colors of gold and green and earth tones, patriotic music, and flag colors of white and red and blue are taking hold in my brain. I'm already part of Pete.

"There's no way we're gonna explain this away too, by Zara saying she was just doing a simple prayer for healing," Dad says while marching east and west in the kitchen.

Mom's heating up water for tea, and she's got a plate of corn bread—enough to feed about twenty people—and a crock of butter and a jar of honey on the table. She says she gets hungry if she stays up past ten o'clock, but I know it's really because she's nervous as all get out.

She's usually in her bathrobe by this time, but tonight she's dressed for action in jeans, a tee, and sneakers. She glances at me, then back at Dad, and blurts, "What're we going to do, Jim? Zara can't keep hiding out here. Sooner or later the news people are going to get some photos of her working around the place. They're going to interview our neighbors and our friends at church, and somebody'll say something they can twist into a freaky story."

"It was just a coincidence," I say with a certain amount of stupidity, because I'm still drowsy from the recovery sleep I've been taking for the last eight hours. I feel weak, like I've just donated a couple gallons of blood. "Pete got banged up by the trailer, but he's tough. He's always getting cuts and bruises." But it doesn't sit well with me not to tell the plain truth, and Dad knows that. I guess that's why he doesn't want me doing any interviews. Dad got a visit this afternoon from the same local news crew that interviewed me at the hospital.

"Can you tell us more about what happened to Pete Hauge after his accident? Did your daughter do the same thing to Mr. Hauge she did to Timmy Horton?" the lady asked and shoved a mic in Dad's face.

"Pete got knocked down by a trailer," Dad said. "Then he recovered and went home. That's all I'm going to say. I wasn't there when the accident happened." And Dad slammed the door.

But Mom says that on the six o'clock news, the story of Pete's miraculous healing is spreading. The big stations in Iowa are broadcasting about me and Pete, and already they're connecting it to what happened with Timmy Horton.

"We've gotta get Zara away from here, at least, until this blows over," Dad says. "I called Arne, and he says she's welcome to hole up on his ranch for a while."

"Uncle Arne?" I make a face. Uncle Arne is not very nice. He uses language and makes comments about women like they're all of a certain kind. "That's so far away."

"South Dakota's not that far. He can drive down here on Saturday and pick you up. That way, since no one would recognize his car, you can escape without anyone seeing our car going anywhere out of town." Dad's already nodding like he's settled on this plan.

"But, Dad, what about my teaching gig at the library?" My stomach knots at the thought of missing my chance to teach. Not to mention how the teaching was going to look so good on my graduate admissions application forms. "And what about the conference I was going to attend in July?" Being with Uncle Arne is bad enough but missing out on these two things was going to decrease my chances of standing out in a crowd of candidates.

"Zara," my dad says with a sad shake of his head, "sometimes life hands us lemons. It was good that you healed Pete and that little kid, but it's put you in a bad predicament. Now, anywhere you go, people are gonna know who you are, and you won't have a moment's peace. You hafta move some place they won't expect."

My dad's words make me want to punch something. *Abba, why are you taking these opportunities away from me?*

I only have one more tiny argument, and I launch it. "But, Dad, Uncle Arne is so rude, and ... and ... and since his divorce, he never goes to church anymore." There. That's the best I can do. Uncle Arne has always been the black sheep of the family, and I'm sure the older women in our church remember him when he was a rough kid, and they'd be horrified I had decided to live with him.

"Zara, Uncle Arne has mellowed a lot since you saw him," Mom says. "He's given up drinking, and he's a hard worker. I think you'd like it there. Don't you remember how beautiful it is? All those acres of pine trees and rocky outcroppings backing up to the national park? You'd get to work with the horses and go riding every day."

Actually, besides my teaching and attending the poetry conference, I was looking forward to hanging out with Abby and Rolf this last year before returning to school, babysitting Cora, and watching her reach all her first-year baby milestones. Being secluded on Uncle Arne's horse ranch for upward of a whole year is not my idea of quality family life.

I'm shaking my head and frowning, but when Dad makes up his mind, there isn't much I can do to change it. And Mom agrees with him. If I didn't live with Mom and Dad, I'd have to find another cheap apartment. That would put me back years. And who would want to hire me considering the risk of having hordes of people seeking my healing during work hours?

Dad reaches across the table and squeezes my hand. "Uncle Arne said he'd pay you a salary too."

Translation: he's going to work the fool out of me and pay me minimum wage.

Dad's pleading eyes are saying he'd be much happier if I didn't try to stick around Titusville. "So, what do you say, Zara? Free room and board and a salary on top of that."

How can I say no to the man who's been the best dad any daughter could have ever had? And if I can practice being normal for a few months, maybe it will be worth it. No one knows me in South Dakota. No one besides close family will know where I've gone, and I won't be bothered by any more media speculation. I can Skype or FaceTime with my friends. And Mom and Dad won't have tons of sick people beating down our front door—like they did to Aunt Evelyn—searching for me, and when they don't find me, storming the house, looting things around the house that I might have touched. And my parents can go on living their quiet, productive farm life. Mom can enjoy being a first-time grandmother and volunteering at the community food pantry, and Dad can go shooting ducks with his buddies, and no one will ask about his "special" daughter and if she's healed anybody lately.

CHAPTER THREE

Finn unlocked the front door of his Manhattan brownstone walk-up and stepped inside. He set his grocery bags and his keys on the table inside the entryway, peeked out the door's paned window to make sure he hadn't been followed, then bolted the door and reengaged the security system.

Before he could turn around, his brother's booming baritone startled him, coming from the living room. "Hey, some girl called from the health club. Says she's the one who gave you her card and offered to get you a modeling job. She wanted me to be sure to say that the agency she represents is currently looking for tall, dark-haired guys with blue eyes."

Finn made a face.

"I don't know why you keep going to that gym," Clooney said. "Those spandex girls are always coming on to you."

"It's an unfortunate liability in health clubs nowadays. I wish we had been born in an earlier generation, before girls got the idea they could chase men with such boldness."

"I'd stay away from 'em. Girls and drug deals don't mix in general."

"But, little brother, who would I get to play Lana Turner or Greer Garson or Olivia d'Havilland at my parties?"

"So, you're saying girls are good for the cinema but not much else?"

"Assuredly so." Finn looked at Clooney sideways. "That's why I require my weekly Reel to Real parties. I get to celebrate life as it should be, where all the men are heroes, and all the women are beautiful and helpless." He patted his pockets, muttering, "Now, where did I stow that business card the man-eater at the health club gave me? Oh yes, it is still in my wallet. Note to self—pitch it in the kitchen garbage with the rest of the sales circulars and junk mail."

Sorting through the mail that had been sitting on a table by the front door, he announced, "I'm meeting Bernard Glouster tonight. He's got a cocaine shipment arriving on the nineteenth and wants our help. He's willing to cut us in for twenty percent. I told him I'd hear him out."

Clooney didn't acknowledge Finn's words. Something on the TV had riveted his attention. "Finn, c'mere and see this. It's that farm girl again." Clooney, reclining on the couch, crushed and tossed his empty beer can onto the pile of fast-food wrappers, ripped and spilled bags of chips, and half a dozen additional beer cans already littering the coffee table. Poking through the mess was a bottle of antacids. Clooney ran Cheetos-stained fingers through his greasy brown hair, leaving streaks of orange residue that resembled Halloween highlights.

Finn snarled at the mess. "Clooney, when are you going to clean up this mess? And enroll at the club? Maybe you can work off some of those pounds?"

He joined his brother on the couch, pushing the coffee table out another foot to accommodate his longer legs.

"She's done it again," Clooney garbled, his mouth full of Cheetos.

"Another healing?"

"Yep. Only this time, it was on the farm where she lives. One of the farmworkers got run over by a trailer. The other farm guy said he almost bled out. The girl was already there when the EMTs arrived, and they couldn't move her away from the guy. But afterward, the guy was fine. No more blood. He just got up and walked around like nothing happened. Weird."

"Is the young lady a member of a religious cult or Wicca or another macabre religious organization?"

Clooney rolled his eyes. "You think everything weird must be tied to witchcraft."

"Well, I've read numerous accounts of such fantastic occurrences. Isn't that how they attract new members? They promise that the obedient and faithful will receive power or the ability to perform miracles." He leaned forward to get a closer look at the screen. The news station kept scrolling through the same footage of a farmhouse, then cut to an exasperated father standing at his front door, trying not to lose his temper while keeping the overeager news crew at bay.

"Too bad we can't see her effing face."

"Why do we have to see her face? She's just a young lady somewhere in the Midwest who performs healings."

Clooney stopped munching and glared at Finn. "You can't be as dumb as you sound."

Finn raised his eyebrow and folded his arms over his chest. "And you make that judgment based on which of my statements?"

"Do I have to spell it out for you? Two people—a little boy and now a man—were dying, and then this girl comes and puts her hands on them, and poof! They're okay. Now listen carefully, big brother. Papa is dying of lung cancer," he said slowly, as if talking to a six-year-old. "The doctors say there's nothing more they can do for him. So, we get the girl. She puts her hands on Papa. Poof! No more cancer. And then we won't have to worry about losing a nine-million-dollar-a-year contract with our Russian friend, Evgeni, because he will only deal with Papa."

"I see." Finn narrowed his eyes and stroked his short beard. "I believe you're saying we should travel to Iowa, knock on the young lady's front door, and say with exceptional courtesy, 'Hello, we are a duo of brothers who make their living by contracting illicit drug deals with foreign actors from the office of our high-rent Manhattan home. But, my dear young lady, we heard about you on the news and are fascinated by your healing talents. We would be pleased if you would accompany us back to New York City with the hope and expectation that you will touch our grandfather and heal him, thus making it possible for him to continue his cordial but illicit deals with his foreign friends? And, by the way, it is necessary for you to come alone—no family members or friends—because it would not benefit our operations if they should later be able to identify us. And also, the only reward we can guarantee for this extraordinary act of charity is a quick, merciful death.'" Finn stood and hefted his grocery bag. "Yes, those words should prove an irresistible invitation."

Clooney swept the Cheetos crumbs off his rounded belly as if he were dusting off his brother's sarcasm, and he swore under his breath. "Papa's got a month, maybe two, to live. And you wanna waste time arguing with me about a simple little kidnap? You're no grandson of Niall Finnegan if you don't work with me on this."

Finn turned and headed toward the kitchen. "Let me ponder on this while I prepare our green salad and lamb chops."

"Yeah, and while you're doing that, I'll put in a call to Hector." Clooney wiped his orange lips with a napkin. "He'll be able to locate the girl. With any luck, we could have her here in less than a week, tops. Oh, and FYI, I hate lamb chops."

Uncle Arne got here late Friday night and bunked in Abby's old room. That night I dreamed about Aunt Evelyn.

She was young and tall and dark haired, just like me. Not the middle-aged woman who had died under questionable circumstances when I was only a little girl.

I'd spent most of Thursday and Friday deciding what I should take to South Dakota. But now it's Saturday morning, and I'm mostly packed. I'm bringing my flute because, as I remember, Uncle Arne doesn't have a piano or any other instruments. I can't understand people who don't like music. Something must be missing in their brains. I hear music in my head most of the time, but the melodies get especially thick and luscious when I'm near specific people. I figure I can take my flute when I hike into the hills behind his ranch in my spare time. If I have any spare time.

A knock sounds on my bedroom door. "Honey, are you ready?" my dad calls.

I grab my backpack and my overnighter and open the door. Dad spies my two big suitcases and comes inside to take them.

"There's also a box that has my books."

He nods. "I'll come back for that."

Uncle Arne's blue Dodge Ram truck is pulled up close to the front porch so we can quickly put my stuff in the backseat and me in the front, just in case any news media is out on the highway trying to spy on us. After we do that, I stand by the truck feeling awkward because my mom is already crying and my dad is acting all efficient and businesslike.

Now that I think about it, I'm surprised I don't feel more emotional. I thought I'd cry. But last night, Abby and Rolf came by to say goodbye, and I held Cora one last time.

Mom wraps her arms around me and holds me tighter than she's ever done before. "FaceTime me tonight, okay?"

I nod into her shoulder. When I look up, I notice the lines around her blue eyes and how they're especially deep this morning.

Dad comes up and puts his arms around both of us and gives me a kiss on the top of my head.

Uncle Arne is already revving the motor, so I disengage from Mom and Dad and climb into the truck, buckling up. Now that I've gotten used to the idea of South Dakota and Uncle Arne's ranch, I'm actually kind of excited. They always say that writers need exposure to different experiences so their writing is authentic. Maybe my life at Uncle Arne's ranch will be an adventure I can use later as a writer and poet. I glance over at Uncle Arne, and I'm surprised that he smiles at me. He hardly ever smiles. I hope this is a sign, a harbinger of good things to come. Maybe he realizes it's hard for me to leave my family.

As we drive out of the farm's long driveway, we see a white van pulled over on the road. There isn't any kind of satellite attached to the van, so I'm pretty sure it's not a news vehicle. All I see is the driver, who's opened the hood to check for whatever's wrong. I look at Uncle Arne. He's a very good mechanic, and it would be easy for him to help the guy. He must have the same thought because he pulls over and parks but keeps the truck running.

I watch him walk up to the guy, who's wearing a baseball cap, but I can see his dark hair and slight beard. They exchange words, but I can't tell what they're saying.

Uncle Arne inspects the motor and pokes around inside. He says something to the driver while pointing at the motor. The tall guy shrugs and shakes his head. After Uncle Arne drops the hood back into place, he shakes the stranger's hand. The dark-haired man looks over at where I'm sitting, says something to Arne, and Uncle nods. Both men trudge toward our truck, and I roll down my window because I can see the guy wants to say something to me.

When he stops at my window, he bends slightly so he can look at me. He removes his sunglasses, and his eyes are especially blue, like glacial ice, and he studies my face almost as if he thinks he recognizes me. He's really cute but way too old for me to be interested in, maybe mid-thirties.

"Miss, I apologize for delaying you." He doesn't take his eyes away from mine. "Your, um, father arrived at just the right time. Otherwise, I would have missed a very important meeting."

Even though he's behaving like the very soul of good manners, he's still staring. I meet his gaze and hold it, feeling stubborn, daring him to keep looking. And I remember my dad's words to me when I was in first grade and got the worst of a fight with a third-grade boy. "Zara, ya gotta remember that discretion is the better part of valor." I drop my gaze to the gravel around his shiny black shoes. I don't like those shoes. A tornado funnel seems to spin around them, stirring dark dust inside my brain. Those shoes don't belong around here. Why is the man having a meeting way out in a farming community? I tear my gaze away from his shoes.

"Well, I sincerely hope you have a nice day. It's fine weather for a drive." He jabs his hand out toward me, and though he makes me nervous, I automatically take it because I've been conditioned from childhood to be polite.

"Thanks. I'm glad Uncle could help."

When his fingers close over mine, I imagine a snake, its cold, muscular body coiled around me like I'm a monkey. Poor monkey that can't breathe. I can't help myself. I whip my hand away so the image will disappear.

He looks startled, takes a step back. He frowns and lifts his hand and studies his palm as if I'd shoved a splinter into his skin. When he looks up again and sees me watching him, his mouth morphs back into a smile and he waves goodbye.

I don't wave back. I roll up my window, shuddering at the bad color rising in my brain. Uncle Arne hops in and pulls back onto the road.

In the rear window, I glimpse the tall man with the python grip as he gets into his van. He raises a phone to his ear while slowly merging onto the highway, going the same direction we're traveling.

It's Saturday, so there isn't a lot of traffic. Within ten minutes, we're past Titusville, past the grange, past the pumpkin farm where they do that maze thing in the fall, and only a few miles from the interstate.

The white van stays with us even when we get onto Interstate 29, going north, but I guess lots of people enter the state highway at this point to travel to Sioux Falls or points north or west. Still, I don't like that the van has been behind us for at least half an hour. My uncle likes to stay in the slow lane. Usually, cars either pass in the left lane or drop back, eventually receding into the distance. I can't help it that I keep checking the rearview mirror. The paranoid part of me comes from my mom. She's always suspicious with strangers or other cars on the road. If she'd been in the truck when Uncle Arne pulled over to help the tall guy in the baseball cap, she would have said, "Oh, please don't stop! He could be a serial killer."

The thought of my mom's hyper-caution shakes me by the shoulders and shoves sense back into me. Big deal … we helped a guy with a broken-down car. He gave me the creeps. What of it? Nothing bad happened.

I have a phone, but Mom and Dad told me to not go all generation Z on Uncle Arne and ignore him in favor of social media, at least during the trip to his ranch. "Uncle Arne, do you mind if I turn on the radio?"

He quirks an eyebrow. "Sure, so long as you don't put on hip hop."

"Uh, gag me." I make a face, and my uncle chuckles. I search for a country channel, because I know Uncle Arne likes that kind of music, and I'm hoping we can make some sort of connection. I find one that plays classic country, and Randy Travis is singing. My uncle makes a kind of grunt sound that communicates he likes the music, and I relax a little more.

It's warm in the cabin of the truck, which is making me drowsy. Since Uncle Arne is the type who does all his talking inside his head, there isn't much to keep me awake.

I fold my arms across my chest and close my eyes. I'm drifting off, but when the truck slows, I wake up and glance out the window. Uncle exits the interstate, then signals to pull into one of those giant truck stops with the convenience store, restaurant, and restrooms. Even showers for the truckers. Out of curiosity, I check the rearview mirror and see the white van zoom by, still on the interstate, and I breathe a relieved sigh.

After we gas up and use the restrooms, we're back on the road in less than ten minutes. I'd grabbed a diet pop and some strawberry sugar wafers, so I'm good to go for at least another couple of hours. Uncle Arne is crunching on Doritos, which seems to put him in a mood to talk.

"Once we get onto I-90, it's only about five hours to Spearfish," he says.

I have a vague memory of going fishing with Dad somewhere near Uncle Arne's property. I didn't catch anything, but Dad snagged a couple of trout. The other thing I remember—I guess I was about ten last time I visited—was the long gravel driveway leading up to the ranch house and how he'd lined it with lots of big stones. I spent a whole afternoon trying to balance while jumping from stone to stone.

"I'm a good cook," I say to remind him of what Mom had told him earlier this morning. "Mom taught me to make all of her favorite recipes, and I've made up some of my own."

Uncle Arne nods enthusiastically. "Your mom's always been a really good cook. If you can cook like her, we're going to get along just fine."

My healthy cooking would probably help Uncle Arne slim down. After his divorce, he gained weight, and it all seems to have settled on his belly. I'm already picturing myself puttering around Uncle's big kitchen with the granite countertops, the farm sink, the six-burner gas stove and double oven, and the giant island. Kelly, his ex-wife, had remodeled the kitchen because she'd said she'd never cook with the way things were laid out when she first married him.

We exit Interstate 29 and take a county road going west. Uncle wants to avoid the traffic around Sioux Falls. "We'll pick up I-90 farther west," he says.

The road we're on is too quiet. Hardly any traffic. Just farms and fields and fields and farms for miles. I'd hate to get stranded around here in the winter. I could freeze to death before I could walk to the nearest farm for help.

I check the rearview mirror again, still feeling like I've been watching a Stephen King movie. Something about the white van and the strange man with the blue, blue eyes and the iron grip causes a shiver. There's a car behind us, and it's coming up pretty fast. I'm guessing it's someone who knows these roads well and is preparing to pass Uncle's truck.

But at the last minute, lights on the side of the vehicle start flashing. Uncle Arne sees it at the same time, and we both groan simultaneously.

"Unmarked police car," he says, frowning and shaking his head. "I wasn't speeding, though. Wonder why he's pulling me over."

Uncle signals, slows down, and pulls over to the soft shoulder. "Zara, reach into the glove compartment and pull out my registration stuff, will ya?"

I do as he asks and hand him the folder with all his info. Uncle pulls his wallet out to show the officer his driver's license. I check the mirror again and see the officer talking on his phone, and that strikes me as weird. Don't they usually use those handheld radios? But maybe they do things differently in unmarked vehicles. My heart pounds even though we haven't done anything wrong. A cop had pulled me over a few years ago, shortly after I'd gotten my learner's license. Mom was in the passenger seat. I didn't get a ticket, just a warning about getting one of the brake lights fixed. But it scared me.

Finally, the officer steps out of his car. His hair is messy brown, and he's not wearing a uniform, either, and he waddles when he walks. His stomach is big, and it bulges out all the way around his belt. Don't police officers have to be in fairly good shape so they can chase criminals on foot or wrestle them down once they catch them? The other thought that makes my stomach go jittery is, I once heard a story of a girl getting pulled over by a guy pretending to be a cop. How would anyone know? You see flashing lights, and you assume it's a real policeman.

As the fat policeman approaches, I have this strong impulse to jump out of the truck and run for my life. He's wearing a gun holstered under his arm, like those detectives wear on TV, not like the officers you usually see around town who wear them on their belts. And where's his badge?

When he comes to the window, I intend to ask, "May I please see your badge, Officer? I have the right to ask to see your badge and to get your badge number." Even though I'm not usually so assertive, I fully intend to show this officer I know a thing or two. Mom would be proud of me for being cautious and for following through on my suspicions.

He comes up to the driver's side. I didn't think they did that anymore. Don't they usually go to the passenger side because it's safer? Uncle Arne opens his window, holding his driver's license out the window with both hands, I guess to show the officer he's not holding a weapon.

Now that the cop is close, even though he's looking at Uncle, his eyes repeatedly flick over to me. And each time he looks, little spears of pain jab me. I stare at my uncle, how the muscles around the base of his jaw twitch slightly. Perspiration has sprouted on the back of his neck. Maybe it's because he had some really unpleasant associations with the law in the past.

Out of the corner of my eye, something big and white—a van—zooms past our truck and pulls over, peppering gravel and dust onto our windshield like BB pellets, which makes me jerk like they're actually coming through the window and hitting me. I'm all hyper-adrenaline.

"May I have your driver's license, registration, and proof of insurance," the officer says.

"Officer." I put my hand on my uncle's shoulder to stop him from handing over his info. "First, we have the right to ask to see—"

The driver of the white van jumps out and hurries over. *Oh, my Abba, it's him.* The tall guy with the baseball cap. I gasp when I see the police officer and the van man exchange glances like they know each other well. I'm panting hard, warnings hurtling through my body, into my arms and legs and down to my toes, making me ready to fight or die.

"What the heck?" Uncle recognizes him too, and his tone of outrage and confusion spills into his body language. He drops his wallet and opens the door.

My uncle is trying to put two and two together, but I've already done the math. I don't know how I know, but this police stop is not about my uncle's driving or anything being wrong with his vehicle. It's about me. I'm opening my door too, ready for action. Should I jump on the van man? I'm strong and athletic. Scratch and claw at him? Try to sock him? Or run?

The police officer whips out his gun and aims it straight at Uncle Arne. "Don't move!"

Uncle Arne freezes. But I'm already yelling, "Put that gun away!" I can't hold it in. This isn't real.

The van man hurries over to my side and pulls my door open all the way. I'm still yelling.

"Shut up!" He yanks on my arm, practically pulling it out of the socket.

I don't feel pain. "No!" I yell, but he smacks me hard on the mouth, and I tumble to the ground. He bends over to grab me, but I roll away. When he makes another lunge for me, he stumbles in the shoulder dirt, loses his balance, and throws his arms out to break his fall. Before he can get to his feet, I jump down into the plowed field and run. Maybe I can make it to the farmhouse. It's only half a mile away.

I don't get more than twenty feet. He catches up and tackles me, and I hit the ground hard. I don't yell this time. I'm so mad I want to punch and punch and punch. But he straddles up my back so I can't roll over and fight. Grabs me under the arms and lifts me to my feet. He's holding my arms behind me, so I all I can do is jerk my shoulders from side to side and kick. I kick any part of him I can reach, especially those awful black shoes. I get in a good shot to his knee, and he snarls. He spins me around, and his eyes are cold and deadly. He lets go of me, cocks his arm back, and the last thing I remember is his big fist rocketing straight toward my jaw.

CHAPTER FOUR

I'm having terrible dreams, but I can't wake up enough to escape them. I'm Aunt Evelyn, and I'm running down a city street with horrible, ugly zombies chasing me. The more I run, the more zombies there are. I turn right, and there are more. I scream, "Leave me alone. I can't help you!" I run into a building and hop onto an elevator, but when I step out in the top-floor corridor, I run into more zombies. The only place I can go now is the roof, but that doesn't stop them. They follow me, arms outstretched, fingers green and gory, decayed black mouths gaping. They've backed me up to the edge. Just before they're about to grab me, I step off and hurtle toward the pavement.

A voice like a documentary narrator says, "She did everything she could, but after all, she was just one person."

I jerk awake, but I don't see anything because there's something covering my eyes. I try to move my hand up to my eyes, but it won't budge. I'm lying on my side, and my shoulders are burning because my arms are held behind my back.

"The girl moved. I think she's waking up," a man says from somewhere behind me.

I'm being jounced around on a hard flat surface, and motor sounds tell me I'm inside some sort of vehicle. I hear movement, and then I start when a hand touches my face, inches my blindfold down. I keep my eyes shut—even though my heart is drumming so loud I'm sure he can hear it—and pretend to be unconscious. He pokes me hard in the ribs several times. I moan because that seems more realistic than just lying there and not reacting to the painful jabs. Also, there's something bound around my mouth.

"Finn, does she need more of the stuff?" This comes from the man who's not near me, probably the driver.

"I estimate that she will require more in another hour," the man close to me says.

I'm guessing this must be Finn. I recognize the voice and the formal style of speech. He's the one who decked me. Part of my brain screams, *Why aren't you terrified, Zara?* From another part of my brain, I snarl, *Dummy, I am terrified.* Some people freeze when they're scared. Me? When I'm scared, I go quiet and focused in the brain, like I'm about to go all mixed-martial arts in the ring. One time a big stray dog on our farm chased me. I was scared as all get out, but I climbed the rope swing that hangs on the tree in our front yard and wrapped my legs around its supporting branch. While the mangy thing was jumping up and snarling, trying to get at me, I pulled out my phone and called 911. The police came and shot the dog. Turned out it had rabies.

"Weren't you terrified?" Abby had asked when I told her about the dog, her eyes big with both horror and admiration.

"I've never been so terrified," I told her.

But I had to do what was called for. Something takes over and tells me exactly what I have to do to survive. I don't have control over it. They say people like that make good fighter pilots because they can keep their wits about them.

Right now, besides being so scared I want to hurl, my brain feels a kind of buzz. Not the buzz I've heard about when people drink too much. This buzz is like an energy. And it's zapping my brain, which turns all bright and rainbow colored. *Memorize their voices*, my brain instructs. *Listen to their conversation. Try to determine where you are. Feel the space around you. Smell them. Smell the environment. Taste the ...* No, all I can taste is the rag they've stuffed in my mouth.

Finn smells like men's cologne. When he replaces my blindfold, I detect a hint of fabric softener in his shirtsleeve. His speech indicates an educated man. But not a gentleman, I note, aware of my throbbing jaw and head.

Finn moves away from me, and I hear both men talking softly up front. They mention cocaine—that much I catch. And words like "shipments" and "expedite" and "bribe customs inspectors."

Then it's quiet. I'm figuring out we must be on a big, well-maintained road, most likely an interstate. I haven't noted any sharp curves, and we haven't come to any stops.

Why did they take me? Are they serial killers planning to torture me and then kill me and throw my mutilated body into a cornfield? That thought kicks my breathing into higher gear. My nostrils flare to get more oxygen. My shoulders ache because my arms are pulled back behind me, and my wrists hurt. I'm thirsty and sick to my stomach, and I could use a bathroom. Even though my legs are tied at the ankles, I'm able to roll over and make some sounds so Finn knows I'm awake. Once more, fingers inch my blindfold downward, a flashlight shines on my face, and this time I glare up at him to show I'm not going to be an easy victim.

He chuckles. "Hello, young lady. How lovely to see those big hazel eyes again."

I whip my head fast from right to left a couple of times and moan angrily so he knows to take this fool gag out of my mouth!

He unties it, and before he can change his mind and retie it, I say, "I'm gonna be sick."

"Clooney, we need a bucket or some other receptacle. Pretty girl says she's planning to be sick."

"We're coming up on a gas station. We can take care of things there."

I focus on keeping my breaths slow and regular, swallowing again and again to keep my nausea from taking over.

Finn puts a bottle of water to my lips, and I drink until I start choking.

"Hold on there," Finn says. "I'll give you more later." He screws the cap back on. Then he turns his back and unzips a bag and messes around with it.

When I see the syringe, it's too late to struggle. "No, don't!"

He's got a grip on my arm, and I know that the needle will pour sleepiness into my veins. He lets me go and watches me for a few minutes.

"Feel better?" he says with a knowing smirk.

"What did you give me?" I'm outraged and terrified but feeling loopy at the same time.

"Just an old family recipe. Isn't it wonderful?"

When I glare at him, he shrugs. "We need you quiet if we're going to let you use the restroom."

He waits and watches. The next time he speaks, I have trouble comprehending his words.

"Good. Very good. I see that you're growing rather relaxed."

The van comes to a halt. Finn unties my wrists and ankles. The back door opens, and the driver, Clooney, reaches in and drags me out. He's the police officer who pulled my uncle over. He's rough, and he doesn't let go of me, which is just as well since I'm so dizzy I don't think I can stand on my own.

He's watching me closely, obviously fearing I'll scream or try to get away even though I don't see a soul gassing up. It's dark, probably way past midnight since there are no other customers. But whatever Finn gave me has made me dumb and dumber.

Bright security lights surrounding the gas station hurt my eyes as we walk around the side to find the restrooms.

Clooney shoves me inside the women's bathroom door and says something like "Be quick," but keeps his foot propped in the doorway while I take care of business. I have to go so bad I don't even care if he can hear. Besides, the man is a pig, so why should I care at all?

Afterward, I wash my hands and face with cold water and cup some more water to drink, and then he opens the door and pulls me outside. He's got his arm wrapped around me like he's my boyfriend escorting me back to our private love vehicle. Yuck. I try to memorize the license plate, but my mind is so messed up I can't even comprehend the symbols on the plate.

In seconds we're all back inside the van and Finn has retied and gagged me. Sleep overtakes me even though I fight it.

I'm dreaming again, and none of it is nice. My body is jostled, and I almost wake up. But it's not enough, and I fade back to the dreams.

Then the movement stops. Hands fiddle with my body, and I feel myself lifted, carried. I try to open my eyes, but they're too heavy to keep open. I've been waiting for Santa Claus while huddled on the living room sofa, staring at the fireplace. But I couldn't stay awake long enough to see Santa arrive. Daddy is carrying me upstairs to my bedroom, tucking me in, giving me a kiss on the forehead. "Sleep tight, little princess,"

I nuzzle my pillow and drift off into the land of Nod. Tomorrow's Christmas.

But when I wake up, it's not Christmas and I'm not in my own bedroom. I'm lying on a single bed in the corner of an unfamiliar bedroom. The aroma of coffee and toast floats in the air and makes my stomach grumble. Then it all comes back to me: the two criminals, running and getting tackled, the man punching my lights out, riding in a smelly van.

All of a sudden, I'm sick again. I hope that door to my right is a bathroom because I'm about to hurl on the floor if it's not. I thrust open the bathroom door and make it to the toilet just in time. My heart is pounding, and I've never had such a terrible headache. Afterward, I move to the sink and slump over it, sipping handfuls of water and splashing my face. Hanging there, gulping air for a few minutes, makes me feel better. I don't bother to flush the toilet. Someone might check on me.

Back in the bedroom, outdoor daylight pours through thick, translucent panes of glass. Another bed—the kind you'd see in hospitals—is on the opposite side of the room. The head of it is propped up and facing away from me. An IV tube is dripping liquid from a plastic bag suspended on an IV pole. Dripping into whom?

I tiptoe over and peep around the head of the bed. At first, I glimpse only the wispy hairs on the head of an old person. But I take another step and see the profile of an old man. His mouth is open in sleep. White sheets and blankets hide the rest of him, but I can tell the figure underneath is wasted from illness. And sick people have a certain odor to them.

I move so I can see the man's face. His eyes are sunken, and his cheeks are hollow. He's on oxygen, and I wonder what is dripping through the IV tube. The skin on his wraithlike forearms and hands is thin and bluish and mottled. A dying man. But I feel no compassion for him. Abba's breeze isn't pushing me forward, urging me to lay my hands on him.

Why am I in the room with him? This doesn't look like a hospital room. And if this man is being cared for, where's his nurse? My stomach jolts. If someone comes in to care for him, maybe they'll help me get away.

It's daylight, and the kidnappers are probably nearby. Are there others?

My pulse hammers my head as I creep over to the door and try the handle, but my stomach falls when the handle won't budge. I'm locked inside a room, and there's no telling how long it will be before my killers come to check on me or do whatever they've kidnapped me for. I tug on the door handle harder. Pull on it, rattle it, but it doesn't budge. I want to pound on the door and yell, but that would only bring my killers. I bend and peek through the old-fashioned keyhole, but don't see anything.

Next, I check the windows. They've all been nailed shut. I pull at the nails, but they're too tight. I jab and jab, trying to shove a fingernail underneath them, but it's hopeless. All I get are ripped nails and one that bleeds. I'm tempted to drive my fist through the window. Is there something I can use to break the glass? I glance around the room, breathing in ragged gasps. Nothing. There's nothing. Even the books on the shelf aren't heavy enough.

The desk. On the other side of the room. I keep my eyes on the old man while I glide silently over to it. But the drawers are empty. No letter knife, no pens, no ruler, nothing I can use as a tool or a weapon. No twine either.

Would the bathroom have tweezers or nail files? I place one foot in the direction of the bath, but then I hear footsteps. I hurry to my bed, climb in, and pull the blankets over my shoulders. My heart beats so fast it makes me breathe hard. I take a few giant breaths to cram oxygen. But when a key is inserted into the lock, I close my eyes and feign sleep. The bedroom door opens and steps approach.

"Hmm. I could have sworn I heard someone pattering around in this room, opening drawers, trying the handle of the bedroom door. Must have been my imagination."

Finn's voice.

If he goes out, it will give me more time to scope out possible escape routes. I wait, breathing deep and even, hoping he'll assume I'm asleep and go away.

"Ah well, I guess I'll have to try back later." Finn's steps recede. The bedroom door shuts.

I barely flick an eye open, don't see Finn, and look again. Good. The man has gone. I sit up and glance at the bathroom door. I need to get back in there and check the medicine chest and vanity for any implements I can use on the nails. Or maybe something heavy to smash the windows. I ease my feet onto the floor, reminding myself to walk softer this time. Just as I think this, the wood floor creaks.

"If you're going to sneak, you'd better learn which spots to avoid placing your feet on."

CHAPTER FIVE

I'm so jolted my head feels like a nail and Finn's voice is the hammer. I whirl to see him sitting on an upholstered vanity chair in a corner of the room, his long, lean legs stretched out on an ottoman.

I can't find my tongue, but my body trembles, and I hate that he can read the fear in me.

He's dressed in black, like he's going to a funeral. Or is this how someone dresses when they're about to cause a funeral?

I have nothing to use as a weapon, just my own hands and feet. And those didn't do much good a day or two ago.

"You're probably hungry, Zara. Ah, Zara. What a pretty name for a pretty girl. Hair like the midnight sky shimmering with stars, and so tall and slender she could be a queen. And just look at that face."

Finn examines me as if critiquing a new painting at the Metropolitan Art Museum.

"Zara is petrified, but she obscures that emotion with a regal tilt to her chin and fire in her eyes. She's young but wise, tall but vulnerable." He stands and performs a slight bow. "I would be delighted if you would join me for breakfast downstairs, fair Zara. I've got some eggs and bacon and toast in the warming oven. Would you prefer coffee or tea, or perhaps milk?"

Now I understand. Finn is more than a criminal. He's a psychopath. He sees the way I stare at him, and I can tell he totally gets what I'm thinking. He's enjoying this minute, enjoying my obvious terror, knowing all the questions that would arise from my victim status, comprehending how my mind might race. How I might be sizing him up, searching for vulnerable areas, and then—remembering how I didn't find any the day he bested me—casting about for a weapon or a means of escape. He's thoroughly enjoying that I have no weapon, that I'm dressed in nothing but a flannel nightgown—who put this on me?—and that when I finger my jaw, I'm remembering his right hook.

He's kidnapped me, and now I'm just going to accept that I'm his prisoner and let him feed me breakfast? Like I'm supposed to surrender and accept that this is the way it's going to be? Is he going to lock me up and keep me prisoner like that horrible guy in Cleveland, Ohio, did to those three girls? He beat them, raped them, kept them in a dependent state for ten years. Is Finn that kind of criminal? And the other man too?

I'm going to be sick again, only there's nothing left in my gut. A kind of wail begins in my throat and starts building. I open my mouth to let it out or it's going to explode through my chest.

Finn jumps up and hurtles toward me, but I fight him with all my strength. Scratching and beating him does no good. His body is hard like granite. He drags me over to the wall and grinds my shoulder blades against it, one hand over my mouth. "Shhh. You don't want to wake Papa, do you?"

I growl through his hand, eyes watering from the pain.

He skewers me with his stare. "Will you be quiet?"

His look communicates he'll make me be quiet if I keep making noise, so I nod.

"Very good." He slowly removes his hand but keeps it poised a foot from my face in case I change my mind about yelling. "I knew you'd be a young lady with the good sense to control herself." He releases me and gives me a few inches of space.

"Who are you?" I whisper with as much ferocity as I dare. "Why did you bring me here?"

"I'll answer all of your questions only after you have breakfast."

"Why? Are you going to drug me again?" I thrust my chin out to stare him down.

"My, but you're a warrior queen." He studies my eyes.

Can he see my "warrior" resolve shrinking? Or is he just thinking about how he's going to enjoy torturing and imprisoning me?

"No, I have no intention of lacing your food with any mind-altering drugs. Unless I find it necessary." He raises one well-groomed eyebrow, still staring.

"All right." I look down at his shiny black shoes, nod, and slump my shoulders, hoping he'll think my body language signifies I've accepted my fate, whatever that is. And besides, if we have breakfast somewhere else in the house, it will give me a chance to explore other ways of escaping.

He backs away, glides to the corner he'd hidden in when he surprised me and retrieves a grocery bag. He's graceful in a kind of snakelike way. "Here are some things for the bathroom. And there are clothes in the closet. Knock on the bedroom door when you're ready."

He leaves as noiselessly as he had entered, but I hear the snick of the lock.

I check the bag's contents. He's picked up a toothbrush, toothpaste, soap, shampoo, hairbrush, even a bottle of Chanel Number 5.

Now that he's gone, my whole body is jittery when I open the closet and see dresses, all my size. I search through the hangers for the jeans or leggings I usually wear, but all I find are chiffon and satin and velvet dresses and some knee-length, tight-around-the-waist, scoop-neck fancy party dresses. Others look more like costumes from older eras. There are underwear items too, in a small bureau in the closet. They're all my size, and this is beyond creepy.

I want to keep searching for things I can use to help me escape. But Finn expects me to clean up before breakfast. I'm obviously stinky, so I need to get past the creeps and keep my mind focused on surviving. He wants me clean, so I'll make myself clean. Anything to put off some horrible fate awaiting me when the murderous mood strikes him.

What's with the Barbie-doll clothes? I'm angry that Finn is making me dress a certain way. Am I part of some sick fantasy? But without clothes, it'll be hard to escape, so I snatch a dress out of the closet and the other stuff I need and tiptoe to the bathroom. I close the door, but I notice for the first time there's no lock. "Crap!" I stomp back into the bedroom and drag the desk chair into the bathroom and wedge it against the doorknob.

I don't like that Finn said I should knock on the bedroom door when I'm ready. That means he's close by.

I hurry to shower and shampoo, peeking through the shower curtain about every three seconds to make sure Finn isn't playing the psychotic Norman Bates, invading my bathroom to slash me into ribbons. My fingers shake from the graphic image from Hitchcock's movie *Psycho*. I turn off the water, towel off, and dress as fast as I can. Then I sneak over to the dying old man's bed.

He's changed position slightly, and his mouth is closed, which means he's probably getting ready to wake up. Finn called him Papa. Could this shrunken, gnarled, old tree branch be someone he cares about? And why am I in the same bedroom as this man? Is he a prisoner too? This is creepier than any movie I've seen.

One of his hands is hanging over the side of the bed. I reach out and barely touch it, but draw back. It's cold, like death, but I can hear the old man breathing. I try again, forcing my fingers to remain in contact because I need to experience him.

Lots of old people have wonderful colors inside. When I was a teen, before my parents disallowed me, I used to visit the rest home on the outskirts of town. I'd go and sit with some of the old ladies. There were hardly ever more than one or two old men. The old ones all remembered stuff. It didn't matter if I wasn't their granddaughter or friend. They were just happy to have someone hold their hands and listen to their memories. Many of the old people were ones I had known in church, and their colors were lovely. After being with them for a couple of hours I'd go home and take a walk outside, just basking in the splashes of warm light still lingering in my brain.

Holding "Papa's" hand, I wait for the old man's colors to rise up in my brain. Maybe he'll wake up and I can help him. But even though I gently squeeze his hand and speak to him, he doesn't respond.

"Old man," I whisper, "do you hear me?"

I lean over and press my forehead to his hand. Sometimes this helps.

I wait for the explosion of color, but instead he moans. Then something whacks me over the head so hard I'm thrown to the floor. I stifle a cry and cower, drawing my legs up so I'm in the fetal position to protect myself, fully expecting blows to continue raining on me. When no more blows come, I hold my head, checking for cuts or other wounds. I don't dare look up but stay still. Finn must have come in and knocked me to the ground.

But nothing more happens, so I move my hands from shielding my face. There are no shiny black shoes or black-trousered legs standing near me. There's no one in the room but me and—I slowly rise to my feet—the old man. He hasn't stirred. But his colors showed in that slap to my head. He must be a very bad man.

I glance at the bedroom door, holding my breath and listening with all my might for Finn's movement or his breathing. What would he do if he found me hovering over the old man? Is this some awful situation where Finn and Clooney—I don't know if anybody else is involved—are holding their papa prisoner, maybe trying to get something out of him? Maybe they've seen his will and want him to change it. Or maybe they're keeping him drugged so he can't call for help. Are they denying him professional care? So far, I haven't seen any indication that they're feeding the old man.

Without any more information, I'll just be shooting at dust motes. It will be hard to hold in my outrage if it turns out Finn's been hurting this old man, even if he is bad.

I turn away and move toward the bedroom door.

A couple of seconds after I knock, the key turns in the lock. Finn must have stationed himself a few feet from the bedroom. He opens the door, then stares wide eyed at me like a teenaged boy at his date on prom night. His eyes skim my outfit, and he smiles.

"Very nice, Zara. You look like Ava Gardner, even down to her famous cleft in the chin."

Ava Gardner, hmm. Famous actress, beautiful, tall, dark-haired. I saw her recently in the movie version of *Showboat*. Am I her surrogate? Ava Gardner always took on tough but feminine roles. In the movies she's nobody's fool. She operates independently of the traditional woman's roll of the fifties. Okay, I'll play the Ava Gardner type. I gesture toward my bare feet. "No shoes?"

"A real queen doesn't need them."

I step out into the hallway, narrowing my eyes at him. "Yeah? Well, just so you know, I'm still a warrior queen."

He chuckles. "Very well, Your Highness, please accompany me." He holds up his arm for me.

I balk and refuse to take his arm. "Why? Where are you taking me?"

He ignores my question, takes my hand, and pulls me down the hall. I want to whip my hand away, but what if he hits me again? He's so confident, so arrogant, I wish I could knee him in the groin and make his face show a world of hurt. But I'll go along with this, and maybe I'll figure him out. Is he a cat that likes to play with his victim before he crunches it? Or does Finn actually believe that I'm his "queen"? It sounds crazy, but if he really is a madman, it might be easier to play into it and somehow build his trust.

As we head toward the kitchen, I'm hoping I'll spot some stairs that maybe lead to a front exit. I'd like to count the number of stairs and see how far they are from the front door. But instead, he nudges me to turn right and to go through a doorway. We're standing on a narrow landing and beyond that is a spiral staircase. I hesitate, aware that Finn is pulling my hand, urging me to follow, and he clearly doesn't appreciate that I'm resisting. The light from behind makes his shadow on the steps long and crooked, and as each descending stair grows dimmer and dimmer, I feel like I'm being escorted by the devil himself down to the blackness of hell. Am I really going downstairs to eat breakfast? Or am I being led down to a sound-proof torture room? My mouth is dry, and I'm hyperventilating. Finn's hand grips mine with that same snake-like power I'd felt on our first meeting down the road from my house.

Every fiber in every muscle is twitching, urging me to break away and run. But where would I go? At the foot of the stairs, I look through the doorway and see a kitchen. I exhale and then take the first normal breath I've had for at least thirty seconds. Everything's stainless steel, even the counters, like a restaurant kitchen. I'm guessing that it's underneath the bedroom where I'm being held, which explains why I smelled the coffee and toast up there.

Finn leads me to a table on the other end of the kitchen. It's been set with a white tablecloth and real silverware, with red roses in a crystal vase in the center. He pulls out a chair and seats me. Bizarre. Okay, so the creep is giving me the royal, or should I say "queen," treatment. I'm surprised he's not serving pâté au foie gras and champagne.

I check the table for anything I could use to defend myself. But there are no knives except for the useless, dull, butter-spreader types. So, I resign myself to sitting still. To be Beauty to his Beast. I daintily place my napkin on my lap.

"Coffee, Zara?" He lifts a silver coffeepot.

"Please." Up until this moment, I've never tasted coffee. When I was a teen, Mom and Dad always said coffee would stunt my growth. Even when I was in college, I never started drinking coffee. I drank lots of herbal tea. But Finn seems to need me to play some character, and I'm willing to try it to maintain the fantasy he's invented. I add a splash of cream and sugar.

I taste the coffee, which, to my surprise, is delicious. "Umm," I murmur. "Thank you. This is all lovely."

Finn looks pleased. He hands me a serving dish laden with scrambled eggs and thick slices of bacon.

"So," I say as I help myself to a serving, while forcing myself to sound cordial, "you spoke of the man in the bed as your papa. By the way he is being cared for, you must love your father very much."

"Grandfather. Mine and Clooney's. His name is Niall."

Finn doesn't say anything else, which makes my stomach tense up again. He's watching me, watching how I butter my toast and spread jelly on top. He seems to be fascinated with my hands. I have long slender fingers with tapered ends, perfect for a hand model. Except my hands bear scars from throwing bales of hay and other farming work.

He spreads his napkin and takes a breath, like he's going to speak, but still he doesn't.

I pause in my jelly spreading and look at him earnestly. "He's your grandfather?"

Finn meets my gaze and nods solemnly. "Yes. He's very ill. Lung cancer. We keep him sedated, or he becomes quite agitated."

"Oh. I wondered why he didn't wake up when I moved around the room."

"Yes, he's very uncomfortable."

"If you'll pardon me for asking, but why isn't he in a hospital?"

Finn's mouth hardens, his whole body tenses, and I get ready to dodge his iron fist.

"Hospitals." He practically spits out the word. "Dirty places. A breeding ground for every kind of bacteria. Sick people are in hospitals. Can you imagine putting your papa in such a place?"

"Well, now that you say that—"

"There's nothing they can do for my papa that we can't do ourselves. I've hired a nurse. Did you know that?"

I shake my head. "No, I had no idea." My heart flutters at the possibility of getting a message to someone outside of this house. "That's wonderful that you take care of your papa. I admire nurses. I wouldn't know the first thing about taking care of a dying patient."

His eyebrow shoots upward. "That is surprising. Have you not been around dying people?"

"Only a few times. It's awful to see people suffer. Nothing bothers me more than that. But nurses know so much about the body and how to ease suffering." Why would Finn want me with his grandfather if he already has a nurse?

"You care very much about others' pain, don't you, Zara?" Finn's eyes are probing.

"Oh, yes. Sometimes I feel as if I need to give my life to save someone."

"Yes," he murmurs. "I thought that the first time I ever saw you."

I shouldn't have said that about giving my life. It made his eyes narrow. I tremble again, like that day Finn and Clooney grabbed me. I shove a hunk of toast into my mouth so I don't say anything else that could be used against me.

"I saw you on the news ... with that little boy who would have died except for you. You put your hands on him, and he didn't die. He didn't die, Zara." He looks in my eyes like he expects me to catch his meaning.

"And that farm hand that you healed. That was amazing."

I chew but struggle to swallow my toast because my mouth is still dry. "You're asking me to do something for your grandfather?"

"Papa is ill. He's going to die unless you put your hands on him."

"You're so sure I can help him. What if I can't?"

"I know you can. You're a healer. That's what healers do." He pours his coffee, stirs cream and sugar into it, tastes it, and nods as if he's doctored it just right. "Besides, I find that daughters who care about their families generally will do much to assure their safety."

"My family?"

"Yes, Zara, your family. You do want to make sure they don't die, don't you?"

"What? You wouldn't ... you're not ... are you saying that ..." My throat dries up. I stare at him, at Finn, the monster. Finn, the man who seems to be saying he'll hurt my mom and dad and other family members. The hair at the base of my neck is up like a cat's, and I wish I had cat claws so I could impale Finn with them.

"Jim and Astrid Nielsen. They're such nice people. Salt of the earth. I can see they love you very much. Just before we locked them inside their eight-by-eight windowless room, sweet Mom said, 'Please don't hurt our baby. Do anything to me, but let Zara go.'"

I open my mouth to take in more air, but it's not getting into my lungs. My head is swimming. "You ... you took my mom and dad?"

"Oh, they're quite safe, for the time being. Not entirely comfortable. But safe."

My eyes flash and I jump up. "I don't believe you. You're just saying that. You ... you're just a small-time thug. How could you kidnap my parents?"

"Would you like to speak to them? I can reach them on a cell phone."

"Get them," I demand, but I'm choking because my throat is closing off. "Get them now!" Tears stream down my cheeks, but they're not from sorrow. They're from rage. Why does Abba let people like Finn live?

Finn rises and saunters over to a high cabinet fitted with a combination lock. He returns with a phone, punches in a series of numbers, and listens. A man answers.

"Put Zara's mother on the phone." Finn hands the phone to me.

My hands shake as I listen for Mom's voice. I hear some scared breathing and then a woman's quaking voice. The reception is awful, and I hardly recognize her voice. "Zara, Zara? Baby, are you okay? Where are you?"

I've never heard my mom sound like this. "Mom," I say in hardly more than a whisper. All my energy has left my throat and gone to my arms and legs. "I'm okay. I don't know where—"

Finn grabs the phone. "That's enough. Now you both know you're alive."

"What are you going to do to them? Where are they?" I'm so mad, spittle spurts out of my mouth.

Finn lays the phone on the table. "Not far from home. Please sit down, Zara. You look positively apoplectic."

My mind is like a wheel's hub, and thoughts shoot out in every direction. *Who are you guys? How could you do this to me? My parents? Where am I? Am I in a city? Which city? What do you plan to do to me?*

But I don't ask because he might think my anger and fear will make me refuse to heal his papa. He doesn't know how my healing works. And I mean to keep him from knowing about it, because his not knowing just might save my life. I have to find out where my parents are. To get away and contact the police. And warn Abby and Rolf.

Finn looks at me like he can read my thoughts. "And just in case you're thinking that you could somehow call the police, you can forget about it. If you try to talk to them—or anyone else, for that matter—we'll execute your parents immediately. Oh, and I wouldn't like to hurt that pretty blond sister of yours or her cute little baby."

His words spear my gut. All the air rushes out of my lungs, and I close my eyes so I can't see the face of my parents' murderer. I need a plan. I need to survive. *Abba, if you want to keep flowing through me, you've got to help me get away.*

"Where are they? What are you doing to them? Let me talk to them again."

Finn shakes his head slowly. "That was enough for today. Perhaps later, I'll give you another tidbit."

Finn escorts me upstairs to my prison. I shake with pent-up rage, and I wish I could throw myself on him and kick and punch him and gouge out his eyes.

When he closes my door and locks it, I run to my bed and throw myself onto it, sobbing.

CHAPTER SIX

After he locked Zara back in her bedroom, Finn sauntered back down the stairs to take care of the breakfast dishes. Clooney pounced on him by the sink.

"Wha'd she say? She gonna put her hands on Papa? Today?"

"It'll happen." Finn soaped up a cup and rinsed it.

Clooney grimaced. "We don't have a whole lot of time. Evgeni is due to sign that contract in two weeks.

Finn set the cup in the dish drainer. "Even if Papa doesn't recover, I'm learning the language, so that old cheater won't be able to use our not speaking Russian as an excuse not to deal with us."

Clooney screwed up his mouth. "There's more than just the language barrier. Papa and Evgeni go way back. Papa told me Evgeni's got tons of other contacts he'd rather use than me and you. What if Evgeni finds some other company to move his stuff in the meantime?"

Finn shook his head and frowned. "Maybe Papa told you that as a kind of life insurance policy."

Clooney made a rude gesture with his middle finger.

Finn sighed. "Clooney, you haven't exactly been clever about hiding your hatred for Papa."

"Whether I love Papa or hate him is beside the point." Clooney snagged a piece of bacon off a plate before Finn could brush it into the garbage, and popped it into his mouth. "Right now, we need him alive. So I'm telling you, the girl's got one week to do her thing. Otherwise ..." He formed his hand into a gun and pulled the trigger.

Finn whipped his hands out of the dishwater and shoved Clooney against the counter, holding him by the shoulders, making him wince. "Look, you sadistic Cheetos-encrusted bowl of jelly, I'm enjoying my little fantasy of the week. So don't go cheating me out of the best fun I've had in years. Zara's a classy young lady, and you know I enjoy playing with the ladies. So butt out"—he gave Clooney's backbone another grind into the counter—"and let me enjoy my recreation."

He grabbed a dish towel and wiped his hands. "And furthermore, don't even think about talking to the girl. She's all mine to deal with. Ladies are convinced by genteel ways and romance, not threats of violence."

Clooney winced when he slid his back away from the counter. "You got one, maybe two of your stupid parties, and then, if she hasn't done her work, I'm stepping in."

Somebody worked on the old man while I was downstairs with Finn. A fresh IV bag dangles above Niall. He's been cleaned up and shaved, and the sheets are fresh. I hang out close to his bed, hoping he'll wake up, and then, I can introduce myself and find out more about him. Maybe he can convince Finn to let me go.

There's nothing in the bathroom I can use to pick the lock on the bedroom door or to jimmy the nails in the window. I wander the room, checking out impossible places where I could hide or break out. My only hope is talking to the old man or asking the nurse to help.

One of the man's frail hands moves slightly. I put my hand on it and stroke it ever so gently. "Old man, can you hear me?" His hand is so cold. The veins stand out like blue cords on top of the shriveled, mottled skin. His jaw is slack.

"Old man, wake up. I need to talk to you. You're the only one I can talk to. Please wake up."

I probably shouldn't do this, but I jiggle his shoulder a little. And then he makes a sound. His voice is husky but deep. It's not a word, just a moan.

His eyes flutter, close, open again, and I get a good look at faded blue eyes. He stares at the ceiling as if it were his mother and he a newborn child. His mouth works, and his teeth are surprisingly okay for someone who looks ninety years old.

"Muh," he says.

"Papa? Niall?" I try, and almost jump when his torso lurches and his hands fly outward. His white caterpillar eyebrows bunch for a few seconds while he stares at my face.

"Papa? Are you Finn's papa?"

He looks down at my hands, then back up at my face, and I see the white all around his pupils, the way a steer's eyeballs widen when it's being led to slaughter.

"My name is Zara." I point to my chest and repeat, "Zara." Does he understand, or is his mind that far gone? "Finn wanted me to visit with you."

"Finn," he utters with difficulty.

"Yes, Finn thought I could sit with you and ... and ... pray for you." I wait to see how he reacts to my words. Will he get more upset, or will he continue to stare as if my words mean nothing?

Abba, Abba, I need this to go well so that the awful men don't get riled and put a bullet through my head.

"... see you ..." The first part of his directive doesn't make it through his throat, but the wave of his hand makes it clear that he wants me to move to the front of the bed so he can see me.

When I'm in his range of sight, his gaze begins at my hair and travels downward to my dress, and he nods in approval. "Pretty girl," he rasps.

It's not a nice look on his face, because it resembles Finn's expression, and my stomach rebels.

I know right away that telling Papa I've been kidnapped is not something he's in any condition to hear. And who knows—maybe he'd approve of my being taken. I can't tell yet if the old man has all his wits and is on heavy painkillers or if he's demented as well as terminal.

I wish I could simply put my hands on him and heal him, and then Finn would be satisfied and maybe they'd let me go.

But that's not how it works. The power doesn't come from me. I'm only a conduit. *Abba, won't you come now and work through me?* I raise my arms in a gesture of supplication and wait. And wait. But no sweet-smelling breeze moves me closer to Papa's bed. No heat blasts through my hands.

Papa Niall's eyes are filled with questions. He forms his mouth into a small round shape, and I know he's asking who I am.

I lower my hands in defeat. "My name is Zara. Zara Nielsen. I'm from Titusville, Iowa. Finn and Clooney asked me to come here and spend some time with you."

He nods slightly.

"Is there something I can do for you? Would you like me to get you some water?"

He shuts his eyes and shakes his head.

Just then, I hear the key in the lock. Finn stands framed in the door, looking surprised and pleased to see me talking to his grandfather. Papa's eyes fly open, and he turns to his grandson.

I move aside. Finn comes up to the bedside and takes his grandfather's hand. Papa makes a motion, and Finn bends close to his mouth. Whatever Papa said to Finn makes him chuckle. It couldn't have been very nice, because Finn looks over at me with that same cold, teasing expression he'd worn this morning.

"No, not yet, Papa."

He lets go of Papa's hand and motions for me to follow him to the bathroom. "Have you talked to Papa yet?" he asks when we're out of earshot.

"We were just getting acquainted when you showed up," I say with a slight edge.

I'm nervous and suspicious about what the two were saying a minute ago. Papa Niall is not some innocent old man, and if he can joke with Finn, then he must have some wits about him.

"Why don't you just let me go?" I blurt out in a fierce whisper. "Do you really think kidnapping me and punching me is going to convince me to heal your Papa?"

"Hmm. I think you'd look better with your hair up."

It's obvious he's heard my question and is ignoring it. He takes me by the shoulders and turns me so that we're both facing the vanity mirror. I freeze when he takes a brush from the bathroom counter and brushes my hair smooth. He takes some bobby pins out of his pocket to pin my hair up.

Aha! After he leaves, I can try one of the pins on the door.

"There, that's much better. It shows your pretty neck. Just like Ava Gardner."

He repositions one of the hairpins. "You were saying?"

I look at his reflection in the mirror. I get it. He means to show me how little I matter. My fear means nothing.

"I'm glad you chose that dress today. It's exactly the one I would have chosen for our date tonight."

"Date ... tonight?" I ask stupidly.

"Yes, tonight is *Mogambo* night. That's why I've been mentioning Ava Gardner."

He waits for me to show him any sign I know what he's talking about. When I don't respond, he sighs and says, "Have you never seen the famous movie with Clark Gable, Ava Gardner, and Grace Kelly set in Africa?"

He sweeps his hands down on either side of me. "You're wearing her dinner-party dress. And I'll be in Clark Gable garb. Oh, I know you're a bit young to play Ava, but with a touch of lipstick, you could pass for twenty-seven or twenty-eight."

Freakin' looney.

"I'll pick you up at seven p.m. Oh, and wear the cologne. Play up your eyebrows too, a la 1950s."

He leaves me, still standing helpless at the mirror.

CHAPTER SEVEN

I hunker on my little bed in the corner, trying to figure out other ways to escape. I'd pulled out one of the bobby pins and tried to pick the lock on my door, but it wasn't strong enough. So, I tried using two, but that was too thick and didn't work. Then I straightened them both and tried again. No luck. And since these two bobby pins were the only ones Finn slid into my hair, I had to bend them both into their original shape and redo my hair.

I wonder what Aunt Evelyn would have done if she'd ever been imprisoned. I only have a few memories of her. One is of Aunt and me sitting on the back porch swing and her telling me how she loved all the "sweet critters on God's green earth." But the other memory isn't so nice. On one of her rare visits, she had stayed in my bedroom, so I'd bunked with Abby across the hall. I skipped into my bedroom to get one of my dolls and found Aunt Evelyn sitting on the floor, unspeakably sad, tears streaming down her face and onto her blouse. I burst into tears, and she held out her arms for me. She held me and rocked me and made a low moaning sound. Of course, at five years old I didn't understand her pain.

"Zara, you'll be a much better one than I was," she had whispered.

I'm pretty sure that's what she said. Sometimes we rewrite things people have said, so I hope I remember that accurately.

She disappeared not long after that. None of us knew where she had gone or why. Later, a letter came from a friend who had been close to Aunt Evelyn. She had died. A few years later, I overheard my mom use the word "suicide." But when I think about it now, years later, I don't know if anyone knew for sure.

But thinking about my aunt's suicide makes me realize it's suicide for me to stay here and not attempt an escape. Finn and Clooney are murderers, and they're not going to let me go even if I heal their Papa. They'll dispose of all of us once I'm no longer needed. If I escape, maybe there's a way to find my parents.

"You look lovely," Finn says while standing at the entrance to my bedroom. He surveys my white party dress, my stud earrings, and my makeup. He's hiding something behind his back, and I tense up when he pulls it out and hands it to me.

"Oh, it's a shoebox."

He looks confused. "Of course. What did you think it would be? These should fit." He opens the box, revealing a pair of red spike heels. He crouches and slips them onto my feet. After he stands, he brushes a stray hair away from my face. I'm five-ten, and with the shoes on I'm nearly as tall as Finn. "We're about to go outside, Zara. But don't think that escape is within the realm of possibility for you."

I don't believe him. My heart is drumming at the thought of all the things I could try once we're outside. I could scream or pretend to have a seizure or do something weird to bring attention to us.

"Here are the rules. Number one, do not try to escape. I have a gun, and I will use it to stop you." He opens his suit coat to reveal the gun holstered under his left arm.

"Number two, do not try to get anyone to help you. Especially the police. Your parents' lives—indeed, those of your entire family—depend on this. Additionally, the people you're about to meet at our gathering love to role-play. So anything you say to them will only be perceived by them as acting."

He pulls a pair of sunglasses out of his pocket. "Number three, do not try to remove these unless and until I say you can." His fits them over my eyes.

The lenses have been painted black, and I cannot see anything but a tiny rim of light that pours in from the sides.

You dumb donkey, I still have my voice.

But as if he's already guessed my thought, he says, "And now for the pièce de résistance ... Open your mouth." He stuffs some fabric into my mouth, ties a scarf around my face just below my sunglasses, and lowers another piece of fabric over my head. I reach up to finger it. It's like a head scarf that a devout Muslim woman would wear.

"Careful, now. Don't mess with perfection."

His fingers straighten out the fabric around my neck and tug it farther down over my forehead.

"Now we're ready to go." He takes my arm and guides me down the hallway. We turn right. "Four steps."

I hold on to his arm, sensing the movement of his thigh so that we step together.

"Turn left. Step down."

I obey and count twenty steps till we reach the end of the staircase.

"Wait here." I hear him walk on carpet, then wood floor. A door squeaks. Hangers are moved. The door closes.

I jump when I feel his hands on my shoulders. My skin prickles at his touch. He slips a coat over my outfit. It's long enough to brush the tops of my shoes.

We go through a door, and currents of air brush my forehead. City smells penetrate through the scarf over my nose. I smell restaurants, wet pavement, my sweat, and Finn's now-familiar cologne.

Freedom seems inches away. My body tenses for the right time to spring away.

I try to count the number of steps we take and how the pavement feels. My heels go click, click, but I can hardly hear Finn's shoes. I keep my breathing steady so he doesn't hear my fear. Where are we going? Is there something more to this little walk than just a party and role-playing? Two hundred and thirty-nine steps, then we take a right.

"You're definitely going to be the most beautiful Ava Gardner at the party," Finn says, and I lose count of my steps.

I can't answer, so I just give him a muffled "Uh."

He sounds upbeat. "I can think of at least three other ladies who'll be Ava tonight. Unfortunately, they're all too old to carry it off. So you, my dear, will be greatly admired."

I fight the gag, trying to get my tongue behind it so I can push it forward and out of my mouth. My knees have that awful feeling you get when you have to stand up in front of a hundred people and give a speech. Cars zing by, and I'm tempted to whip my right arm out of his grasp and dash into traffic. Something diesel passes, probably a bus. I make a little movement to check how tight he's holding me.

Finn's grip tightens. "Don't even think of it," he hisses. "Just remember rule number one."

Using my left arm, I pretend to scratch my forehead but shift my blacked-out sunglasses so I can see out the side. I wish I could see people coming toward us, but a side view shows only bits of parked cars and whizzing vehicles.

Finn stops suddenly, guides me to the right, then downstairs. He pulls me through an entrance, and I hear music and peoples' voices.

He stops. "Okay, you can take off your sunglasses."

I squint in the glare of bright lights, music bombarding my ears. Twenty-five or thirty people mill around, talking, gesturing, dancing.

Finn removes my headdress and unties my scarf.

I claw the wad of cloth out of my mouth and fill my lungs so I can launch a screaming "Help me!" missile. But Finn is watching me closely. He grips my shoulder, squeezing hard enough to make me wince, and tears spring into my eyes.

"None of these people give a flying fig that you've been kidnapped. None of them will help you, so don't waste your breath."

I release all the stored air in my lungs in one giant exhale while he removes my long coat. There's a hush in the conversation, and several people look my way. I was wrong. Close to forty people are in this crowded little basement room.

A short man in a British uniform rushes over. "I say, Mr. Finnegan, where did you find this delicate flower? She makes Carolyn look like a cactus in comparison."

Finn still has his hand on my shoulder. "Caruthers, if I told you, I'd be giving away a trade secret."

Caruthers stares me up and down, as if he were a fashion designer. "The fit is perfect. Simple and elegant, the hemline exactly where Ava wears hers, just the right kind of jewelry. Your lady really doesn't even need makeup, her skin is so gorgeous." He leans in close. "Tell me, sweetheart, are you a college theater student?"

"I ... uh ... I ... I mean ..."

Finn interrupts me by sliding his arm around my waist. "Let's keep the illusion alive, Caruthers. She's Ava, plain and simple. No more questions."

"Who's the new girl?" A red-haired woman in a white dress asks while dancing up to Finn in a provocative way. She snakes her fingers up to his collar and strokes the fabric. When she turns her head to me, her eyes glow with curiosity but not friendliness. "You didn't tell me you were bringing a date, Finn."

She's got rings on all her fingers, purple and black nail color, and four piercings on her face.

"At a party this size, I figured we need another Ava," Finn replies, and the woman gives me an insincere smile before dancing back into the group in the middle of the room.

Finn steers me to a bistro-sized table against the wall.

A young woman walks by who's about the same height and size as me, with long dark hair. She's wearing a khaki top and skirt. Most of the people are middle age, and I wonder why this young woman is participating. I wish I could talk to someone, but Finn is closely guarding me.

The music stops, and the dancers head to their tables and turn their chairs to face the left wall, where a screen has been set up. Lights are turned off. The opening credits begin for *Mogambo*. As soon as the action starts, people call out the lines of the characters in the scene. It's hard to hear the real actors' voices over all the posers. Everybody's so into the dialogue, I wonder if I can slip away and find the women's restroom. Maybe there's a way to escape in there. Or maybe there's a kitchen with a back entrance.

I start to rise, but Finn clasps my arm. "Where do you think you're going?"

"I ... I need the restroom."

"No, you don't." He doesn't even look at me. He's glued to the screen and the real Ava Gardner.

My mind and heart race with alternative plans. What if I just dash to the front entrance? No, that won't work. Finn would be on me before I could even reach the door. What if I play sick and he has to take me to the restroom? Wouldn't work. He'd know I was faking, and then I couldn't use that excuse again if I ever needed it. What if I faint or have a seizure? Something to get other people's attention. Then maybe, if someone gets close enough, I can whisper "Help. I've been kidnapped."

Finn's calling out Clark Gable's lines. He's totally into his tough-man part, giving Ava Gardner some hard looks. I stare at the screen, then back at Finn. It's like he's in another zone. Mrs. Nordley, who's played by Grace Kelly—I recognize her from some other movie I'd seen—and her husband arrive on a boat. Sounds of African animals bawl in the distance. The couple come up the wood stairs to Clark Gable's ramshackle house. The women in the room who are dressed in Mrs. Nordley's costume call out her dialogue. One tall, heavyset lady stands up to say her lines. She doesn't look like Grace Kelly, but she's into Grace Kelly's fake British accent.

Finn is clearly annoyed because she's blocking his view. A man—I think it's Caruthers—says, "I say, Athena, kindly sit down please."

Athena looks angry, but she weaves through the tables and stands on the side so she can still say Mrs. Nordley's lines.

I'm claustrophobic in this little crowded room with a madman guarding me and crazy people acting crazy. I can't breathe. I jump up before Finn can stop me, and shout, "I've been kidnapped! Somebody help me."

Finn grabs me and claps his hand over my mouth. "That's not the right line, my dear," he hisses in my ear and drags me down onto my chair again.

A man dressed in khakis turns and glares at me. "If you can't do the right lines, then just don't speak at all. Be considerate of the others."

That's it. No one else even acknowledges my cry for help. It's like they're zombies or live in some alternate universe where reality doesn't exist. I gasp for air, tears running down my cheeks.

"Oh, for heaven's sake, go get yourself cleaned up. Your mascara is running down your face." Finn pulls me to my feet and escorts me to the back of the room, around a wall, and down a corridor. We pass a door marked *Gentlemen* and come to the women's restroom.

"You've got five minutes. I don't appreciate missing *Mogambo*." He shoves me through the door and slams it shut.

I'm alone in a two-stall restroom. I take in the walls, the one sink and vanity. There's a small window high up.

Maybe I could use the trash can to reach it. But once up there, would I be able to open it wide enough to even fit through? I check the ceiling in case there's an attic, but no luck.

I flush a toilet and run water so Finn will think I'm doing what he wants. I dry my face. When I come out of the restroom, he hurries me back to our table.

The rest of the movie is a blur because I'm thinking about what I saw in the back corridor—two extra doors. One was clearly an emergency exit. The other? Don't know yet. Finn mentioned that these movie parties are a weekly event. If I'm still alive next week, I'm going to find a way to get out that back door.

The next morning, Finn arrives to Papa's room with my breakfast tray. He gives me a "shame on you" look. "That was very foolish of you last night, Zara."

"Foolish, because I tried to get free from a kidnapper?" I keep my voice low because of Papa Niall sleeping a few feet away. "If you were in my shoes, wouldn't you try to get away?"

"You know what you have to do to gain your freedom." He pours my coffee and stirs in cream and sugar.

"You promise you'll let me go, and my parents too, if I heal your papa?"

He doesn't even blink. "Of course."

I won't go near him. I don't believe his promise. Last night he was rough and threatening, and I'm afraid he'll lash out and hurt me worse. The bruises from when he gripped my wrist are still throbbing, and I can feel his black heart and tension.

Staying at least ten feet away, I say, "Finn, you seem upset. Last night, you were enjoying the movie and speaking the parts."

"It's you, Zara. You trouble me."

"Why is that?" I inch a little closer.

"You're so kind, so gentle. It's like there's a light shining through you." He trudges over to the boudoir chair and slumps onto it, leans over his knees, and puts his head in his hands. When I follow him, he peers through his fingers, then closes them around his face again.

"I am kind, Finn."

"But you won't help me." He turns away from me, as if the sight of me wounds him.

His shoulders tense and his fingers turn white as he presses them into his skull.

"I will help you in any way that is good."

"Don't you want to save my life?"

"Is ... is your life in danger, Finn?" Funny, I sense no fear in him.

"I need Papa Niall to get better." His voice breaks. "If he doesn't, bad things will happen to me. Bad things will happen, Zara." He turns and looks up at me, and actual tears well in his eyes. "It makes me ... It makes me ... afraid." He drops his head back into his hands, takes a huge shuddering breath and lets it slide out accompanied by whimpers of fear.

Insincerity drips off him like sewage from a cracked pipe. But what if there's a small percentage of real fear in him that I missed? I have to know.

In spite of my fear and loathing of the man, his wet eyes ignite compassion in my chest. I ease my hands onto his shoulders. If only I could believe him *Abba, please help me know the truth.*

Finn's shoulders are like a sculpture. It's hard to believe the man is human. My fingers tremble from just touching the monster who kidnapped me and threatens to murder my family. Colors swirl in my brain. Gun-metal gray, browns of dying weeds, murky underwater depths, currents making dead things sway back and forth. In spite of his cologne, other odors flow into my nostrils, all awful, like skunk and stink beetle and carrion mixed together in a witchy brew.

I jerk my hands away and back up cautiously, like from a rearing cobra. There is no sorrow or fear in him. I want to sneeze on him, to release the awful odors of death filling my nostrils.

The colossal phony.

CHAPTER EIGHT

For the last twelve hours, Papa Niall has been awake for longer periods. Finn said he'd asked the nurse not to drug his papa so much. Where is that darned nurse? How could I get a definitive message to this elusive person, to let him or her know I'm here, a prisoner, threatened with death?

While the old man slept last night, I used some lipstick to scrawl a message on the underside of his hospital gown's hem, hoping the nurse, who comes in every day, will see it when changing his sheets. *Help. Please call police. Kidnapped.*

Clooney takes me out of the room regularly—probably so the nurse can work on their papa—and holds me in the kitchen. Unlike Finn, Clooney doesn't talk to me. He hardly looks at me. Just stuffs his face with whatever he can find in the fridge. Doesn't he ever bathe? His hair is greasy, and he has bad breath. And he doesn't even try to hide his murderous thoughts from me. He takes phone calls and curses and threatens and practically spits at the people he's talking to. The fact that he doesn't hide his criminal plans tells me I'll never get out of this house alive. Unless I make it happen myself.

I've tried talking to Clooney, but he ignores me. He looks at me like I'm a chicken or cow and he can't wait until it's slaughter time. Also, he won't come near me once he has me in the kitchen. Maybe he thinks I'm a witch and my touch might do something weird to him. Or maybe he suspects I can feel people's intents, so he tries to put distance between us. It's a good thing he doesn't know how much I've already read in him.

After an hour of being around him, I'm almost relieved when Finn comes downstairs and takes me back to my room.

I rack my brain to figure out a way of escaping from the basement room where we attended the Reel to Real party—Finn spelled it out for me, to make sure I understood the wordplay—a few days ago. That room seems to be the only spot I could possibly make my move.

I'd wondered if there was a way I could put something in Finn or Clooney's coffee. But there's no aspirin or sleeping pills in my bathroom and nothing remotely useful for drugging that I can glimpse in the kitchen cupboards. Besides, Clooney watches me like a predator, and Finn is way too clever to let me 'help out' with food preparation.

Finn is about halfway up the back staircase with me when he receives a text. He stops to read it. "Excellent, truly excellent. Zara, you're going to love this news. We've got another movie party coming up."

My torso reacts, but I keep myself from jumping up and down in excitement. My stomach does the butterfly thing, and adrenaline zips through my arms and legs. But I make my voice sound bored. "What?"

"*The Big Sleep.*"

I shrug. "Okay, so what's that?" Actually, I've seen this movie, and I absolutely loved it.

"Don't they ever watch movies in Iowa?" He looks at me like I live under a rock. "Humphrey Bogart and Lauren Bacall. Now that's some dynamite duo. Lauren Bacall plays Vivien, this beautiful, sophisticated, spoiled rich girl. When Vivien says, 'You've forgotten one thing. Me.' And he says, 'What's wrong with you?' And she says, 'Nothing you can't fix.'" Finn sighs. "The way she says it." He licks his lips like he's savoring a wonderful dish. "What a girl."

He starts walking again, but he doesn't tell me if the party will be at the same location as before, and I'm afraid to ask, in case he might get suspicious that I'm plotting something.

"Have you touched my papa yet?" he says. "He really needs your healing touch, Zara."

"I, uh, I've needed him t-to be conscious," I stutter, trying to think of an excuse.

He stops and looks confused. "But you touched that little boy and the farm guy, and they weren't conscious."

"Well, uh, they … were …"

"I thought you said the boy was in a coma."

My brain sends alarm signals all over my body, and my mouth goes dry. I need to be careful what I say. "They're all different. I never know when I can touch them. It's … it's like a drive … that comes from outside myself. I … have to wait for it."

Finn's eyes narrow, and he studies me like he's sure I'm playing him. "Because if I thought you were simply refusing to heal my papa, I'd—"

"No, no, I wouldn't do that," I say quickly, electric shocks jolting my brain. "I care for him. I want him to be well." My hands fidget, so I put them behind my back. "This thing … that I do. It's something I don't understand. I don't seem to have control of it. It … it comes when it comes."

"Well, you'd better make it come pretty soon. I don't know how much longer I can protect you from Clooney."

"What?" I back up against the stairwell wall and glare at Finn. My throat closes off, and I picture Clooney's hands squeezing the life out of me. When I'm dead, no one will find me. No one will ever know whatever became of me. And Mom and Dad will die too.

"Little brother likes to snuff people," he adds, slowly swiveling his head back and forth with a concerned look on his face. "Zara, I want to help you, but you've got a day or two, three at most."

He takes me by the arm and leads me upstairs. The sickness in my stomach churns like the ocean in a hurricane, and I feel like I'm going to faint. *Why, Abba? Why won't you make this right? Where are you?*

When we get to my prison door, he reaches out like he's going to caress my cheek, but I jerk away and turn my head. It's not only that he disgusts me—the big fake—and that he just threatened me. It's so I can wipe away tears and force myself to look fearless. For whatever good that does. Whether I'm fearless or not, he's still going kill me.

"Have it your way," he says softly, as if my rejection hurts his feelings. He opens the door and waits for me to enter, then closes it after me and keys the lock.

Papa is awake. I can't hold it in. I run and throw myself onto his feeble chest, sobbing. He makes a surprised sound, but I know I haven't hurt him. "Help me, sir!" I take one of his hands, stroking his wrinkled skin. "Please don't let your boys hurt me." I feel his other hand on my head. He pats it softly.

"You're a good girl," he says while continuing to pat my head. "A good girl."

I look up and see he looks sad. "Please, sir, won't you tell your boys to let me go home? I just want to go home." I can't say anything more, because I'm sobbing again.

I almost can't hear him, he's speaking so softly. "My Finn, he loves the ladies. I can see why he loves you, pretty girl."

Papa doesn't have a clue what's going on. Is it the meds, or is he senile? "B-but, Finn's keeping me here against my will, sir. That's ... against the ... law." I try to control my sobbing. "He's going t-to hurt ... me."

I lift his hand and keep stroking it. "Papa, Finn intends to kill me." I stare into his face for any sign that he comprehends what I'm saying. But he lifts one side of his mouth into a kind of mocking smile.

"That boy. He loves his movies. He said you're his best Ava Gardner."

"No, no, no!" I raise my voice, looking over my shoulder to make sure Finn hasn't snuck into the room. "This is not a movie. It's for real. Papa, this is real. Finn is going to kill me. Really kill me, in real life. A real-life murder. Not a movie. Please tell him to let me go!"

I press his cold hand to my cheek, and my hot tears roll over it. Papa makes a strange moan and tries to pull his hand from mine. My tears on his hand have turned into ribbons of ice. When he moves his hand, the ice cracks and crackles, and the chips fall onto the mattress.

"Go away," he murmurs. "I'm cold, so cold."

I'm still crying, but I stand and cover him with the extra blanket at the foot of the bed.

The key turns in the lock. My body trembles, and I jump away from Papa's bed. I'm expecting Finn, but it's Clooney, and his movements spell trouble.

"So, you're waiting for the right time, huh?" His face is red, and his nostrils flare like a bull ready to charge. "You—" He calls me a horrible name. "How 'bout I make it the right time?" He pulls out the gun he keeps holstered under his arm, points it at me, and advances.

"I-I'm. I-I-I'm trying, Mr. Clooney." He's like that rabid dog underneath the tree, lunging and frothing at the mouth. I back farther into the corner of the room, but he keeps coming. He grabs me and stuffs me under his stinky arm, holding the gun to my head. Dragging me toward Papa's bed, he snarls, "Yer gonna do it now or yer gonna be dead. No more excuses."

He's crunching me so hard I can hardly breathe. When we reach the bed, he shoves me down over Papa, his foul breath blowing all over my face and hair. The room goes dark and cold, like I've been transported into a cave and light is way up high at the end. Clooney's breath is like poisonous smoke, and Papa's breath mixes with his. Around me, photos of dead people float on strands of smoke, moving in and out of focus. Photos of families standing beside coffins. Sounds of weeping.

I try to draw air, but my lungs are tar-filled and cancerous. I open my mouth to gasp, and I throw out my arms to hold on to something or someone. My nails scrape the sides of the cave. But it's slimy, and I can't hold on. No one can rescue me.

"No, no, no. Get her off me. I can't stand it," Papa cries.

"Do it! Do it, you witch!" Clooney yells. He's pressing me so hard into Papa's side that I can't even scream.

But Papa screams. An awful sound, part hiss, part high-pitched shriek.

"Clooney!" It's Finn's voice. My eyes are tight shut. Papa's darkness has manacled me to him.

Another set of hands pulls at my hands. "Get her off of him. She's killing him."

Clooney lets go of me, but it's too late. Together, Papa and I are being sucked downward, father and farther away from Abba's light.

When I wake, I'm lying on the floor next to Papa's hospital bed. I pull myself up and look around. Finn and Clooney are gone, thank Abba. When I get to my feet, I find Papa is missing. My head is fuzzy, but one thing I remember is Clooney's gun and touching Papa and feeling like hell was licking at my heels.

I glance at the door. Maybe he had to go to the hospital, and maybe they left in a hurry and didn't turn the lock. I hurry to the door and try the knob.

Locked. I pound on the door and scream out of frustration and don't care if anyone hears.

But when it's quiet and no one comes up to check, I scurry back to Papa's bed and search in the sheets for anything I can use as a tool to work on the lock. Nothing.

If only I could break a window and climb out. But they've thought of everything. Even if I could get the window open, they've got a security system—Finn told me—that would alert them.

The hairpins Finn had put in my hair for the *Mogambo* movie party were useless on the lock. And he made sure nothing else in the room could be stuck into the lock. A tweezer would be perfect. Just unbend the two ends and stick one end into the lock. It's stiff enough to turn a lock. Last year I locked myself out of the house. My mom and dad hardly ever use the deadbolt during the day, but I had a pair of tweezers in my purse, and it worked like a charm. I made it inside in just a few minutes of fiddling with the door lock. It's scary how easy it is to break into a house.

I go back to the window and examine the nails for the millionth time. I'd already thought to pull a couple of longish threads from a dress and had slid them under the nailhead. But that didn't work because the nails were embedded too deep.

Then I remember the small chest of drawers inside the closet. What if I could use one of those drawers to smash the window? I'm over there in a split second, throwing the door open. I pull out a drawer and dump its contents onto the floor. The corners just might do it. Solid wood. I carry it over to the bedroom window. How hard do I have to smash that glazed glass? And how many seconds do I have before someone comes running? Clooney with his gun, or Finn with his granite fist?

I raise the drawer over my head, taking a big breath, feeling the muscles in my arms and the power of my farm-girl grasp.

A door slams downstairs. Steps mount toward the upstairs hallway.

My courage goes cold at that sound. I run back to the closet and stuff the drawer into place. Finn opens the door before I can get all the stuff back inside the drawer.

He looks at me, at the drawer, then back at me, his eyes narrowed. Then he smiles. "Good. You're already getting ready."

He's not rushing over to beat me or threaten me, so maybe Papa is okay. I'm afraid to ask where he is. "Ready for what?"

"The party, of course. What else would it be?"

"Oh, you mean the movie with Humphrey Bogart and Lauren Cabal."

He rolls his eyes. "That's Bacall, sweetheart. Lauren Bacall. I've been waiting all year for this one." He reaches into his pocket, and I flinch. But instead of a gun, he removes a three-by-five black-and-white photo of a beautiful young woman with chiseled features, long hair, and icy blue eyes. "Too bad I don't have a wig for you, but just wear your hair like that. And wear the slinky beige gown."

"But?"

"Yes?"

His tone has an edge to it, and he raises his left eyebrow like he does when he's riled, so I hesitate. But I have to know. "What happened ... t-to your papa? Is he okay?"

"Oh that. He'll be fine. We took him to the hospital, and they treated him for mild hypothermia and low blood pressure. It happens to very old people, especially when they've been in bed a long time."

He looks over at Papa's bed and screws up his mouth like he's trying to figure something out. "I guess you weren't ready."

"No, the power didn't come over me."

"Something came over you." His eyes say he thinks I'm some kind of mutant.

"When I touch people, I read them."

"You mean like a medium or a fortune-teller?"

"No!" I say it so loud it's almost a shout. "I'm not one of those."

His eyes widen at my outburst. "Okay, so you're not a clairvoyant or a seer."

"He's dark, your papa. He has not had a good life. I sense death and betrayal and hatred."

"Is that stopping you from healing him?"

"No. I told you before—I have no say in this. Maybe your papa needs to pray to God for forgiveness. Your papa's darkness ... and yours and Clooney's are a big barrier to God's healing."

"You can forget about us praying," Finn says and adds a kind of demonic growl to emphasize his statement. Then, after regarding me thoughtfully for what seems like forever, he says, "So Clooney threatening you with his gun isn't going to work?"

"Absolutely not. It'll scare the crap out of me, but it won't bring the power."

He looks away and mutters, "That idiot Clooney."

"Cursing doesn't do any good either. Prayer helps though. Those people I touched. People were praying."

Finn's lip rears up like the head of a cobra. "Are *you* praying?"

"Always."

He doesn't say anything more, so I change the subject. "So where is Papa? Why isn't he here?"

"They're keeping him overnight for observation." His eyebrows lower. "I'm sorry about Clooney. He's kind of hotheaded. I lectured him about being rough with you. That won't happen again ... at least ... until ..." He trails off on purpose, I'm sure, to scare me.

"Oh, I almost forgot." He takes a small box out of his pocket. "Let me put this on you."

It's a pretty necklace, but I shiver at the thought that he's going to touch me to put it on. I'm still shaky and upset by what happened with Clooney. But I don't have any choice. I lift my hair and hold my breath while Finn's murderous hands work to connect the clasp and then drop the chain onto the back of my neck.

"There, that looks so nice." He takes a lock of my hair and arranges it along my neck. "Almost like the picture," he says, glancing at the photo in my hand. "Be ready by seven.

I can hardly wait." He turns and steps out the bedroom door.

"You bet I'll be ready, Mr. Monster Finn," I mutter. "I can hardly wait too." In my mind, I'm seeing the Reel to Real room, imagining how many steps I'll need to reach that emergency exit and possible freedom. And if I die, at least I died trying.

CHAPTER NINE

We do the same short walk, going two-hundred and forty-three steps, then a right turn and about the same amount of steps before we take the stairway down into the basement room. Finn had put the same oversized coat and the scarf on me. And the whole walk, I'm thinking about how I can escape during the movie.

The mood in the Reel to Real movie party for *The Big Sleep* is different. They've decorated the walls with movie posters. *Mogambo*'s posters were in color, but these ones are in black and white. They're playing music from the 1940s. I recognize the style because my grandparents liked to play records from that era.

The men are wearing baggy waist-high trousers with suspenders and suits with wide lapels. The women are wearing long gowns that cling to their bodies, though three or four of them are wearing gangster suits, just like the men. They've slicked their hair back with grease and topped their heads with men's hats. It looks awful, but whatever floats your boat, I guess.

I recognize the slim girl I saw at the *Mogambo* party who was wearing Mrs. Nordley's khaki outfit. She's one who opted to dress like a gangster. I guess it makes sense, since there aren't too many women's roles in *The Big Sleep*.

She comes up right away and barely gives Finn a glance. "Hi, I'm Calista. Well, actually I'm Eddie tonight."

Finn has his arm around my waist, and he squeezes me. I'm sure it looks affectionate, but it's a warning that anything I say can and will be used against me ... or my mom and dad.

"My name's Zara. Nice to meet you." I make my face express enthusiasm. But I shake with the realization that tonight is escape night.

"I love your dress. You wear it just like Lauren Bacall. I was gonna wear a gown tonight, but the cleaner ruined it, so I had to do this." She indicates her outfit and puffs out her lips like a child pouting over spilled milk.

"I think it looks great on you."

"You really think so?" Calista's eyes light up.

"Yeah. The way you have your hat dipped down over one eye. It looks cool."

"The movie's about to start," Finn says.

Calista winks at me, then heads to her table near the front, near the screen. Finn leads me to the same table we'd sat at for *Mogambo*.

The opening credits give Humphrey Bogart top billing. I glance over at Finn, wondering if Bogart is the actor he's trying to imitate. Just like the last party, when the action begins, the men and women start speaking the lines too. It's like a drama class I took in which all the actors sat around and read from their scripts. Except these people have their lines memorized, but they're not moving around. I don't get it. I thought the point of a drama was so you could move around on stage and use props and be in front of an audience.

I look at Finn again. He's totally into this thing, like he's entered an alternate universe. He even has Humphrey Bogart's strange speech down.

About halfway through the movie and way before Lauren Bacall gets to say her line, "Nothing you can't fix," the screen goes all pixeled. Groans and complaints go out all over the room.

"Sorry," someone says. "Lemme see what I can do."

I see Calista get up and head for the ladies' room. I turn to Finn. "I need to go to the restroom please."

He makes a kind of impatient movement with his shoulders but stands up. "All right, but don't try anything."

"I know, I know," I mutter.

He follows me to the back hall. "I'll be right here." He stations himself a few feet away from the restroom door, and I leave him there. Calista is just coming out of one of the stalls. When she sees me, she smiles. "That dress is so perfect. Wherever did you find it?"

I shrug. "Finn bought it for me." I fiddle with the shoulder straps and shoot her a look that says my dress is causing me discomfort. "Wish I'd had the chance to try it on though. It doesn't quite fit right."

Calista comes closer. "What's wrong with it?"

"Well, first of all, the bust is a bit too big for me, and the straps keep falling down." I pull one of the straps higher so she can see the problem. "Now, you could probably wear this much better. You're more, uh..."

"A bit bigger?" She giggles.

"I should've worn a gangster outfit. That feels more like my style. But Finn wouldn't let me."

"Finn? Who says he's the boss? You can wear anything you like."

"It would be kind of fun, uh, you know, showing him I can wear something I chose."

"Dang straight, girl." Calista puts her hands on her hips.

"Hey, we're about the same size. What if ..." I hesitate and shrug.

"Are you thinking what I'm thinking?" Calista whispers.

I can tell she really wants to try on my dress.

"Why don't we switch outfits? We can change back at the end of the movie. I think it would be so fun," she says.

I mold my face into a look of consternation, like I'm thinking it over. But then I relax my face and widen my eyes. "Okay, let's do it." I slip out of Lauren Bacall's gown, and Calista removes her jacket and trousers.

When we're all switched, I wipe off my lipstick and she applies lipstick to her lips. "There. You look great, Calista. By the way, Finn's waiting just outside the restroom."

She gives me a look. "Man, is he possessive."

I roll my eyes. "Totally. So, I suggest you hurry right past him. I'm wondering how long it'll take him to realize you're not me."

"If he's like most men, it'll take at least half an hour."

We both giggle. Calista's so busy admiring herself in the mirror that she doesn't see my shaking hands. My mouth is numb and tingling. If this doesn't work, I'm dead.

"Here I go," Calista says, and bursts out the door.

I wait two seconds and open the door a sliver. I see Finn's big shoulders walking away toward the main room, hurrying after Calista in my dress. I don't have another second to waste. I turn right, dash to the back entrance I'd spotted last time, thrust the door open and enter an alley with a big green dumpster partially blocking the way. I race around it and run for my life. Just as I round the corner and reach the actual street, I hear the back door open again, this time with a bang.

Finn's after me.

Without Calista's man-type shoes, I'd never have made it this far. When I hit the street, I turn right and look desperately for a place to hide. A breeze kicks in and practically forces me to turn into another alley. I'm pushed along about twenty-five yards, and that's when I see it. A dumpster at the end of the alley. I hear the sound of Finn's footsteps change from running, to fast walking. Then they slow to an amble. He must know where I am. In another second, Finn will round the corner and see me. My heart hammers in my throat. I run to the far corner of the dumpster, jump onto a collection of pallets, open the lid, and throw myself into the stink.

The dumpster is half-full of garbage bags and boxes. I burrow down and cover myself with as much as I can grab, then wait, my hands over my mouth so he can't hear me breathe. Finn's steps slow to a creep when he comes around the corner. I can almost hear him thinking, *Where would Zara have gone? Did she run down this alley? If she didn't come down here, where else could she have gone, because I would surely have seen her? She must be here somewhere.*

He walks slowly. His steps come up to the dumpster, and he stops. He must be listening, like a fox listening for the mouse under the snow. Ears perked, head tilting back and forth.

"Zara, I know you're in there. Come on out right now. If you come out, I promise I won't hurt you," he says.

Yeah, right. The snake.

He waits. I can hear his breathing. "I'm waiting, Zara." More silence.

He steps up onto the pallets and opens the lid. It's dark in the alley, and he doesn't have a light. I don't move. I don't breathe. He stands there, looking, listening. I can't hold my breath any longer and exhale silently. He's there for what seems an hour. Finally, he drops the lid. Jumps off the pallets. But he still doesn't leave. He's standing there, probably listening, hoping I'll climb out because I think he's left.

Finn starts talking to someone. He must be on his phone. "Zara got away."

I can't hear what the other person says, but Finn responds, "No, of course I didn't. She's got to be nearby. She doesn't have any money. Call Hector and tell him to get the guys out here. We'll find her. And then you can do whatever you want with her."

No more talking. Finn must have ended the call. He curses.

Oh, Abba, please make him leave.

"Zara? Come out, come out wherever you are," Finn calls with a menacing tone. I almost squeal when he kicks the side of the dumpster hard. Then his footsteps move away in the direction he'd come.

Still, I don't move. He might be waiting down the alley. Waiting for me to move, to climb up and swing that lid open and pop my head out and look to make sure it's safe. Then when I climb out and dust off my garbage-scented clothing, thinking I've gotten away, really gotten away, he'll burst out from around the corner and use those big fists to shut me up forever.

It's morning. A sliver of light pours through the top of the battered rim of the dumpster. I hear traffic increase. Somebody opens the lid and dumps a couple of trash bags on top of me. Two men talk in Spanish. I smell cigarette smoke. Then a door bangs shut.

I'm thinking through my moves. Did I do the right thing by escaping? Yes, I did. If Finn and Clooney think they can still get me back, they're not going to hurt my family. At least out on the run, I have a chance at returning home and working to find Mom and Dad.

I shift, wait, shift some more. From one of the garbage bags comes the scent of last night's tacos and grease and refried beans, not yet spoiled. I move the mushy bag out of the way and prop my arm onto a bag with harder contents. When I move to stand up, it rips a hole in the bag and cigarette ashes puff out and pepper my clothes. I'm sure my hair must stink of smoke, and rotting fruit peels, and everything else that's covered me for the past eight or nine hours. I scramble upward and lift the dumpster lid and peer out, scanning the area. Finn is nowhere in sight. The alley seems empty. I climb out, lower my feet onto the pallets, and jump down.

I don't go to the street. Finn might be there. And if he's not there, it could be Clooney or somebody else he's hired to watch for me. I need to find a safe place and change my clothes. But I don't have any money. I throw the jacket in the dumpster. That is obviously a costume. I can't get rid of the suspenders, because they're the only thing holding up my baggy trousers. The hat might be useful for hiding my greased hair.

I look at the tops of the buildings, wondering if there's a way to get inside and go upstairs. The one building next to the dumpster is a Mexican restaurant. But next to it are some apartments. They're brick and about four stories. Sometimes apartment buildings have connecting hallways. My hands are cold, and I stuff them into the trousers pockets, and that's when I feel the bill. I pull it out. It's a twenty. Calista must have stashed it in there. At least I'll be able to get a meal or two out of that.

I try some doors in the alley, but they're locked. But then I see a fire escape in the corner where the two apartment buildings meet. There's an open window on the third floor. If I get caught trespassing, I could get shot or beaten up. But it's either the fire escape or the street, and Finn has people looking for me.

The scent and color of flowers—orange blossoms and gardenia and jasmine—curls around my head and sends tendrils into the open space. It wants me to move to the fire escape. I look over my shoulder to make sure no one's seeing me. Once on the fire escape, I scoot up like a cat burglar, past the second-floor window and on to that open window on the third floor. When I reach it, I lean inside. It's an apartment. I don't see anyone. Maybe whoever lives here has already gone to work. I slide inside and tiptoe across to the front door. I hear water running somewhere. It shuts off before I can open the door, and someone comes around the corner.

"Alfie? Alfie, is that you?" she calls.

CHAPTER TEN

My hand's on the doorknob, but something tells me to stop.

"Oh, you're not my Alfie." She doesn't sound scared, just disappointed.

"I'm ... I'm ... I'm sorry. I got ... lost." My mouth tries to make words come out that sound reasonable, but my brain is not cooperating.

"I was looking for—"

"Are you looking for 3B? Lots of girls come up here looking for 3B. They're always walking in here thinking they're in 3B. But, my dear, this isn't 3B. It's 3A. 3B is on the other side of the hall. I live in 3A." She shuffles toward me with determination, and I back out of her way. She opens the door and points to the door. "See, dear, it's 3A."

I'm ready to bolt past the old lady, but she closes the door. "But I don't think you're a 3B type of girl, now that I look at you. No, I don't really know what type of girl you are. Yer kinda cute in that getup, though. Reminds me of my uncle Gus back when I was a little girl. He always wore suspenders. And greased his hair back, jes' like that. I think yer too pretty to wear men's clothes, dear. If you wore some lipstick and did your hair in a nice do, you'd look like a showgirl. Yer so tall."

She nudges me away from the door. "You look like you need to sit down, dear. How about I make you a cup of tea, and we can sit and visit for a bit. As long as Alfie isn't here, we might as well spend some time getting acquainted. Did Alfie send you here?

I open my mouth to give her a lame answer, but she goes on before I can say anything.

"It doesn't matter. Any friend of Alfie's is a friend of mine. I was kinda hoping he'd come with good news about the auditions down on Forty-Second. I've been studying my part, and I think I got it down cold."

She points to a chair and waits for me to sit. Once I do, I know I'll have to sit for a while because I'm so tired after my wretched and stinky night in the dumpster. She doesn't seem to notice that I smell.

The old lady shuffles back into the kitchen, still talking nonstop. "I've got just the right getup for the audition. I'm gonna wear my red dress. The one that's cut down low. Oh, it's still decent and all. Rosie, in 3B, said it was elegant. And that's just what this part is about. An elegant lady. If I wear the blond wig, I look a little like Marilyn, don't you think?"

She doesn't wait for an answer, just keeps gabbing. The chair I'm sitting in, or rather sinking into, is the kind that's made for napping. She's chatting away, and the teakettle wheezes like it does when it's about to start whistling. It goes *whizz*, and I hear her taking it off the stove. The fridge opens and shuts, and a package rustles. They're comforting sounds. The kind I remember my mom made when she was getting lunch ready. I should be escaping, but this is the first feeling of safety I've had in two weeks, and I don't look forward to stepping out of this apartment building and maybe facing Clooney or Finn or some other thug.

"... and then Alfie said, 'Ruby, you're a keeper, yes you are.' And he's been gone for a while, but, you know, I'm a stand-by-your-man woman, so I just keep waiting. That's why my door is always unlocked. Don't tell the neighbors that, dear. But I never know when my Alfie will come back, and I'd feel terrible if the girls in 3B heard him knocking on my door late at night. That would be so embarrassing. Because I'm a good girl. Always have been. Even when I was real busy being a showgirl. Did I tell you that I'm making a comeback? I've already gotten my hair done. Do you like it?"

She comes out of the kitchen, carrying a tray with a teapot and cups and a plate of cookies and sets it on the coffee table. "I just love red. Red dresses, red shoes, red lipstick." She reaches up and plumps her frizzy crazy-red hair. She's wearing an awful shade of red lipstick, and her skin is wrinkled and ruddy like she's been a lifelong sun worshiper. She's penciled some dark eyebrow color up high on her brows, and it makes her look surprised all the time.

"Let's have our tea and get acquainted. Did you say Alfie sent you? It doesn't matter. Any friend of Alfie's is a friend of mine. I'm expectin' him back any day." She pours tea into a cup and hands it to me.

I'm so thirsty, I down it in seconds. "This is really good, ma'am. Thank you."

"Aw, call me Ruby. All my friends call me Ruby. That was my stage name. Ruby Star. My real name's Pamela Laycock. But that's not a name for the stage. So I changed it. I thought up the Ruby part. Alfie added the Star part. He said I just shine like a star. And since you're a friend of Alfie, you should call me Ruby. All my friends call me Ruby. Ruby Star. I was a good dancer, but I wasn't tall enough to be a Rockette, so I danced lots of other shows right here in Manhattan."

Manhattan? I know next to nothing about it except that it's a borough of New York City and it's an island. And I know it's big and crowded and the people here are supposed to be rude and aggressive. And I've always dreamed of flying here to see a couple of Broadway shows and to visit some museums. But how in the world am I going to get out of this city without money? And do I dare ask to borrow Ruby's phone to call Abby and tell her I'm all right?

No, no, I couldn't do that. Abby has a big mouth. She'd squeal to Rolf, and he'd call the police for sure. No, it's too early. I'll find a way out there. Then I'll think some more about who to call.

Ruby's still talking. "Yep, I even danced in Las Vegas, but I didn't like the desert so I came back. New York's the place to be if you're gonna make it in show business. So why are you lost? Are you running from someone?"

I hate making up stories, but what else can I do? "Um, my, uh, boyfriend is trying to find me. He's been really mean to me and—"

"And you need some space from him, right?"

I nod.

"Well, you just let Ruby take care of you for a bit. I won't let that man find you. You're safe here." She sips her tea and shuts her eyes and makes a *mmmm* sound. "Have a cookie, dear," she says with her eyes still closed.

I can't resist. I'm hungry too. I stuff two cookies into my mouth while Ruby's still unaware. I pour myself another cup of her really good tea.

My mom is an expert at making tea. She doesn't use those tea bags you buy at the store. She goes to a specialty store and buys the loose-leaf tea, the kind that costs a lot. Mom likes to have her friends over for tea. She'll put up some card tables and decorate them with tablecloths and flowers and use her best china. And all the ladies from church come, bringing canapés and petit fours and cookies and sandwiches. I only got to attend when it was a mother/daughter tea. At the time, I was glad because I would much rather have been riding my horse or helping Dad drive the tractor. But in college, I'd invite my friends over and do my own kind of tea and study get-togethers.

The delicate scent of Ruby's tea is making me unbearably homesick and worried for Mom. Dad too.

I don't even know if Mom is okay. I'm having a hard time swallowing my mouthful of cookie, thinking about her and Dad and where they might be, and if they're still okay, or what if Finn called the bad guys who are holding them and told them to kill my parents? I get the cookies down, but then I can't stop the tears that have been threatening this whole time I've been in Ruby's little apartment. Now that I'm safe—well, for the time being—I'm so worried. The police must be searching for my parents. They're smart. They have all sorts of ways of finding missing people. They have to know something bad happened to them. And what happened to Uncle? Did Clooney kill him? Probably. They couldn't just let him go. He witnessed Clooney and Finn kidnapping me.

I cry, but quietly. If Ruby opens her eyes and sees me crying, she's going to wonder what I'm crying about. I can't tell her. I can't tell anybody. Not even the police.

Where are Mom and Dad? What happened to Uncle Arne? How can I get some money so I can escape? These are all thoughts I've been having for two weeks. It's driving me crazy that I don't have any answers. Finn wouldn't tell me anything. I'm terrified of being recognized by the police. Finn said that if I went to them, he'd kill Mom and Dad. And they'd make me hurt, bad. I don't know what to do. I don't even know how I'm going to get out of this city and get back home to Titusville.

I must have dozed off, and when I wake up, Ruby is gone. I jump up and peek into the kitchen, but she's not there. Has she gone to the police and reported me as a burglar? Maybe all that time she was talking to me, she knew I was trespassing, and now she's gone and contacted them and they're coming up here to arrest and question me. And then I'll have to tell them what happened, and all heck will break loose.

My heart pounds, and I'm gasping for breath. I have to get out of this place. Quick. Before they get here. There are still cookies on the tea tray. I think about stuffing the whole mess of them into my pants pocket.

Slow, thudding steps plod up the stairs outside Ruby's apartment. I know that whoever is outside her door is coming for me. I race to Ruby's open window, but before I can even put a leg out of it, the door opens and it's Ruby. She's carrying a grocery bag, and she's breathing hard.

"I'm so glad you're awake, dear. You looked tired, so I thought I'd just let you sleep a bit."

"What time is it?"

She juts her chin over to the mantel. The mini grandfather clock there says it's just after noon, but that can't be right.

"Just add five hours, more or less, and you've got the right time. But now that you're awake, you can help me get dinner on. I really splurged today, on account of having you as my guest. And of course I always make extra just in case Alfie shows up. You never know. I can't keep calling you *dear*. What is your name, dear?"

"My name's Za—" No, I can't give my real name. What if Ruby watches TV and sees my face on the news? She might call the police.

"Zza-zza, did you say?"

"Uh, no. I, uh, got a frog in my throat. My name is Zoe." I hope she doesn't ask for my last name too, because I feel bad lying about my name.

I follow Ruby into her kitchen and wait for her to tell me how I can help. But the whole time, I'm wondering how to get out of her neighborhood without being grabbed by Finn or his bad guys.

"So tell me about this naughty boyfriend that's hounding you," she says out of the blue, and it couldn't have come at a better time.

"W-well ..." I picture Finn's icy eyes and his big hands balled into fists, and it makes my voice shaky. "I thought he was nice, but he turned out to be mean, and he doesn't want me to get away from him, and—"

"Um-hmm, I know all about bad boyfriends. Maybe you wanna get out of town till he cools off, is that it?" Ruby's hand is poised over the package of lamb chops, and her face is filled with understanding.

I try not to cry, because she's so right and she's such a sweet, crazy old lady. "Yes. I need to get out of town quick. He's got friends who are helping him, and if he finds me, he won't be nice to me."

"Ugh, men. We sure need them, but they can be an awful bother sometimes." She plunks the lamb chops onto the heated pan and watches them sizzle. "Let me think for a bit, dear. I mean, Zoe. That's probably not yer real name, is it?"

She looks at me with her surprised eyes, and I nod. "No, it's not."

Ruby sighs. "Oh, I remember one time, before I met Alfie, there was this man. I thought he was a gentleman, but he turned out not to be. Kept pestering me after we had one teeny-tiny date. He kept bringing me flowers after my shows. Called me all the time. Waited by my apartment. At first, I was kinda flattered. But later it wasn't so nice. I mean, he wasn't so nice."

"What did you do?" I wipe my eyes and am ready for her advice.

"I got me a big, gaudy ring. It wasn't a real diamond." She giggles and strokes her ring finger. "I told him that a gangster named Ray, a killer, had asked me to be his girl, and he didn't like it when anyone messed with his girl. Well, everyone knew who Ray was, and no one ever tried to pull a fast one on a man connected to the mob. So my would-be boyfriend quit bothering me."

"Oh." I screw up my lip because I don't know any mob guys.

"But don't you worry, dear. We're gonna have a good dinner, and you're gonna sleep well tonight. Then tomorrow we'll figure out how you can get out of Manhattan without your boyfriend spotting you. Don't you worry. Too bad Alfie isn't here. He'd be able to drive you out of town. Maybe he'll show up tonight. You never know about Alfie."

CHAPTER ELEVEN

"Are you awake, dear?" Ruby waits at her bedroom door, in her bathrobe, her hair in curlers.

I stand, clutching a sheet around me because I'm only wearing my underwear. "I'm awake."

Ruby had made up a bed for me on the sofa. I'd slept fitfully, wondering about Mom and Dad and how to make some money so I could buy a bus ticket out of here and away from Finn and Clooney. The same thoughts still swirl through my brain this morning.

Abba, please help me. And even if I can get back to Titusville, there's no guarantee I can do anything to find my parents.

I'm willing to hitchhike if I have to, even though Mom had warned me about how dangerous it is for a woman. I told her I could save some money coming back from college for a visit if I just hitchhiked. She was horrified. But now I don't care. I have to get back to Iowa.

"Now, dear." Ruby takes my hand. "I've got it all figured out. You come with me."

She leads me into her bedroom and to her closet door. When she flips on the light inside, I see a good-sized walk-in closet filled with colorful clothes, like the stuff Finn had put in the closet in Niall's room, except these are more like the costumes a lady would wear on stage.

"I've got some great outfits that I'm sure you could fit into." She steps into the closet and rummages through the items. "They might be a bit short on you, but that wouldn't be a problem, considering that kids today wear all kinds of crazy things. Hmm, how about this outfit?"

She pulls out a beige jacket and matching pants. "And here's a scarf I used to wear to give it a bit of color. And a hat that I think looks just nifty with the suit. So chic. What do you think, dear?"

"It's very nice, Ruby. Really nice. Thank you."

"And don't worry about the pants being too short. I never wore them because they're too long for me, so they should be perfect for you. How tall are you, dear?"

"Five ten."

Ruby whistles. "Just perfect for a showgirl. I was always a bit short for the lineup. They put me on the end."

She hands me the hanger with the suit. "Now, why don't you slip into this? And I'll try to find some shoes. What size are you?"

"Eight."

Ruby squeals with delight. "This is so much fun. It's like dressing a model." She bends and peers at the line of shoes on the floor. "I think this pair should work with that suit. Here, sit down on the bed and try these on."

I've just gotten the slacks on and transferred the twenty-dollar bill into the pocket of the pants.

When I sit to slip on the sensible shoes, I notice a photograph on her nightstand. "Pretty photo. Is that you, Ruby?"

Ruby looks pleased. "That was taken the day Alfie proposed. We were at Coney Island for a show he was in, and he bought me a little silver ring. I've never taken it off." She flashes her ring finger. "That Alfie. You should have seen him dance. He was dancing in a variety show there. Better than Tommy Tune, if you ask me."

I stare at the photo because it's at least fifty years old, probably taken some time around the sixties or early seventies, judging by their tie-dyed T-shirts and the bell-bottoms. "Did you and Alfie ever get married?"

Ruby looks surprised. "Oh, we couldn't do that. My mama always said you had to be engaged at least six months. Time to make the wedding plans and all. But as soon as Alfie gets back, we'll set the date. He got drafted, you know. Had to do his time in Vietnam. But I expect him back any day now."

I look up at Ruby's sweet old face and back at the photo of her and Alfie as young people, probably still in their teens, and I finally get it. My heart squeezes for her and how her heart must have broken—her mind too—when Alfie didn't come back from the war. And my heart hurts for the wedding that never happened. "Well, that will be great when Alfie gets back."

Ruby smiles and nods. "How do those shoes feel?"

I stand and wiggle my toes. "Perfect."

"Why don't you go in the bathroom and wash off all that Brylcreem in your hair. And while yer doing that, I'm gonna put together a little overnighter for you with some other odds and ends you might need for your trip out of town."

I nod like a dummy because I realize for the first time that Abba's breeze led me to 3A and Ruby and her closet filled with costumes. And I tear up again.

"Now, now, everything's gonna be fine." Ruby's eyes are filled with tenderness. Her eyebrows are nonexistent without pencil, and it makes her look more like a proper grandmother. She wraps her arms around me and lets me cry. "That mean ol' boyfriend isn't gonna find you." She releases me and gives me a gentle nudge. "You go and get cleaned up."

Later, after breakfast, Ruby presents me with a pretty leather bag with tooling of cowboys and horses and lassos. It's heavy, but I'm too polite to ask what's in it.

Ruby sees the look on my face and guesses correctly what I'm thinking. "Every girl needs a change of clothes. And there's some travel things inside too. But don't you peek until you get to a safe place, okay?"

"Okay."

She's still wearing her rollers, and her face is coated with cold cream, but I don't care. I throw my arms around her and give her a kiss on the cheek. "Thank you so much, Ruby. Why are you being so kind to me?"

"Why, silly girl, don't you know? Alfie told me to take good care of his friends. He has so many friends. He'd be so disappointed if he got back from 'Nam and heard I hadn't done a good job."

She backs away. "Oh, I almost forgot." She hurries into the bedroom and comes back seconds later with a blonde wig. "We can't have you stepping outside without the most important part of your disguise."

Ruby takes a comb to my hair, pulls it back away from my face, and stuffs everything under the wig. Then she fluffs the waves around my face. It's one of those blonde shoulder-length layered styles, and when I check myself in the mirror, I'm surprised at how different I look. It gives me a little more confidence that I could walk down the street and not be recognized.

Then she plunks a pair of sunglasses on my nose. "I think you're ready now." Ruby nudges me toward the front door and opens it. "If you see Alfie, you tell him I miss him."

My throat is tight, but I manage to say, "I will, Ruby. Goodbye. God bless you."

"God bless you too, dear."

I step out, take a big breath, and head down the stairs.

Once I'm away from Ruby's neighborhood, I walk for a couple of hours. Tons of people go down to the subway, but I don't even consider that. I don't know where to go. I wish I had a cell phone, but I'm not crazy enough to ask someone if I could borrow theirs. Maybe there's a library or store where I can check out a map.

My arm is tired from carrying the overnighter, and I'm curious what Ruby put inside. But I'm nervous about exploring its contents with all sorts of people walking around me. I spy a coffee shop and head that way. Inside, I buy a slice of lemon loaf and a coffee, dumping tons of sugar and cream into the dark liquid, just like when I had breakfast with Finn. It's crowded in here, but I snag a small table in the back by the restrooms and sit so my back is to the wall and I can view the entrance. I snarf the lemon loaf and sip my coffee. The caffeine revs me up, and I'm ready for more travel. But first I need to find a map. I down the last of my cup, then pick up my bag and unzip the opening.

What I see inside gives me hope that I can get out of this scary city. Ruby had put in a change of clothes, toothbrush and toothpaste, comb, and bar of soap. She'd rolled up a lightweight windbreaker with a hood. In the inside pocket, she's stuffed a subway map and schedule. There's a manila envelope in the pocket too, with a message scrawled on the front: *You might be needing a little "mad" money, dear. I hope this gets you to a safe place. Ruby.*

I open the envelope and see cash, lots of it, by the thickness of the wad. I glance around me and stuff the envelope back inside the bag. I'm nervous about counting money in such a public place, so I keep my fingers inside my overnighter and flip through the bills. Two hundred dollars. I can hardly believe it. *Thank you, Abba.* I tear up again. It was clear from being in Ruby's apartment that the sweet old lady didn't have much to live on. The two hundred dollars had to have been a tremendous sacrifice. If I weren't in such danger, I'd run back to her apartment and thank her.

Now I can get a bus ticket back to Iowa. Where's the nearest bus station? I zip up my bag and head to the counter to ask.

"Port Authority," the lady at the counter tells me. "It's not far. Down four blocks, then turn right and go another two or three blocks. You can't miss it."

When I say, "Thanks, ma'am," she raises her eyebrows like I'm from another planet.

Outside, I've never been surrounded by so many people, traffic, and noise. My ears hurt from all the sounds, and I wonder how anyone can keep their sanity living in the city for more than a couple of weeks. A big clock on a tower bongs the time—10:00 a.m.

I wade through pedestrians, my stride quick and hopeful for the first time in weeks. But then the obvious jolts me. Why I hadn't thought of this before makes me want to pound my forehead and shout, "Duh."

How am I going to purchase a bus ticket without ID?

Think, Zara. What kinds of transportation don't require ID. A taxi, but I can't take a taxi all the way to Titusville. A train requires ID. So does a plane.

The only other mode I can think of is to try to get on a private bus or get with a bunch of students who need to pool their money to get somewhere cheap. I did that from Northwestern University to Titusville for spring break one year when I was low on funds. Got home for twenty-five dollars.

But where am I going to find information for one of these rides? *Abba, I wish I had a cell phone so I could do a search.*

A pigeon flutters so close to my face that I throw my hands up to block it. When I do, I notice a sign on a brick building that says Manhattan College of Nursing. Beyond is a paved pavilion with benches and trees and several students milling about, carrying books, others sitting and studying. If they are students, there must be some who are trying to find cheap transportation home or to visit friends.

Outside a building that's labeled Student Union I spy a kiosk with slips of paper pinned to its walls, flapping in the breeze. I hurry over and peruse the messages. Most are messages offering tutoring. About knee high, a red eight-by-ten sheet catches my eyes. It advertises "RIDES to Boston, Miami, Chicago. Cheap fares. The Pigeon. Call this number."

I pluck the page off and stuff it into my bag. If I can get to Chicago, I could use the same carpool that got me to Titusville back when I was an undergrad at Northwestern.

Inside the Student Union building it's surprisingly quiet. A girl and two guys are down the hall, checking their mailboxes. A lounge area is empty except for one girl who's curled on a sofa, taking a nap. I'm standing in the intersection between the mail hall, the lounge, and an office, trying to decide who I could ask about the 'cheap travel' bulletin, when a woman's voice calls, "Miss, can I help you?" I turn and find a middle-aged woman sitting behind the office counter.

"Well, I uh, need to use a phone."

"Local call?" she asks.

I nod.

"Here, use this one." She lifts the receiver on her phone and hands it to me.

"Thanks, Ma'am."

The woman smiles like she guesses something about me, then leaves me alone so I can talk in private.

I punch in the numbers from the bulletin and after about ten rings a man's gruff voice answers with a "Yeah?"

"Hi, I'm calling about the ad I found at Nurses College for cheap travel. I need to get to Chicago.

"Bus leaves tomorrow. You gotta pay a deposit first." He gives me an address. Then he hangs up.

I scribble the address, muttering, "Aw, c'mon, Mister. What's the fare? When does the bus leave? From where?

The lady who lent me her phone is watching me with a curious expression. She's got wavy brown hair cut just like my mom's, and she has kind blue eyes. "You're looking confused. Can I help you?"

Her resemblance to my mom is making me feel weepy again. I swallow and clear my throat. "I'm just visiting Manhattan, and I have no idea how to get to 8th Avenue."

"Oh, that's easy. You're really close. Just go north a couple of blocks and turn right and you'll hit the avenues."

She smiles, and I thank Abba for a friendly face in this mass of humanity crowded into such a slim piece of land.

"So north is ...?"

She leans over the counter and gestures toward the door I came through. "Go out the front doors and make a right."

"Right?"

"Yep. All the avenues go north and south, while the streets go west and east. Once you got that in your head, you can get around town. 'Cept, there are certain neighborhoods to steer clear of. But all cities have those, right?"

I nod like I know all about big cities. But really, the only cities I know fairly well are the suburban ones around Northwestern University. All those years there, working on my studies, I didn't even go into downtown Chicago more than a handful of times.

"My name's Pam."

"I'm ... Zoe."

Pam extends her hand and I take it.

"So, what brought you through our doors today? Are you visiting someone at the school?"

I shake my head. "Just trying to get my bearings, Ma'am."

She chuckles. "Now I know you're not from around here."

"Sorry?"

"The last time someone called me Ma'am, I was in Kentucky visiting my son."

"Oh, I get it now." I laugh, but my face is heating up. It must be obvious to everyone I meet that I'm a country bumpkin, not a sophisticated city girl."

"Hey, I'm just finishing up for the day, and I'm free for a bit. I'd be happy to help you find your address on 8th Avenue."

My eyes go wide. "Are you a New York native?"

She looks surprised. "Yes. Why?"

"Well, excuse me for saying this but I've always heard that New Yorkers are kind of hard and aggressive. But you're so kind."

"We're not all like that," she says almost tenderly. She pauses to grab her purse and sweater and come out of the office. "C'mon, let me show you the softer side of New Yorkers."

We reach my address in less than half an hour. The name of the place is 'Ezee Pawn.' Just the run-down look of it makes me feel as if I'm about to perform some sort of illegal transaction.

Pam's wearing a wary expression. "Are you sure this is where you were supposed to come?"

I check my scrawl again. "Yes, this is what the man said."

"Okay." She looks doubtful. "But I'm gonna wait outside until you come out. And if you don't come out in ten minutes, I'm coming in after you."

I give her a nervous laugh. "Be right out." The door jingles when I step inside. The place has a smell I have to think about to describe. I think it's partly the hundred-year-old wood of the doors, the paneling, the trim. But it's the stuff in the business too. The room has too many aged and oiled leathery items that have become encrusted through time with the salt and pepper of book dust and foot traffic.

An older man pushes his face through a curtain near the back. "Can I help you?"

I recognize the voice as the man who spoke to me on the phone. "Yes, I'm here to pay a deposit for the, uh ... Pigeon?"

He doesn't say anything, just indicates for me to come behind the curtain. I should be nervous about this, but the man seems more interested in the money I'm going to give him than anything more nefarious.

After I give him the cash, he hands me a receipt and gives me another phone number to call tonight so I know where to meet up tomorrow morning. Weird. I wonder what kind of passengers are going to be riding with me. Obviously, I'm taking a risk riding in a vehicle that most likely has no insurance or registration for carrying passengers. But it's got to be better than thumbing a ride.

Pam is still waiting for me when I come outside. "Whoo, that made me nervous when you went back behind that curtain. I was about ready to run inside."

"I know. But nothing happened."

"If you don't mind me asking," Pam's voice is almost a whisper, "you're not into anything shady, are you?" She puts her hand on my arm. "Are you in trouble?"

Careful, Zara. Pam doesn't need too much info. I stuff the receipt into my pocket and compose my face so there's nothing in my eyes or crimping my mouth to make her doubt my words. "Nothing shady. It's just a deposit for riding a private bus to Chicago."

"Oh." She still looks doubtful.

"Pam, I'm just a Northwestern University graduate student, looking for a cheap ride back home." All true.

"Well, that's a load off my mind. When does your bus leave?"

"Tomorrow morning." I can't meet her eyes, so I stare at the debris and the cigarette butts beneath my feet. She's got to be wondering where I'm staying in the meantime.

Pam turns and stands directly in front of me, practically commanding me to look up. When I do, she's wearing that tender, motherly look that so resembles my mom.

"Do you have a place to stay tonight?"

"Not exactly." I'm staring into her eyes, trying hard not to let her see my fear of being on the street for the next twenty or so hours.

"Now look, Zoe." She puts her hands on my shoulders and gently squeezes them. "I know we're practically strangers, but you seem to have fallen on some lean times. Now, I'm a nice, normal woman, who is always looking for my next God appointment. I live close to here in a nice, normal apartment with my sweet old mom and a cat and two fish. They'd all be happy for you to stay the night, if you're willing."

CHAPTER TWELVE

Pam picks up a few things at the neighborhood grocery mart and then we walk another couple of blocks. Her apartment is in a nice neighborhood, and I wonder if she's lived here awhile, maybe before rents went sky high. Her apartment is on the fourth floor, and it's a hoof because there's no elevator.

"Mom?" Pam calls. "I'm home. Got a friend for you to meet."

I follow Pam into the kitchen where she drops off her grocery bag. Beyond the kitchen countertop is the living room. An old woman reclines there on a Lazy Boy. She's wrapped in an afghan, and the only part of her I can see clearly is her white hair. One of her legs is elevated and by the careful way she shifts to get a look at me, she's clearly uncomfortable.

"Mom, this is Zoe. I met her at Nurse's College." Pam gestures for me to follow her into the living room.

I hope I won't have to take the woman's hands. I don't have my gloves.

"Come on over here and let me get a look at you, young lady," the woman says in a surprisingly young voice. But I can hear in her voice she is in pain.

I stand directly in front of her chair so she can study me.

"Well, what do you think?" Pam says, standing right next to me. "Isn't she just like I described her?"

"Welcome, Zoe. My name's Emma Joy, but everyone just calls me Mom. Sorry I can't get up and give you a proper welcome. My foot's hurting right now. Gout, the doctor says. Stop eating red meat, he says. You know what I say to that?"

I'm smiling at Emma Joy because she has the most lovely aura. Royal purples and lavenders and violets dance themselves into a braid that trails down her neck and then splits into multiple ribbons of color that cascade down onto her shoulders. Her eyes are green. And I mean green like a tropical forest. Her snow-white hair is styled and softens her big, handsome face. "What do you say to the doctor?"

Emma Joy looks like she's going to laugh. "I say, 'Pooh.'"

I can't help but laugh too. I get the feeling she could say just about anything and get away with it.

"My daughter called about an hour ago and told me about your needing to go to a pawn shop. I said, 'Well, get that girl out of that place as quick as you can.' And she said she's gonna bring Zoe home, and I said good 'cause it'll help distract me from my darned gout." She looks down at her elevated foot and puffs out her lower lip like a five-year-old being sent to her room.

And I can't help laughing again. She reminds me of my grandmother, the one we used to visit in Chicago. Granna always made everything seem fixable. Whenever I got upset, she'd say, "Oh my, that *is* something we'll have to deal with, but you know, it's not the end of the world." I miss her.

If I weren't in such a hurry to get back to Iowa, it would be nice to get to know Emma Joy better.

Emma Joy leans toward me. "D'you want to see a gout-y toe?"

"Mom!" Pam puts her hand to her mouth. "She doesn't want to—"

"No, I'd like to see it, Pam. Really. I've never seen what gout looks like." I'm getting tiny prickles from my back all the way up to my scalp, and a floral breeze is swirling around my head.

"Spoken like a true nurse," Emma Joy says as she carefully pulls the afghan away from her foot.

It looks just awful. Her big toe is swollen and red. There are no good colors anywhere near her foot.

"We've got everyone at the church praying for Mom," Pam whispers. "When she has an attack, she can't come to church. And everyone says she leaves a really big hole when she's not there to teach Sunday School."

"Do you mind if I touch your toe, Emma Joy?" I fully expect her to say, please don't touch it, it hurts too much. But she's quiet for a few seconds. I look up and meet her eyes. She nods. Her purple and lavender and violet colors blaze off her head and send streaks of them all the way to the ceiling.

Abba. Emma Joy is praying.

I kneel in front of her, reach out and make contact. I take a big breath and hold it. Her skin is hot, like it's infected. But my fingers are cool, as cool and refreshing as a mountain stream in July. Emma Joy gasps when the cooling seeps through her skin.

"What am I feeling? What is that?" she cries.

I keep my fingers there for as long as the cooling flows through them. Emma Joy is weeping, and the sobs are making her head and shoulders bounce.

I'm vaguely aware of movement around me, but I cannot tear my focus away from the woman's foot. Time has frozen. I feel as if the breath I took when I first touched Emma Joy has nourished my heart and lungs for the duration of the healing.

I close my eyes and exhale. Daddy is carrying me upstairs to my bedroom. I nuzzle my head into his shoulder and I'm warm and protected. My brain feels like cotton candy clouds, and I'm drifting way up high. "Go to sleep, little princess. Tomorrow's Christmas."

"Zoe? Zoe? Are you okay?"

Someone is tapping my wrist, squeezing my hand.

"Zoe, wake up."

When I open my eyes, I find Pam leaning over me, gently patting my hand. "Zoe, are you okay?"

I sit up, and the quick motion makes my head pound. There are many people in the room, so many I can't even see Emma Joy in her chair. Pam helps me stand, and as soon as I do, they all surround me, touch me, stroke me, embrace me.

"That was amazing," a woman exclaims.

A tall man says, "Praise the Lord! He poured healing through you, Zoe,"

"Thank you, Zoe," Pam whisper close to my ear. "I knew God had a plan to bless my mother through you. As soon as you touched Mom, I knew I had to hurry and invite my friends to witness the healing."

"H-how long have I been sleeping?"

"Not long, maybe half an hour." She takes my hand and leads me forward. "Look." She points at her mother who is sitting up, an expression of rapture lighting her face.

"Zoe," Emma Joy calls. "Look at my foot. It's all better." She kicks the footrest down and stands in one fluid motion.

Everyone cheers, laughs, claps, rushes over to surround Emma Joy.

But Emma Joy is moving toward me, focused only on my face. The crowd parts and lets her come to me.

She wraps me in her arms and kisses me on the cheek. "I had faith, Zoe. Our God has sent you at just the right time. Thank you, sweet girl."

I don't know what to say, especially when there are so many men and women witnessing this moment. "It-it was Abba," I whisper close to her ear. "He did it, not me."

"Of course, it was our Abba," she whispers back and kisses me again. "But he chose you to do his work."

Someone exclaims, "We need to get the word out about Zoe. There are so many needs in our church for her healing."

A woman responds with, "Yes! We should call Pastor and tell him what happened tonight."

I pull away from Emma Joy and practically shout, "No." But my voice is drowned out by the throng's excited voices, each one suggesting ways I could minister to their church and the community.

"Just imagine," a man close to me calls out, "how this is gonna silence all those voices that say we Christians are all phonies."

"This'll make 'em stop and consider," another man agrees.

"No, you mustn't do that." Finally, my voice breaks through the crowd.

There's silence while they stare at me like I'm a space alien. And now I'm thinking fast, trying to decide if I can trust this loving, enthusiastic group of friends to keep my story secret.

Emma Joy puts her arm around me. "Let's listen to Zoe. She must have a very good reason for us not sharing what she did tonight." She gives my shoulder a gentle squeeze. "Go on, girl. Tell us why we need to keep quiet."

How should I begin to tell them what has happened in the past couple of weeks? Images of my parents, my uncle, Finn and Clooney, and sweet old Ruby zip through my mind. "There are bad men who are looking for me. They want to kill me."

A collective gasp ripples across the room, followed by murmurs of, "That's awful," "What happened?" "How could someone kill Zoe?" "Why?" "How can we help?"

I put my hand up for silence. "You're all asking the right questions, so please let me answer them."

I have their attention now. Pam and Emma Joy and the rest are hanging on my words, except for a pair of whispering women. Pam stares them down and they quit talking.

"A couple of weeks ago, God poured out healing through me on a little boy and then one of our farm employees. The story was broadcast on national news, and these drug dealer guys saw the story on TV. They thought they could kidnap me and force me to heal the head of their cartel. They threatened to kill my family if I didn't heal him. I escaped, and I've been running from them, but they'll do anything to find and kill me.

"They're holding my parents hostage. And if they think I've talked to anybody, they'll execute my parents."

Emma Joy is gripping my shoulder, a grimace twisting her mouth. "Oh, my dear, dear girl, we had no idea you were in danger. We'll keep quiet about my healing. We *all* will, right?" She straightens and scans the faces of her friends. And they all nod.

"We'd hate to put your life in jeopardy for doing God's will," she says. "But what are you going to do? Where will you go?"

"I must get back to Iowa, secretly, and find my mom and dad."

"We want to help you, but we don't know how," Pam says. "Should we call the police?"

"No." I say it so loudly that everyone in the room jumps. "Don't do that. It's imperative that you don't call them. When the time is right, I'll call them myself. But not now. That would only put my mom and dad and me in danger from the bad guys."

One of the women who had been whispering now has tears streaming down her face. "Zoe, we'll all be praying for you."

"Yes," Emma Joy says. "We'll have the whole church praying for you, but we won't tell them about your situation. Only that you have a dire need for prayer. Is that okay, Zoe?"

I smile at Emma Joy, and then turn in a circle so my words go out to each of them personally. "Yes, please pray for me, but be very careful how you share my need. Any mention of a healer is sure to eventually get out to outsiders. The men that are chasing me are dangerous, very ruthless. They have eyes and ears everywhere. You could put yourself in danger by mentioning me or what I did."

By the sober looks on the faces of Emma Joy's friends, I can tell my words have had the desired effect.

"Then, we'll pray," says the tall man who had earlier exclaimed, "Praise the Lord."

Emma Joy and Pam place their hands on me, and seconds later, the rest of the group has encircled me. "Lord," Emma Joy says in a strong voice, "Our Zoe has done your will, and now we're asking you to please take care of her as she travels to Iowa. We know there are bad men trying to find her. We ask that you hide her and give her wings like an eagle to flee from them. We know she has many more healings to perform in your name. Bless her, speed her to her destination, and help her find her parents. Amen."

After the prayer, everyone touches me on the shoulder one last time. Then Pam escorts them all to the door, reminding them each, "Remember, don't tell anyone what you saw tonight."

CHAPTER THIRTEEN

When I wake up, I have a hard time figuring out where I am. Then I recall yesterday's events, and the memory of them shoves me into full consciousness. I'd had a hard time sleeping last night. It could have been my full stomach from Pam's "light" supper of pork chops, Yukon Gold roasted potatoes, applesauce, green beans, sour dough bread, and coffee. Or maybe it was the anxiety caused by thirteen strangers witnessing a healing and then promising not to tell a soul. How was that going to work out in reality?

People at the Titusville Hospital blabbed what they'd seen in the ER when I touched Timmy Horton. Medical people are supposed to keep a patient's health records completely safe from public scrutiny, but all sorts of information about me had been leaked to the media within a couple of days after Timmy's healing.

The more I obsess about what Pam's friends might say to other people, the more my heart pounds. I have to get up. Get out. I shower and dress hurriedly. I figure I can sneak out of Pam's apartment without disturbing them by trying to make breakfast. It's Saturday, and Pam is most likely sleeping in.

My phone call last night reached a woman who furnished me with an address and a meet time of 8:30 a.m. I am to bring no more than two suitcases—hah, I wish—and a carry-on, and refrain from wearing cologne or using scented hairspray. Also, I'm not supposed to wear any jewelry, including a wedding ring. Oh, and the bus will have a pigeon painted on its side.

The instruction to not wear jewelry has me worried. Not that I'm wearing any, but what kind of people am I going to be sharing this ride with? Pickpockets, muggers, killers?

Grabbing my bag, I tiptoe down the hall toward the front door, but a sound halts me. Pam's already in the kitchen, fully dressed, softly humming while scrambling eggs.

"Good morning, Zoe, "she says when she notices me standing in the hallway. "I thought you could use a little breakfast before you leave to catch your bus."

Now I feel guilty for trying to sneak out. Pam has shown me wonderful hospitality. How dare I disappoint her by disappearing before she could send me off with a full meal? "That's so kind of you. May I set the table?"

"Already done," Pam says, smiling like someone who's accomplished something really important. She divides the eggs equally between two plates, adding slices of toast. "All you have to do is sit."

She's set the table with glasses of orange juice, strawberry preserves, a small pitcher of cream. She says a blessing, and we eat in silence until I realize Emma Joy hasn't joined us yet. "Isn't your mom going to have breakfast with us?"

"Not today." Pam pours coffee for both of us. "She had to do some things at church to get ready for Sunday School tomorrow. She left super early this morning, but she said she'll keep on praying, and to not forget to keep in touch."

That's the Emma Joy I read in her lovely colors last night. The kind of woman who lives to serve others, eagerly shows hospitality to strangers, and who is loved by everyone she meets.

The doorbell rings and Pam jumps up to see who is at the door. I feel a strong urge to run down the hall and hide until her visitor has gone, but I control myself. A deep voice greets Pam, and she opens the door wider to admit one of the tallest men I've ever seen.

He looks to be in his late twenties or early thirties. He has to duck slightly to pass through the door, so I guess he's close to seven feet tall. I must have failed at hiding my shock, because he chuckles at my expression.

"Zoe, this is Craig. Craig Montague. He's going to walk us down to your bus stop. Just to make sure nothing weird happens along the way."

"Craig, do you want some coffee to go?" Pam holds up the coffee pot.

He shakes his head. "No, thanks. I'm already tanked up."

"Tank" is an excellent choice of words to describe Craig. The guy probably weighs close to three hundred pounds, no fat, just solid muscle. I feel better now about walking to my bus rendezvous. Who would want to mess with Craig?

He joins me at the table, and I have a hard time not staring. The giant man has wavy auburn hair, a couple day's growth of an equally auburn beard, and dark, dark eyes—and something indefinable about him makes my insides go mushy.

I tear my eyes away from Craig, take one last sip of coffee, and move to collect my dishes.

But Pam intervenes. "Don't you worry about this stuff. I'll take care it of later."

Craig lifts my overnighter, and it looks like a purse in his giant hand. "This all you've got?"

"That's it. I travel light." I make a goofy face, and he grins. Craig is almost handsome, but it's the radiant smile that grabs me. And I'm charmed by his New York accent. His colors are happy, and I wish I could hang around and get to know him better. I wonder how Pam knows him.

"So, I hear you're going to Chicago?"

"Yes. Actually, I plan to go to Evanston. Northwestern campus. I've got friends who might be able to help me."

Craig shakes his head. "Don't involve your friends if it means they'll be put in the crosshairs of some criminals." He seems adamant about this.

"Then, what can I do to arrange a ride to Titusville?"

"I've got better friends. Ones who are experts at avoiding public exposure. Here's what you do, Zoe. Ask your bus driver to let you off as close to the Field Museum as possible. Then, make a phone call to this number." He hands me a business card with the words, The Field Museum, printed on the front, also bearing the address of the building. On the back, he's scrawled a phone number.

"After you call, someone will meet you."

"But who will I look for?"

He frowns. "I can't say."

I'd thought Craig was just Pam's friend, but now, all of a sudden, he's turned into some cloak and dagger spy.

When I stare at him, he says, "Trust me."

I do trust Craig. But he knows way more than he's saying, and that makes me nervous.

We all step outside Pam's apartment and tromp down the stairs. On the sidewalk, Craig makes a sign for us to halt. He looks up and down the street. Even though it's Saturday, the city buzzes, booms, and bangs with the sounds of traffic and construction. Music and hip-hop beats whoof from passing cars. From a distance, a woman and a child are walking at a leisurely pace in our direction, probably enjoying the beautiful weather. Behind them, others appear to be walking to work. A couple of joggers with earbuds trot by as we wait. A red car slows as it passes, but the windows are tinted, and we can't see if the driver is watching us. Aside from that, nothing seems out of the ordinary. Craig motions for us to follow.

In about ten minutes we pass the Ezee Pawn shop, but we still have to walk a couple more blocks. Craig is moving fast, like he's a football lineman clearing the field for us. Pam and I have to trot to keep up with him. On the street where my bus will be, delivery trucks and cabs clog the streets by double-parking, and angry commuters gesture and yell and honk in frustration. I can't wait to get out of this noisy city.

At last, I see the spot where I'm to meet the bus. "There's the address, Craig." I point it out, and he slows. The meeting place is in front of a florist's shop, but there's no sign of any bus with a pigeon on its side. For some reason, now that I've arrived safely, I feel especially anxious. My stomach is knotted, and every muscle in my body is taut as if in preparation for a race for my life. But I'll calm down once I board the bus, and it starts moving.

I check up and down the sidewalk, fearing I'll see Finn and Clooney stalking with guns drawn. But right now there's no one but the same woman and girl we'd seen outside Pam's apartment building. And in a flash, I know why I'm anxious. I know they're heading straight for me. My mouth goes dry.

When they get close, the woman, out of breath, says, "Miss, you don't … know me, but … I go to Resurrection Chapel … and my friend, Mara told me about … you, how you can heal."

Pam gasps, and Craig thrusts himself in between me and the woman."

"Jean," he says in a quiet, respectful tone, "Mara was not supposed to say anything about a healer. She needs to—"

"I-I know, she warned me," Jean says in tears, "but I thought as … long as your healer is here, she could …"

She's looking way up into Craig's face, but he's clearly communicating a command to stand down.

Pam takes Jean's arm gently. "Dear, this young woman is in grave danger right now, and your showing up will bring attention to her. This is the last thing she needs."

"But," Jean persists, "my daughter's sight. She needs to be—"

Pam puts her arms around Jean and tries to lead her and her young daughter away from me. "Jean, this is not the right time."

But the woman will not be moved. Craig leads me away from Pam and the mother and child. But while I'm hiding behind Craig, I see a man moving toward us with a noticeable limp. Did he follow us from Pam's apartment too? He's hurrying, thrusting one arm forward with each stride for momentum, dragging the bad leg in reckless haste. I'm gritting my teeth, fully expecting him to lose his balance any second and fall.

Even though he hasn't reached us yet, his eyes have already homed in on me, and he calls, "Zoe? Are you Zoe?"

Where's that blasted bus? It's 8:30 a.m., and it's supposed to be here now.

Craig intervenes again. "Zoe needs to catch a bus. She can't help you at this time."

But the limper is trying to get around Craig, who puts out his arm to block the guy.

A man who's unlocking the florist shop comes between the limper and Craig. "Hey, I don't want no trouble here. You guys looking for trouble?" He's maybe average height but he goes onto his toes, flexes his just-okay muscles and thrusts out his jaw like he really would like some 'trouble.' He checks out Craig, then the limper, then Craig again.

"Mister?" I sidle toward the florist shop front door. "Do you mind if I go inside to wait for my bus? It should be here any minute."

"Not a chance, babe," the shop guy growls over his shoulder. He backs up a pace to show me he means business. "Last thing I need is a fight inside my store."

Jean and her daughter are both crying. She's pleading with Pam. "Please let me speak to her. If Zoe could just see my sweet Maddie, she'd want to help her."

The limper is shouting over the voices of Craig and the florist, "Hey, Zoe. Hey, Zoe. You can see my limp. Bomb almost took most of my leg in Afghanistan."

A red car with tinted windows pulls over and a man jumps out. When he gets closer, I see that his face is horribly disfigured, probably from fire. "Zoe!" His mouth is barely a mouth, and he has trouble pronouncing my name. His nose is mostly gone, and one eye is covered by scar tissue.

When the scarred man gets closer, the limper sees him and sets his body to muscle the man from getting in front of him.

"Zoe, Zoe!" they're all calling. A jogger tries to navigate through the gathering crowd. "Move over, dudes," she says irritably. "You're blocking the whole sidewalk."

They ignore her, so she stops to study the crowd. "What's going on here?" she demands as if she's the town mayor.

"It's Zoe," the disfigured man says. "She's gonna make my face normal."

"What?" the jogger screws up her mouth. "Who's Zoe?"

"Her," the limper and Jean say simultaneously while pointing at me.

The jogger whips out her cell phone. "I gotta catch this."

"No," I shout. "Please, just mind your own business and jog away."

"Oh, yeah?" Jogger approaches, her eyes narrowed with spite. "No one tells me to go away, you witch."

I've turned away, and I'm trying to cover my face. That's when I hear the sound of a diesel engine. I look through my fingers, and there's the bus with the pigeon on the side pulling up to the curb. The bus driver opens his door and comes out. "What's goin' on here?"

Pam rushes over to the driver and points me out. "My friend is trying to get on your bus, but these people are harassing her."

"Why the heck are they doing that?" He glimpses me cowering by the florist shop. "Ya wanna ride or not?" He motions for me to get into the bus. Only I can't. I'm blocked by desperate people, an irate jogger, and a belligerent shopkeeper.

And when I peer through my fingers again, at least four or five more people have joined the crowd, and they're all asking what the hoopla is all about.

Even if I could fight myself through them, there's a danger I'd end up hurting the very people who need healing. I couldn't live with myself if I ever hurt a person.

Colors are swirling in my brain, all turd browns and spoiling yellows. It hurts, like hot iron pokers jabbing at my brain.

"C'mon, Zoe." Craig stuffs me behind his back and starts pushing through the crowd. "I'm gettin' you on that bus."

Cell phones are clicking as more and more curious onlookers try to document the disturbance.

"Hey," the bus driver yells at an obnoxious man who's pushed his way in close. "What're you doin? You better delete that photo, I'm telling you."

The man barks something rude.

"Oh, yeah?" the bus driver responds. "Well, stuff it in your mouth."

I can't see the rude man, but I hear him. "Hey, jerk bus driver, where's your certification for that pigeon piece of crap yer operating? I jes took a photo of your license plate."

The bus driver's mouth snaps shut like a trap. He turns and runs back into the Pigeon bus, and slams the door. A second later, the bus guns it into traffic, belching black exhaust.

"My bus," is all I can say before I'm drowned out by voices all clamoring for me to place my hands on them. I look up. "Craig, how am I going to get to the Field Museum now?"

A man is taking a video of me and Craig on his cell. Craig puts his arms out and attempts to block him.

"I'm sorry, Zoe," he says, wrapping one arm around me and pressing my face close to his jacket.

Jean has managed to thrust her daughter in close to me. So does the limper. And other people are pressing in close. Their colors are a mish-mash, flowing from the spectrum of desperation, need, and fervent prayer. I can't breathe. I wish I could take each desperate person one at a time. But they won't wait, and the task now becomes overwhelming. The crush of bodies encircling me tears Craig away, and the current of their desperation washes him farther and farther away. And then, they take me down to the cement. They're pressing in on me, stealing my breath, tapping into my energy. *Abba, help me.* Power is pouring through every pore on my skin, burning me alive. A woman is loudly exclaiming, "Maddie can see. Zoe healed my daughter. Praise God, Maddie has been healed."

The flesh on my face is melting like wax, dripping off my skull. I try to scream but no air remains in my lungs. I'm a dead thing.

CHAPTER FOURTEEN

Aunt Evelyn cradles me in her arms. "It's okay, sweetheart. It's just a little boo-boo. But remember, Christmas is tomorrow morning."

Aunt's heart pulses slow against my ear and the sound of the steady beats comfort me. Her beautiful colors flow through my mind like a dancer skillfully employing multi-hued scarves to enhance her expressive motions. Slow, like Evelyn's pulse, slow, like a Sarabande.

A faceless man invades our peaceful embrace, jouncing me and pulling me out of my aunt's arms. I don't want to leave her, and I try to push him away.

"Three more steps, then turn right. The bed's to the left."

I open my eyes just long enough to recognize Craig and realize I'm being carried down a hallway. Another man, a stranger, guides Craig into a room awash in sunlight. A bed comes up to meet and cushion me. My eyes are too heavy to keep them open any longer.

When I wake up, the room is dark. A light from outside is shining through a slit in the curtains, focused directly on my face. I'm curled up on a big bed, covered with a quilt. When I sit up, my head spins and I feel terribly weak. If I weren't so hungry, I'd lie down again, but I can't deny my aching stomach. I can't find the light, so I fumble across the room to the sliver of light under the door.

Voices from another part of the house guide me to them. Craig is sitting at a kitchen table with a middle-aged man and a younger woman, probably close to my age. When Craig sees me, he stands and hurries over, concern puckering his eyebrows.

"You need to sit," he says gently and guides me to a chair. "Lynette, do you have any more coffee?"

"No, that's okay. No coffee for me," I say to the pretty blonde woman. "But I'm really hungry."

The middle-aged man fixes me with compassionate eyes. "How 'bout I heat up some of my famous meatloaf and mashed potatoes and gravy?"

"That would be great. Thank you, Mister ...?"

"I'm Frank. And Lynette's my daughter."

Lynette appears to be about my age, and although it's clear she's interested in Craig, she turns her attention to my side of the table long enough to smile and say, "You're welcome to stay here as long as you need, Zoe." Then her eyes are back on Craig, who looks uncomfortable with her attention.

Frank arranges a couple slices of meatloaf on a plate along with the mashed potatoes and puts it in the microwave. He also pours me a tall glass of milk.

I take a big gulp of milk, then another, and another. I hadn't realized how thirsty I was. The microwave goes ding, and Frank moves to fetch my plate.

"This sounds stupid, but since I've been asleep for a while, can you tell me which state we're in?"

Frank sets my plate in front of me. "You're in Pennsylvania. Doesn't matter which town or the street you're on. Just remember that Frank and Lynette, whose last name you can't recall, gave you a meal and a bed for a night."

Craig scratches at his auburn beard. "Frank and Lynette like to show kindness to strangers in need, 'specially the ones who are running away from evil. If we had more time, they could tell you stories you almost wouldn't believe about some of the people who've come through their doors."

I glance at Lynette, and she's wearing a mysterious smile, but she doesn't say anything.

Between shoveling in bites of Frank's delicious meatloaf, I ask, "What happened today? I can't remember anything past meeting you and leaving Pam's apartment."

Craig's eyebrows shoot upward. "You really don't remember anything?"

I shake my head. "I feel exhausted and weak, so I suppose something pretty big happened."

"I'll say. You were mobbed by people, all wanting you to put your hands on them. Zoe, what I witnessed was amazing. You should have seen them after they touched you. A lame man got up and started dancing and yelling that he was whole. A little blind girl got her sight back. And a man whose face was badly scarred—well—to see his face kind of like, melt, and then his eye and his nose move back to where they should be. Unbelievable.

Craig is gazing at the ceiling as if he's seeing the scene all over again. He looks down and his eyes refocus on me. "Zoe, God has done a work through you. I hope you thank God every day for such a gift."

Yeah, right. I guess that's what a good guy like Craig would think about my healing. Praise God. Easy for him to say. If what he tells me actually happened today, my ambitions and my life's plans are dead on arrival. I'll never have another normal day for the rest of my life. This sober realization makes the food in my stomach sit like a pile of bricks, and I feel the urge to run for the bathroom.

I stare at my plate. "Craig, did anyone take photos?"

"Yes."

"And? What happened after the healings?"

"Someone called NBC to ask if they could send a news crew over. Luckily, Pam overheard, and she phoned a friend who raced on over before the media could get there. We put you in the car and got the heck out of there."

The thought of the media putting photos of me on the news makes my whole body react. My brain lights up, and the whole street scene in Manhattan comes back to me. I see it all in high definition. "B-but, if everyone was taking pictures, how do we know they didn't get a shot of the car, and the car's license plate number?" My racing heart is making me breathless.

Craig rests his hand on my shoulder. "Don't worry, Zoe. Even if someone posts it on Facebook or whatever, we changed cars a couple of twisty-turns later while still in Manhattan. Then we changed again once we got into New Jersey. And again in Pennsylvania when we met Frank. I very much doubt anyone could have tailed us."

"Yes, but someone might have heard me when I said I was going to the Field Museum."

Craig's face falls, and I'm sure he's scanning his own mental video of the event. Then his face brightens. "I doubt anyone could have heard you say that. There was a lot of shouting and scuffling bodies, all trying to get close to you."

Despite Craig's reassurance, I'm not convinced. They don't know Finn and Clooney and his network of savvy criminals.

Overnight, I woke many times, reexperiencing the feelings of helplessness I'd felt when needy people had crushed me. I remember Jean and her blind daughter, Maddie, as they pressed into my shoulder. The limping man had grabbed hold of my leg and held on like a bulldog. And the scarred man had thrown himself over my torso, and my body had immediately glued him to my chest. No wonder I couldn't breathe. Some onlookers—maybe those simply wanting to experience a healing up close and personal—

had found unoccupied places on my arms or legs to feel my energy.

I don't want to diminish what it must be like for someone who's been assaulted, but this morning, I'm shaky and angry and resentful. I feel like those people violated me, taking what I had but not asking my permission. And my Abba had let them do it. What sort of God approves of this kind of supernatural rape?

I'm angry enough to not eat, but I force down the eggs and ham that Lynette serves me. I need to recover from my assault and keep up my strength. Who knows what else I'll face on my way back to Titusville?

We get an early start because Frank and Lynette have business to discuss with Craig. Around noon, Frank shows us his back yard where several vehicles are parked on his semi-rural property. Some of them don't look fit for the road. He gives us keys to a white minivan, and Craig and I climb inside. He can take me as far as Youngtown, Ohio. Then someone else will offer up his or her car for the ride to Chicago. Frank says they may have someone who can meet me there and drive the rest of the way to Titusville. He'll text Craig with more information as if becomes available.

I urge Craig not to take Interstate 80. If someone were trying to follow us, they'd likely think our car would be traveling that route. We plot our route on an old map Frank has given us and opt for some county roads before merging onto Interstate 70/76. We gas up in town, grab some snacks, then relax—kind of—on the county road. Our route will take a little longer but it's worth it for safety's sake. I purposely don't look around to mark which town Frank and Lynette live in. That way, if someone asks me, I can honestly say I don't know where I spent the night.

We talk about our hometowns, and then it occurs to me that I really don't know much about Craig besides the fact that he grew up in Brooklyn.

"What do you do when you're not rescuing damsels in distress?"

My question makes him grin. "I'm a teacher."

I like that. I can see him standing up in front of high school students and them totally respecting him. None of the guys act smart in his class. And the girls worship every word he says.

"High School?"

"Nah. SUNY."

"State University of New York? You're a college prof?"

"Yep. History."

I shake my head, and he tilts his in response, a question in his eyes. "There's a little bit of cognitive dissonance going on here." I tap my skull.

"How so?"

"Well, most of my professors at Northwestern were pretty agnostic, at best. And they'd be awfully skeptical of anyone claiming to be a healer."

Craig chuckles. "Not all of us. Although, for most of my life I was a skeptic and agnostic. Then I traveled overseas, working on my doctorate. Asia, Africa. I saw some things happen that I couldn't explain. People being raised from the dead, healings, stories of angel visitations. I came home with questions. A student put me in touch with Resurrection Church, and the pastor there explained about the Holy Spirit. I became a believer pretty quick, and I've been serving at the church ever since."

"How long have you been teaching at SUNY?"

"Three years. I did a year at another college as a fill-in for a tenured professor. Then SUNY hired me."

Not at all the kind of job I would have guessed Craig did. He looks more like a basketball coach. Or maybe a Viking warrior. I turn and watch Craig, who's focused on the road. I wonder if he has a girlfriend. I wonder if he'd ever consider teaching history on the west coast. I wonder how tall our children would be.

As if he hears my thoughts, he looks up and meets my eyes. His smile makes my cheeks heat up. *Zara, stop it. You aren't falling for Craig. It's just that he has the kind of life you want for yourself.*

And just like that, I'm angry again. "Why can't I have what other people have?"

"Sorry?" Craig's eyebrows slant with concern.

I give him an exasperated huff. "I didn't mean to say that out loud."

"What do you think other people have?"

"The freedom to do their own thing."

Craig looks confused. "You really believe that? Most people have expectations placed on them every day. From their families, their job, church, whatever."

"I get that." I'm not saying it right, and this is beyond frustrating. I'm usually better at expressing myself.

"So?" He waves his hand as if to say, "Go on talking."

"It's just that, I didn't ask for this gift. Why couldn't God have found someone more willing?"

He barely touches my wrist. "Help me to understand ... how life is ... to be a healer."

His touch tells me I need to turn and face him because he needs to see my eyes when I talk about my Abba. "I can't compare it to anything I know. Abba takes over, and it's the most frightening thing I've ever experienced. It's like being pulled out to sea, and you know you're going to drown. Then a power from outside fills me up like it's coming from a giant nozzle. I can't contain it. It pours out, and wherever there's a hole, that's where the energy goes.

"Sometimes—just before the energy comes—I feel an exhilarating breeze. I know it's him announcing his arrival. But when he gets closer, he's too much, he's too big. He's terrifying."

Craig's expression says he's filled with the wonder of my words. "I can only imagine what you endure," he whispers. "It is a fearful thing to fall into the hands of the living God."

I nod. "Even if it's not for judgment or punishment."

He looks like he wants to say something, but the words don't make it past his trembling lips. He takes my hand and warms it in his. "I'm honored to know you, Zoe."

Later, Craig has the radio on, and he sings along in a big baritone. He can't carry a tune and he knows it, so I help him. Not that I'm much better, but our voices together sound decent. He beams after each song, and his eyes seem to say I'm his best friend. Which makes me sad because, after today, I'll probably never see him again. I stop singing because my heart hurts. Is this what it was like for Aunt Evelyn, always running, never being able to settle in one place for long? Always saying goodbye?

I've only known Craig for a day and already, I'm feeling the sting of having to say goodbye. His honesty and willingness to listen have touched me deeply. And even though he could act high and mighty about being a college professor, he's humble and dedicated to serving me in whatever way he can.

I notice a small leaf clinging to the shoulder of his jacket. But when I try to pick it off, Craig's colors shed onto my fingers and twirl and twirl upward till they're twining around my entire arm.

Craig's colors aren't the happy blues I'd sensed in Pam's apartment. "You're worried. Is it me that's causing your concerns, or is it something back home?"

Craig's eyes grow round. "Man, it's a bit unnerving having you as a travel companion."

When I don't say anything, he shakes his head. "How do you know what I'm feeling?"

"It's your aura. A healer can sense it."

He tilts his head as if trying to comprehend this new piece of information. "So, do you read everyone's aura?"

"If I touch them. But sometimes a person's aura is so strong, I can sense it even if he's just walking by. So why are you worried?"

He sighs. "You're determined to have an answer?"

I nod.

"I'm concerned about all those people in New York City who witnessed your healing. Obviously, one or more of them ran to our church right after you healed Emma Joy and blabbed what they saw. And the next morning, Jean brought her daughter, Maddie, and someone must have told the guy with the limp. And word spread to the man with the disfigured face. I'm concerned that if they all post on social media or tell others about what they saw, they're going to become targets of the criminals seeking you.

"But Pam told them what's at stake," I say. "By now, she's warned them again not to say or do anything to bring attention to themselves." I say this not because I believe it, but because I need it to be true. Abba will make it be true. He'll warn them to keep quiet.

Craig looks like he's finding comfort in my words. "Maybe you're right. I'm sure you can predict things way better than I can."

We're not on Interstate 76 yet. We're on a winding road that parallels a river. The map says we'll come to 76 in about forty miles. Rain is splattering the windshield and the wiper is not going fast enough to clear the water. Craig slows down, squinting to see the road. Sometimes we hydroplane, and I grip the armrest even though I'm buckled in.

The rain doesn't quit. Spring leaves, driven by the wind, fly onto the road and our windshield and the wipers seem to angrily sweep them away. Rain has collected in low-lying areas and Craig tries to avoid them. But as the rain continues, water floods the road and there's no way to avoid the barrage. I glance at the river and note how high it is. It wouldn't take much more rain to bring it to a cresting level. The terrain on our right is hilly and rivulets pour down onto the road, as well. We drive around a curve and are met by a lake in the road. In this low-lying area the river has crested and is rapidly spreading. Craig brakes sharply, but not fast enough. The van plows into the flood, sending plumes of water cascading onto the windshield. Craig tries to reverse, but the engine stalls.

"We have to get out. Now," I shout over the storm. "We'll climb uphill."

Craig is a city guy. His wide-eyed stare says he's probably never been in a flood. "Shouldn't we just stay in the car?"

"Not if the flood's going to wash the car away ... into that." I point toward the river. Then I open my door and prepare to jump out. "C'mon, while we still can."

Craig doesn't wait to think. He pulls the van key, exits, and slogs around the front of the vehicle. The water level has risen to my thighs. Craig joins me and together we struggle to reach the base of the hill. When we begin our climb, our feet slide in the mud and we have to grip rocks, branches, roots, anything that still holds firm. Higher up, shrubs give way to trees, and we have something more substantial to hold on to.

Halfway up the hill, we pause to catch our breath. Craig looks down onto the road. "Look," he says, pointing. "The van's gone."

I look where he's indicated and see the backside of the van snared in between trees next to the river. Rain has soaked our hair and it's dripping down our faces. I'm chilled to the point of shivering, and I'm sure Craig is feeling the same.

"We gotta get out of this rain," he says with a quivering jaw. He reaches for my hand. "C'mon, we'll climb this hill and see if we can find a farm or something."

"Where's your cell?" I'm studying his pockets, hoping to see the outline of a cell phone.

His big shoulders slump. "Back in the car."

I can't help but make a defeated sound.

Craig forces an upbeat expression and pulls me closer to warm me. "We'll find something."

It's another fifty yards or so until we reach the top. We're both breathing hard from the steep climb. Gathering gloom makes it hard to see ahead more than a few yards. I tug at his arm. "If we don't find shelter soon, we'll be walking blind."

He nods. "I know. But I saw a farm sign a couple of miles back on this side of the road. If we keep heading north, we should run into it eventually."

"North?" I give him a giant shrug. "How the heck do you know where north is?"

He points to north and starts walking.

"Okay, wait for me." I catch up, grab hold of his arm, and sidle up for warmth.

The wind down in the valley isn't quite as strong, and in spite of the rain, Craig's body is warming me.

We hike steadily downhill, and the mud sticks to our feet and slows us down. The sun has sunk below the level of the trees, and we're stumbling over plants and debris. I wonder why we're not seeing any indications of a farm. So far, we haven't come across pastureland, or fences, or signs of farm animals.

What are we doing out in this forest, alone? *Oh Abba, help. We're going to freeze if we don't find shelter soon.* My foot catches in a tangle of branches and I stumble. Craig tries to catch me, but I go down too fast. I've wrenched my foot and I'm hoping it's not a sprain. It hurts like a son of a gun, and tears spring from my eyes. "This is awful."

Craig is kneeling by my side. "I'll carry you."

"No, you won't. You should go on and find help."

"And leave you? Not a chance." He opens his jacket to try to shield me from the rain. "I'm staying right here."

"Hello?" a man's voice calls.

We both jerk our heads in the direction of the sound. A faint light waves at us.

CHAPTER FIFTEEN

The faint light grows larger. I wince when Craig lifts me to my feet, but we try to hurry toward the light. The shape of a man emerges from the darkness, holding a lantern. He's bent slightly, as if trying to see where we are.

"Hello?" he calls again. "You folks lost?"

"We sure are," Craig calls back.

When we get closer, the man holds the lantern higher so we can see our way. "Awful weather, eh? Sometimes the river floods the highway. That what happened to you folks?"

He trudges in front, leading us through a clearing in the trees. My foot feels better, and I'm grateful it's not a sprain. We come over a ridge and see a farmhouse, all of the windows ablaze as if to exclaim, "Come on, come on in, we're so happy to welcome you!"

Wood smoke rises from its chimney. Craig squeezes my shoulder. "Thank the Lord," he murmurs.

We get off the soggy ground and onto a graveled drive, where we scrape off some of the mud.

As we follow the farmer up the porch steps, he says, "Jes' take off yer shoes an leave 'em here." We do as he instructs while he holds the door open for us.

When we step inside, the aroma of roast turkey, pumpkin spices, and everything else I associate with Thanksgiving fills the air.

We stand in the entrance staring at the homey place, and I can hardly believe this is real.

The farmer takes Craig's wet jacket and hangs it up. "Supper's almost ready, but you'll be wanting a shower first, I suspect."

"Really, we just need to use your phone," Craig says.

The old man shakes his head. "Sad to say, my phone isn't working right now. But we can check on it later. Now, about that shower. You can do that upstairs."

"We don't want to trouble you, sir," Craig offers, being way too polite, and I wish I could kick him.

"That's so kind of you," I say before the man can rescind his offer.

"And it's no trouble," the farmer adds. "You're wet and cold. And I got two nice showers upstairs." He waves for us to follow him up the stairs. "There're towels, cloths, and soapy type things in the shower. Mister, you go there," he says, gesturing for Craig to take the hall bath. "And you, ma'am, can use the bath in the master. There're robes hanging up on the door. I'll see you when yer done."

I'm not going to argue. My hair is a straggly mess and hot water is going to feel amazing on my still-chilled skin.

Half an hour later, I'm warm and clean and wrapped in a thick, terry bathrobe, the kind you'd find in an expensive hotel.

In the kitchen, Craig, dressed in his own robe, is helping out by slicing the turkey. The farmer is pouring coffee into mugs. "My name's Herb," he says when he sees me. "Guess I fergot to introduce myself when I first saw you."

I hurry over to help Herb place the rest of the dishes on the dining room table. "I'm very glad to meet you, Herb. My name's Zoe."

Herb looks surprised. "Zoe, is it? You sure your parents named you that?" We meet eyes as we both bend to set food on the table.

I can't think of a response so I just shrug. Herb seems average in every way, and yet, there's a vitality to him and his eyes crinkle with good humor. He doesn't seem curious about us, though. But some people are like that. They just accept you at face value.

"Well, anyway," I say, hoping to get Herb off the subject of my name, "I'm wondering, how did you know we were lost in the woods?"

Herb smiles, and his teeth are as white as a cloud on a sunny day. "I was out, picking up pieces of wood for my wood-burning fireplace, and I heard your voices." He smiles. "Good thing I was low on wood or I'd 'a been huddled inside where any sensible soul should be on a night like this."

"Sounds like a God-appointment," Craig says, coming out of the kitchen, carrying a platter piled with turkey.

"Eh? God-appointment?" Herb laughs and the sound is surprisingly young-sounding coming from an older man. "That's a new phrase. I kinda like it."

"You must have good ears, though," I add. "I could hardly hear my own voice out there in the storm."

"That I do," Herb says with another laugh. "Well, let's set."

When we're seated, he reaches across the table for our hands and clasps them in a warm and firm grip. "Lord," he says softly, "Thank you for gittin' these pleasant strangers out from the storm. All good things come from you, so we're thankin' you fer the good food too. Amen."

"Amen," Craig repeats.

It's a Thanksgiving meal in early summer. Way before the harvest. But that's okay because I know Abba has sent this kind stranger to help us. I can't stay angry at Abba, even though he allowed desperate strangers to pile on top of my body and suck me almost dry of energy. Because now he's feeding Craig and me, sheltering us. Who am I to question his ways?

Herb has put out a spread a farm wife could be proud of. The turkey is moist and flavorful, and there's not a single lump of unblended flour in the gravy. It's way better than any gravy I ever attempted. "Herb, how come you've made so much food? Were you expecting company?"

Herb pauses to swallow. "Well, you see, I like to make a big meal, then store the leftovers fer later. And, in the meantime, if someone shows up unexpected-like, I'm happy to share my food."

I nod, but I'm not convinced that's the whole reason for this feast.

Craig, however, is not looking a gift horse in the mouth. He's had at least three helpings of turkey, mashed potatoes, and gravy. And now, he piles four dinner rolls on his plate too. I can't imagine having to feed Craig's giant appetite every day.

Herb directs his attention on Craig. "Phone's working now. Maybe you'll want to call friends or family and have 'em pick you up tomorrow morning. Things will be dryin' up—

Craig jumps up before Herb has even finished speaking. "Thanks. I'll do that right now. What's your address?"

"It's 22364 Crescent Drive."

Craig picks up the phone and dial's Frank's number.

I want to follow Craig and listen to his phone conversation, but Herb is keeping me prisoner with his conversation. "Yessiree, these storms keep me watching out for travelers. Cell phones are a good thing, but when you don't have one, you need someone like me to come fetch you."

"You've done this before?" My eyes are wide, and my gut clenches. What if Herb has a kind of racket here in this lovely warm farmhouse? What if he lures people inside, promising to take care of them? Then, in the morning, he presents them with a ridiculously huge bill for the meal and the shower and a bed for the night.

"Yep. Last year, late at night, a man's car broke down on the county road. Well, it's at least five miles to the nearest station, and who'd be open to fix his car at three o'clock in the morning? So, I invited him to stay the night. In the morning, I fed him breakfast. Then we waited down the hill fer the tow truck to arrive."

Okay, Herb isn't a crook. He's just a kind man with an awesome gift of hospitality. My gut relaxes, and I take another sip of coffee.

"Now, fer tonight, you got yer pick of two bedrooms. I have to leave early, but I'll make sure to have some breakfast things set out for you and Craig."

Now that I'm not afraid anymore, my heart overflows with warmth. "How can we thank you? If we hadn't seen your light, we'd be in a really bad predicament by now."

"No need to thank me, Zoe. Jes' pass it forward to the next needy person you meet." He reaches across the table for a handshake, and I gladly meet him halfway. Somehow, I know that my fingers will not zap him. I'm hoping to read his colors, but the only thing I feel is an assurance that everything will work out. I'll reach Chicago safely and friends will help me get home.

Craig returns and digs into his pumpkin pie. "Everything's fine, Zoe. Frank's going to meet us and see about arrangements for towing the van. He'll see that you make your next stop." His eyes and the dip of his chin emphasize that I have nothing to worry about.

After the meal, Herb seems delighted that we help him clear the table and load the dishwasher. He nods, grunts approval, and instructs while we take care of the clean-up. "Yep, that goes there. And I wash the gravy boat by hand. My, you're good helpers. I should hire you next time I have company."

After I hang up the dishtowels, Herb says, "I turn in early, but yer welcome to stay up and make yerselves comfortable by the fire." He turns and heads for the stairs.

"Thanks again, Herb," I call after him.

"Welcome," he says over his shoulder.

Now that we're alone, I have a dozen questions for Craig concerning his phone call. "What did Frank—?"

But he holds his finger up to his mouth while he tiptoes past me and glances up the stairwell. Herb's bedroom door is closed.

"I'm a little concerned that I had to call Frank. I don't like that a stranger—even a nice guy like Herb—has Frank's number now. Frank doesn't like to be traced. Some guy trying to track one of Frank's clients could get his number and come looking for a girlfriend or wife."

"It couldn't be helped. And I don't think Herb would ever give out anyone else's private information."

Craig's face relaxes and he grabs a fresh mug from the cupboard and pours himself more coffee.

Poor Craig. He obviously thinks I read Herb and determined that he's a reliable guy. In fact, I couldn't read a single color coming from Herb. The man had no aura, either bad or good. I decide to keep quiet about Herb. Craig needs to rest tonight. No sense in giving him information that will make him toss and turn.

We're both exhausted so we turn in early.

In the morning, we eat the oatmeal and fruit Herb left for us. I write a note thanking him for his hospitality and leave it on the kitchen counter.

Frank had told Craig he would call for a tow-truck to meet us where Herb's road meets the county road. We hike down the hill and find the truck already waiting for us.

He lowers his window. "Did you call for a tow?"

"Sure did," Craig says, trotting up to the door. We climb inside and the driver starts the motor.

"Some storm last night," he says. "Had tons of calls. People stalled in intersections, stuck in ditches, some couldn't get out of their own driveways. Crazy."

Craig nods. "That's for sure. We almost floated into the river. I hope our van is still where we left it."

"Where's that?"

"Up the road a mile or two," I add. "It was so flooded we had to jump out and climb to safety."

"Wow, like I said, that's crazy." He puts the truck in gear, and we pull onto the road. "Where'd you stay overnight?"

"Just up that lane where you met us." I point backward, but we've already gone around a curve. "A farmer let us stay with him."

"A farmer?" The truck driver screws up his mouth like he doubts my story.

"Yes," I say, "There's a nice farm up the hill. The farmer saw us wandering around looking lost and he took us in."

The driver gives me the kind of tolerant smile you'd reserve for someone with dementia. "Miss, I don't want to argue with you, but I've lived here for more than fifty years and there isn't a farm within ten miles of here."

Craig and I exchange glances.

"Then whose house—?"

"Well, I take that back. Years ago there used to be a dairy farm, but it's all gone now. Nothing but a few logs to mark where a barn used to be."

"But ... but, there was a house." What's wrong with this tow-truck driver? He plainly saw the road we had come down. "It was a farmhouse. And a nice old farmer cooked dinner for us and let us stay overnight."

"Really," Craig says, his tone a little put out. "We're not joking. We did stay in a house and sleep there too. 22364 Crescent Drive is the address. You can drive past it again when we're done and see for yourself."

The driver raises his eyebrows and tugs on the brim of his baseball cap. "Okay, if you say so." He focuses on the road, the condescending smile fading into his fleshy jowls and graying stubble.

Craig takes my hand. "This makes me think about some of my experiences in Africa."

"This makes me think about Abba," I say, and thanksgiving is already buzzing in my chest.

CHAPTER SIXTEEN

Frank and Lynette meet us at the car repair shop in the nearest town. There isn't much the service man can do for a van with a flooded motor, so Frank decides to donate the vehicle. After Frank takes care of business, we all pile into his Buick and continue west to our next meeting spot in a town in western Pennsylvania.

We pull into a church parking lot and idle. I scan the lot, wondering what our next rendezvous car will be. Except for a VW bug parked close to the entrance to the church, there are no other vehicles.

"Zoe," Frank says, "we're waiting for George. He'll be driving a blue church van."

Craig brushes my hand. "Let's wait outside."

I grab Ruby's leather bag and follow him outside. He's shedding gray and beige colors that reveal a bleak mindset.

I walk further away from the van so we can't be overheard, and he follows me. "You know that thing that happened last night?" I ask as we walk. "Herb and the farmhouse and the meal. You want to share this with your church body, don't you?"

"But not right away," he says quickly. "Not until you're safe and you've found your parents."

We reach a brick retaining wall filled with flowers and bushes and we sit. Craig's usually happy face is solemn. Maybe he's dreading saying goodbye as much as I am.

"I'm writing a book about supernatural events and miracles in the church," he says. "It's about time the western church grapples with the reality of what happens on the other side of the world. If you give your permission, I'd like to add our experience to my research."

"Could you change my name for my privacy?"

"Absolutely. But I'm hoping you'll help me recall every detail of Herb and that night. I don't want to leave anything out."

"You have my consent. Just let me see the edited manuscript before it gets released."

"Which means we'll get together again, right?"

I shrug. "We could do this all via email, you know."

Craig's not looking at me. He's studying his hands, folded on his lap. "But then I wouldn't see you again. I'd like this to be an in-person collaboration." He raises his eyes to meet mine. "Please."

I hardly know the giant man sitting next to me, but we've lived half a life together in only three days. "I'd like that ... very much." I feel his need to express his growing affection, and I'm ready.

Craig leans close, cups my face and gives me a tender kiss. "I won't forget you," he whispers.

I'd like another kiss, but the sound of an approaching vehicle forces us to separate. A blue van with the words, The Rock, pulls up. There's a flying dove painted on the side, and I chuckle at the irony of catching another 'bird' but with nicer occupants for the latter half of my trip to Chicago.

Frank and his daughter come over to say goodbye. "You'll be fine," Lynette says when she hugs me. "George will make sure of that."

Craig walks me over to the van door. "Remember, we *will* see each other again."

He bends and wraps his arms around me in a final embrace. I climb inside the van and George shuts the door.

The van pulls forward, and I catch a final glimpse of Craig waving. He presses his palms together in front of his chest to say he'll be praying, but I lose sight of him when we turn onto the road.

My heart hurts.

The Dove, I call it, is closer to a small bus than a van, like the ones that carry handicapped people. So far, there are only George, the bus driver, an older woman, and me. I guess I'm safe inside the Dove, headed for points west and ending at Chicago.

The farther I get from the wretched city where Finn and Clooney operate, the better I feel, even though it's taking me away from a man I think I could love.

Still, what future would Craig have with me if I have to continually hide from hordes of healing-seekers? *Oh Abba*.

We should be in Chicago late afternoon or early evening, so George says. We stop in a town in the middle of Ohio, and I feel a sliver of anxiety while we wait for another rider to arrive and come aboard. Finally, a man drives up and helps a young woman climb into the front passenger seat. She's heavily pregnant, keeps her head down, and as soon as we drive away, she falls asleep.

I've only been on a couple of bus trips before. One time, my mom and I took a bus to Indianapolis to see her aunt Tina. I was about eight. Mom kept warning me not to talk to anyone. The bus station was dirty and the bathroom stank, and even though I washed up, Mom kept applying hand sanitizer to my hands. Most of the trip was boring.

This trip is different. The bus is clean, and George plays lovely music on the radio. Still, I feel terribly alone. I wish my mom could be here with me. Or my big sister. We'd talk about normal things. Abby would talk about her diet and her best diet recipes. Then she'd grumble that it's not fair that I can eat anything I want and never get fat. And I'd say, "I don't hear Rolf complaining about your weight," and she'd giggle. Then I'd talk about books I'm reading and my plans to study at Oxford for my doctorate.

It seems to take forever to get out of Pennsylvania. It's beautiful, but it leaves me cold because of my need to get to Chicago.

I open my overnighter and paw through the contents, doing inventory. The blonde wig is on top, reminding me of my first scary hours of freedom while wandering Manhattan. I shove it under the extra clothes. That's when I discover that Ruby had stuffed a Tupperware box filled with crackers and some string cheeses under the clothing. So, I munch on a couple of crackers and cheese, and my stomach relaxes. Drowsy, I wrap my arms around my bag and lean my head against the window.

The bus stops in a town in Ohio, I think, where the older woman gets off. I go back to sleep. I keep dreaming about being in an empty office building. There's a crowd of people outside, with guns. Soon they're going to barge inside to search for me, and when they find me, nothing good will happen. My stomach knots, and I listen for all I'm worth for sounds of invaders. I creep down an empty hallway, trying doors. They're all locked. Just in time, I find an unlocked door. A closet. I slip inside noiselessly, but there's a dark-haired young woman hiding there.

She holds her finger up to her lips, and whispers, "I've found a ventilation pipe we can climb through to get out of the building. But we have to wait until the people actually get inside before we can escape."

It's a terrible gamble. Escape now and risk being seen and attacked. Or wait until the rabble gets inside and risk discovery before we can get through the pipe.

I jerk awake, my heart pounding and extremities tingling. My bag slips off my lap, and the movement startles me even more. I throw my hands out to grab the bag, and that wakes me up all the way. A man has taken the empty seat next to me. He's holding an iPad and seems engrossed in whatever's on the screen.

I wonder what he's escaping from. Out of the corner of my eye I see that he's dressed in a sweater and nice slacks. His watch is on his right wrist. I sneak a peek. His watch says it's a bit after noon. The man looks about thirty-five, clean-shaven, decent looking. Average in every way. Doesn't look like a victim or a deranged man.

I sure wish I had something to read to make the miles pass.

And then the man turns and gives me an acknowledging smile. He reaches down and pulls something out of his briefcase and offers it to me. "Want something to read? I just finished this. Pretty entertaining, if you like history and suspense."

I stare at the book and then at him. The air that's stirred around him when he moves fills my lungs like a spring breeze through a pine forest, and his eyes have the kind expression of someone who's been a friend all my life.

"Oh, that's okay. I mean ..." I glance down at the book. "It does look interesting, though. I'm, uh, sort of more into poetry and literary novels."

He's smiling like he knows something.

"But thank you, sir."

He nods in a good-natured sort of way and slips the book back into the case. "I usually read books on my iPad, but a friend gave me the paperback, so how could I say no? He said, 'Ian, my friend, make sure you hand off this book to some other reader before they get to Chicago.'"

"Well, in that case, may I read your book?" I say with forced enthusiasm.

"Thanks." He retrieves the paperback. "You've done me a big favor. Now it's your book. And Matt—that's my friend—said to tell the next reader, when you're done, hand it off to someone else." He hands it to me, and now he's grinning like a football player who's just scored a touchdown.

"I'll do that."

"Literary novels and poetry, eh? Ever read Jane Austin's books?"

I sniff. "Of course." That sounds arrogant, so I blurt, "I mean, they're great and all. But lately I've been reading twentieth-century authors, like Salman Rushdie and Virgina Woolf. Last month I reread *To Kill a Mockingbird.*"

"Sounds like some heavy reading."

"How so?"

"Well, that Harper Lee novel, *To Kill a Mockingbird*, is such a sad book, for the most part. Atticus Finch is quite a hero, but it's tragic how prejudice destroyed lives back in pre–civil rights days."

"Still does today."

"Absolutely. And I don't see things turning around anytime soon." He sighs. "We need healing for the world, for our nation, for friends and neighbors and enemies. We need people who are willing to be healers."

Why did he have to bring up that word? "What kinds of healers?" I half expect him to point his finger at me and say, "You, Zara. We need you to be a healer."

He shrugs. "Any kind that's needed at just the right time for just the right kind of needy person."

I don't like the direction this conversation is going. Right now, I need to think about staying alive myself, not helping someone else.

I nod like I'm considering what he'd said, then raise the book. "Thanks for the book. I'll try to get this read before I reach ... well, before I get to my destination." No sense in letting this stranger know where I'm going. Nowadays, I'm mighty suspicious of everyone.

Ian smiles and turns back to his iPad, and I open to the first page of *Blood Stains*. What a dumb title.

The book isn't as bad as I'd thought it would be. Turns out the story is about a civilian outside Paris, France, during World War II who tries to hide Jewish children. But he takes awful risks to get them to safety. I take a breather from reading to watch the farmlands zipping by. It reminds me of home, and my eyes mist again at the thought that things will never be the same. Even if Mom and Dad come out of this alive, I'll have to live far away from them so danger never comes near them again. I won't see Abby and Rolf and Baby Cora very often either.

I glance over at Ian. He's not reading. He's looking out the opposite window. I'd like another handful of crackers, but I don't want to eat in front of Ian. What if he doesn't have anything to eat? That would be rude.

I dig into my bag and pull out the box. Giving Ian a timid touch, I hold up the crackers. "Would you like some? I have plenty." Not really. The box is already more than half-empty, and I still have many hours left in my trip. But at least I can offer some.

"Hey, that would be nice." He smiles again, and his eyes take on that father, older brother, favorite uncle— whatever—kind of warmth.

He cups his hands together, like he's begging alms. The bus jounces us, so I carefully place a handful of crackers onto his palms. The touch of his fingertips as I withdraw my hands is so slight, it's more like a breath. What happens is immediate. A canopy of brilliant white flies upward in front of my face. It's a sail unfurling at a gust of wind. I'm a little girl, and I'm looking upward, and sunshine dazzles my eyes. I turn and look below the sailboat at the pretty sparkling water. I want to splash my fingers in the shiny liquid. It looks so cool and fun, like green bubble bath. I lean over the railing, but my body is too small, so I lean farther, farther. All of a sudden I'm falling, and I hear my mother scream. I know she's too far away to catch me. But my lips don't even graze the cold salt water. My body halts in midair, and something pushes me back. Not pulling. Pushing. Right back over that railing in an impossible, against-the-law-of-physics way, and then my mother is hugging me close and crying, "Thank you. Thank you, Jesus."

My mind snaps back to the present, the bus, and me handing Ian crackers.

"You look like you're three thousand miles away," Ian says.

My hands are still poised over his cupped hands, only his hands are on his lap, and he's eaten half his crackers already.

"Oh ... uh, guess I was caught in a memory. Something that happened a long time ago."

"Memories are wonderful things, aren't they? They keep us thankful, especially when tough times come."

"Yeah, I guess so. Some of them." I stare at Ian because he looks like he knows what I was remembering.

"Thanks for the crackers, by the way. They were really good." He smiles again with such a warm "I've always known you" expression that my cheeks flush, and I get busy closing the box of crackers and stowing it in my overnighter.

I wonder if Ian is a con man. When I was a child, my parents used to tell me not to trust strangers. Some are good at making you to think they're nice. And then they do something like cheat you out of your money. Not that I have a lot of that to steal.

Ian nods at the book on my lap. "What do you think of the book so far? Is it what you were expecting?"

"Well, when I saw the title, *Blood Stains*, I thought it was going to be some cheap thriller about a maniac roaming foggy city streets looking for victims to slash."

Ian laughs a big, manly laugh. Kind of like my dad's laughter, and my heart squeezes at the thought.

"Sorry. I guess I should have clued you in."

"That's okay. I like surprises."

He laughs again, and his joy is infectious. He makes me want to laugh at my circumstances, which, er, under the circumstances, doesn't seem rational. I catch another whiff of pine. It must be his aftershave.

I open the book to the last page I read. "I've often wondered what I would do if some occupying military force ordered me to do things that my conscience couldn't abide. Like turning over innocent children to Nazis."

"We all like to think we'd be a hero and do the right thing."

I shake my head. "Well, I must be atypical. I doubt I'd be really brave. I think I'd mind my own business, try to be normal, not do anything that makes the enemy suspicious. I'm not the heroic type."

"Really." Ian says this more like a statement than a question. "What if you had to disobey the enemy authorities in order to protect your family or close friends?"

"I'd be so scared."

"Being scared isn't the same thing as being cowardly. I have the feeling that if push came to shove, you'd do the right thing."

"How can you be so sure since we've just met?"

"Because I'm like you. I just know." He smiles and his eyes shed such sincerity that, unless he's the most brilliant con man that ever lived, he must be telling the truth.

I can hardly contain myself. My heart is racing at the realization that I might be talking to someone with the same gift. "Are you a ... healer?" I whip my head around and scan the interior of the bus to make sure no one's trying to listen in.

Ian doesn't answer right away. He seems to be deliberating about what to say. Then he leans closer. "Abba gives me ... uh ... jobs to do."

"Jobs?"

"Yes, like the jobs your Abba gives you. Only a little different. My jobs are usually watching out for someone."

Like my friend, Craig, and that father and daughter who help people in need?"

He laughs. "Yes, like Craig."

Thinking about Craig makes me tremble. What if Finn and Clooney manage to find me and I never get the chance to build a relationship with him?

Ian's still smiling. "You're a brave woman, Zara. Abba will have his way in you."

Does this man know things I can't possibly imagine? "Mr. Ian, will I be okay?"

He pats my arm. "You'll be fine. If you have eyes to see, look. Your helpers are all around you."

He reaches for his briefcase and stuffs his iPad inside. "My stop's coming up."

We exit the interstate and come to a small town. We're in the middle of Indiana, I think. The bus pulls into a parking lot, and Ian stands and looks down at me for a second without speaking. Which makes me feel awkward, so I blurt out, "It was nice to meet you, Ian. And thanks for the book … and for the reassurance."

He nods, smiling in a satisfied way, like I'm a movie and he's just seen the happy ending. "Chicago's rough. But a good person like you will always find friends. So long, young lady. I'll be praying for you." He steps out, and I watch from the window. But Ian does not walk away from the bus. He's vanished. My breath catches. Did Ian cross in front of the bus and go the opposite direction? I jump up and hurry to the other side of the bus. No Ian there, either.

Tingles zip down my legs and into my toes. Ian has God-jobs to do. Then, he disappears. Just like Herb.

I return to my seat and pick up the paperback book Ian had given me. Even though it's been in Ian's possession, the book bears no lingering Ian scent. No pine aftershave, No refreshing breeze swirling around it. It's just a book. But Ian wasn't just a man.

I puzzle over what he just said about Chicago. Did he mean that Chicago is a dangerous city for a young woman? Was he telling me to be careful? And I don't remember telling him my name or my destination. Did he read my thoughts about that, too? I feel sad that he's gone, and now I have no one to talk to.

George helps the pregnant young woman get off. A woman meets her and together they trudge toward a rusted and dented car.

Two women hurry from a café and come over to speak with George. They hand him an envelope which he reads over, then ushers them inside our bus.

We're back on the interstate in less than ten minutes.

CHAPTER SEVENTEEN

We're in the outskirts of Chicago, and now I'm nervous. What if Finn knows I'm on this bus? But that's impossible. I hung out in Ruby's apartment—practically a stone's throw from Finn's three-story house—for almost a day. Then I walked away in a disguise so weird, not even my parents would have recognized me. And next, I spent the night with Pam and Emma Joy. I hope Finn and Clooney haven't seen any social media posts about me.

I borrow George's cell to dial the phone number Craig has given me. I tell the man on the other end that I'll be in front of the Field Museum in less than half an hour. He says, "okay," then hangs up.

My stomach is knotting because there are so many uncertainties. My own words might have clued in Finn and Clooney to where I'll be waiting. If the man in Manhattan who took a video of me posts it, I'm in trouble. Craig clearly heard me say I was supposed to be at the Field Museum.

I take a couple of deep breaths to try to relax my stomach.

Finn has probably ordered his goons to scour New York City, looking in places where homeless people hang out. They couldn't have figured out I'd found some money and had been driven out of the state with the help from new friends.

I glance out the window, watching the ugly parts of Chicago fly by. If my ride doesn't show up, I don't have a plan once the bus drops me off. I only know I have to find a ride to Titusville

My heart pulses in my ears as the bus meanders through downtown Chicago. In a few minutes, I'll find out if I've been followed.

I put the horrible, scratchy blonde wig on and feel to make sure I've stuffed all my dark hair underneath and cover my eyes with the sunglasses. The bus pulls over and stops. My heart is practically jumping out of my throat. I peer through the windows, searching for Finn or Clooney.

George gets out and stands on the sidewalk, arms folded across his chest. Craig told him about my bad guys and that they might be waiting for me.

The moment of truth comes. I hold tight to my overnighter as I step off the bus and look right and left. I'm not leaving George's side until I've made sure it's safe.

The wind off the lake nearly blows my wig off.

"It looks safe," George says. "I wish I could walk you over to the museum, but I can't leave my van here."

"It's okay." Already, I'm feeling confident. There are tons of people out on the sidewalk. The sun is shining, and I feel strong, almost as strong as the day I fought off the rabid dog.

"George, thank you so much for the ride. I'll be fine. The museum's just steps away."

"Be safe, young lady." He smiles and turns to get back into his bus.

Behind me, George's bus goes 'toot, toot' and I wave goodbye to him.

Several people are headed for the museum, so I follow them. I'm not sure if I'm supposed to wait outside or inside. The guy on the phone didn't say. Maybe I could go up the steps and wait. From there, I can keep an eye on the whole front of the building. I'm just about to take the steps when someone startles me. "Excuse me, miss," he says. "Would you be able to direct me to the Miracle Mile?"

I snap my arm toward my chest. "Sorry, I don't know." I try to run but the man's grip pulls me up short.

I'm in trouble. I force my eyes upward, and my stomach lurches when I see Finn's bearded face next to mine, his blue eyes cold and threatening. I almost drop my satchel.

"Don't even think about screaming if you want to live," he growls, and shoves something hard against my back. A gun? "Come on, sweet Zara."

He guides me toward the curb, away from the crowd. I can't let him do that. I can't let Finn get me in some spot where no one sees. Is he leading me to a car? I'm toast if he pushes me into one.

"Zara, keep in mind that all it would take is a phone call to some really nasty guys to turn you into an orphan." He snaps his fingers to illustrate how quick the process would be.

That snap does something to me. The me who climbed a swing rope to escape a rabid dog—that kind of me—marches to the front of my brain and takes charge.

An idea pops into my mind, about a girl. A girl being kidnapped right in broad daylight—it was on the news—and what she did to get away.

We're walking south, and a crowd has joined us. There's man in front of me, and he throws off a hideous color like green bile from his head and shoulders. Perfect. We're walking quicker than the stranger. Finn is in a hurry to get me away from all these people. He can't get around them yet. Too many hem us in. We come up close to the man with the ugly colors. I feel Finn's grip tighten in preparation. He's going to pull me to the side so we can pass ugly-color man. I take a breath and throw my bag. Perfect aim. It hits him right behind the knees and makes him stagger.

He stops immediately, whirls around, and glares at Finn. "Hey, what the ...?"

Finn lets go of me, slips the gun into his coat pocket so fast and smooth no one would have seen it. "Pardon me, sir. It was an accident."

"Yeah, well, back away from me."

"I assure you, it won't happen again." Finn snatches up my bag and thrusts it into my arms, shooting me a hateful glance and mouthing, *Don't mess with me.* Again, he shoves the hard thing—most likely the gun—into my back.

But now that I've seen the stranger's ugly colors intensify, I tense my muscles and get ready for my next move. I feel like a warrior, ready for anything the rabid Finn can use against me. I am cold steel with a sharp blade. My mind is quick, my body prepared.

We don't get more than five steps farther, when I launch my bag again. This time it hits the guy square in the butt. The man whirls, his face red, nostrils flaring. He doesn't even wait for an apology, just sends a right hook to Finn's jaw so hard my kidnapper's head snaps back. Finn's eyes roll upward, and he goes down on one knee. Some pedestrians move aside, some stay to see if there might be a fight. Others flee. The stranger's punch has freed me from Finn's grip, so I take off running. No time to look back. I run for my life, like I'm running again from that awful frothing dog.

I cross against the light, several cars almost mowing me down. Horns blare and drivers gesture angrily, but I keep running, dodging pedestrians, dashing through more lines of cars stuck at traffic stops. It's like a dream where you're running but you never get out of breath. My thighs pump speed into me. I run faster than I've ever done the one-hundred-meter dash.

When I stop to look back, a man catches my eye. He's about fifty yards behind me. He's a lumbering guy but just as dangerous. It's Clooney, swinging his hefty arms to help him along, huffing with the effort. Everything about his movement says rage and determination. He presses a phone to his ear.

How far could Clooney follow without having a heart attack? The fat guy is not made for running. Is Finn coming after me too? No time to stop and look back. I cross a street and turn down another. I don't have time to notice street signs. Cross again. Down another street. A patch of green comes into view. I home in like a pigeon. Trees, walkways, bushes. A playground. A small building that might be restrooms. But I can't hole up there and risk getting trapped.

I sprint down the sidewalk, cross the street, and jump over a low-growing hedge. I can't run anymore. I have to rest. I throw myself down behind the hedge. The foliage is dense, but I can peek through it and see if Finn or Clooney are anywhere near. Some kids playing nearby stare at me because I'm lying on my stomach in the dirt, like an army recruit on field training, desperately trying to catch my breath. Out of the corner of my eye, a kid tugs at his mother's elbow, points at me. She sees me, grabs her little boy, and hurries him away. I watch for my pursuers. After ten minutes, my breathing is normal, and I still don't see Finn or Clooney.

I stand and slink farther into the park and down a path. The park is bigger than I'd thought. I sometimes veer off the path to hide and check if anyone's behind me. I'm not sure if I'm safer in the park or back on the streets. Finn or Clooney could be anywhere. They could have other guys out there too. Finn had no trouble recognizing me even in the blonde wig and sunglasses, so I may as well ditch those. I wait until no one is in view and then rip that thing off my head and throw it into a trash bin. I decide to change into the spare clothes, but then realize that I don't have the overnighter.

My stomach plunges again. Everything ... everything was in that bag. Almost all the money, my crackers, my change of clothes. The phone number Craig had given me. I can't help it. I start crying. I push through the bushes lining the path for several yards before I collapse onto the ground and sit with my head in my hands. I don't even try to muffle the sound. I'm hungry. I'm tired. I'm scared almost witless. Every muscle in my body is tense and twitchy. And now I have no money to get a motel room, and no way of getting away from my kidnappers.

My mind is blank. What does someone who lives on the streets do? I've volunteered at food banks and served meals to homeless people, but I've never experienced having no home for shelter. No place to get warm or to be safe from predators.

At least it's warm today. Not much chance of freezing to death in Chicago in late spring unless we have a freak snowstorm.

How am I going to hitch a ride toward Titusville? I've never driven around here. The last time I was here was a couple of years ago in the summer with my church college and career group, and I sure wasn't paying attention when our van exited the interstate and took us downtown.

At least, I'm hundreds of miles west of New York City. That has to count for something. If not for Ruby, I'd still be wandering Manhattan, probably panhandling for change so I could get some food. I think I'm better off here—that is, if Finn or Clooney don't spot me.

I'm a lot less noticeable in this park, away from the path. They'd never figure I'd hide in the middle of some trees and bushes for the night. What would a woman do without money in the heart of Chicago? Well, if she's smart, she'll go to the nearest police station and tell them all about being mugged and losing her bag and about being stranded in an unfamiliar city without any money. But this young woman can't do that. Or maybe she'd head for the local YWCA or a church or homeless shelter or mission. That's what she'd do if she didn't want to explain to the police who she is and how some bad guys have threatened to kill her if she talks about their criminal enterprises. She's not dumb. She knows she needs to get to a place where bad dudes and criminals and predators can't get to her.

I fully intend to find such a place. Just not now. Not when Finn and Clooney are probably still walking around the streets near the Field Museum hoping I'll return. They've probably gone into some of the public buildings to see if I'm hiding out there. Then when they can't find me, they'll go hole up at a hotel. I can just see them, lounging on their hotel beds. They're arguing over what to watch on the TV sitting on the dresser across from the bed. Clooney wants to watch one of those reality shows. Finn rolls his eyes because he wants to watch Turner Classic Movies. They're probably flipping a coin to see who gets his way. Maybe flipping a coin over who gets to kill me once I'm in their hands again.

My body shakes again, and I fight tears. Not too many bright and innocent college graduates are running for their lives from rich, successful drug-dealers-slash-cold-blooded-killers who've likely lost their grandpa to lung cancer by now and want to silence me before I can tell the police about them.

If anyone needed a miracle right about now, Abba, it's me.

CHAPTER EIGHTEEN

Outside the park, about half a block down, a roach truck advertises tacos, burritos, enchiladas. I buy a burrito and a Coke and return to my hiding place. I sure wish I had a blanket or even a tarp to sit on. It's going to get cool as the night wears on, and the ground already feels moist. I scrape up some leaves and make a thin bed. I'm surrounded by bushes and sheltered by trees. As the sun goes down, the chirping of birds ceases, and all I hear are the sounds of cars and buses. Does anyone ever sleep in this city? It's not much different from New York City.

I unwrap my burrito and try to keep myself from eating the whole thing. The Coke tastes amazing after a day spent running and hiding. I wrap up the rest of the burrito and curl up on my bed of leaves.

When I wake up, I have no idea what time it is. It's still dark, though, except for a park lamp's dim rays coming from the concrete path I'd wandered many hours ago. I don't know why I woke up, but all of a sudden, my body is on high alert. I'm not alone.

Human breath, crinkling paper. I whirl around and sit up. An old man is crouching near me, his space dimly lit by a flashlight. He's found the leftover burrito and is stuffing the entire thing into his mouth. He snuffles and chews like an animal, and all I can do is stare.

People have told me they're scared of homeless people. But I've been around them a lot, spent time sitting with them when they came in for lunch. Most of them are harmless, except for the ones who are on drugs. Those are the ones I don't trust. But this old man doesn't look like that sort. His eyes are watery, and he's so skinny he's practically a skeleton.

When he finally swallows his mouthful of burrito, he meets my eyes and smiles. "Thank you, miss." He tips his hat. "Sorry I didn't ask, but you looked so peaceful, sleeping like a baby. I didn't want to wake you." He crumples the wrapper and drops it, then sinks down onto his behind and stretches out his pitifully skinny legs. "My name's Bernard. Pleased to meet you." He extends a blackened hand, and I shake it.

"I'm happy to meet you, Bernard, and I'm happy to share my food. But you should have asked first."

Bernard shifts his eyes back and forth. But then he must have come to a decision, because his eyes settle on me, and he sighs contentedly.

I guess I'm okay with sharing the rest of my burrito. Obviously, Bernard needs it more than I do. But I have a problem with sharing my bedroom with the man. I'm about to stand and say goodbye, when sounds nearby make me freeze.

"Eh, Bernie. I smell food." A big middle-aged man, followed by another man, step into the clearing. The bigger one is carrying one of those solar-powered lamps and has a huge backpack. "Got some to share?" They're standing close now, hovering, their predatory eyes roving over me, then roving the area around my makeshift bed and around Bernard.

"Didn't know you'd be bedding down in the park tonight, Boar," Bernard says, "or I would a saved a bit for you. Hi, RB."

RB, the smaller man, nods but says nothing.

But Boar's hungry eyes and not-too-friendly voice force me to my feet.

"Hold on there, girl," Boar says. He throws his arms out wide like he's blocking a basketball player. When he smiles, I can see why he's called Boar. The lamp in his hand makes his face appear almost monstrous. "Why're you runnin' away? Did I scare you, girl? I'm not scary. D'ya think I'm scary, RB?"

"No," RB rasps. He doesn't smile. His unblinking eyes are pale, and he reminds me of something that lives in a cave. He moves in a circle to block me from running.

RB and Boar close in on me. The closer they get, the more I sense their dung-like colors.

"Got any more food? Maybe some change on you, girl?"

The hair on the back of my back stands at attention. "Would I be sleeping in a park if I had any money?" I thrust my chin out like I did with Finn. Maybe my bluff will work with these guys.

"Now, don't get all testy with me, girlie" Boar growls. "We all share with the group."

Bernie struggles upward to his knees. "Boys, boys, let the girl alone. Can't you see she's in a bad way?"

"Just wanna see what's inside her pockets."

I back away from Boar's dirty outstretched hands. I reach into my hip pockets and pull them inside out. "See, nothing in them," I say, grateful I'd slipped everything into my bra earlier in the evening for safekeeping. Mom had always warned me about pickpockets in the city.

Boar sneers and drops his hands to his sides. "Yer new around here. What's a girl like you doing hanging out on the streets?"

I may as well tell him. It's not as if Boar's going to run to the police and tell them about finding the kidnapped woman from Iowa. "Some really bad guys tried to mess with me. They took everything I had."

"Bad guys, hmm?" Boar scrunches his bushy eyebrows like he's trying to figure out if I'm telling the truth. RB rubs his beard and looks at Boar.

Boar narrows his eyes, "How'd you get the money for the food I smelled then?"

"It was the last bit of money in my pocket. And now I'm just as homeless as you guys are. And I could use some friends ... that is, if you've got the guts to help me hide from my kidnappers."

Bernie manages to make it up to his feet. He stands next to me. "I believe her. I say, let her stay, at least for the night."

Boar opens his mouth to speak, but he doesn't get the chance. A woman's voice cries out from somewhere nearby. Shuffling footsteps follow, and two women emerge from the darkness, one practically dragging the other.

"Bernie, you got some of those sugar packets? Irene's gone all low in sugar."

Bernie hurries over and helps lower Irene to the ground. "Quick, guys, any of you got some sugar? Something sweet?"

The other woman grabs hold of Boar's backpack. Boar whips around, snarling at her. "Hold your horses, Glory. I ain't got nothin' you could feed Irene." He slips out of the pack and lowers it to the ground. "I'm fresh out of food. Don't even have a cracker or cookie or nothin'."

Bernie's all hunched over Irene, holding her hand, talking to her, patting her cheek. But Irene is so far gone, she's not aware of anything.

My head hurts. The pressure builds, sucking at my skull. For once, I don't try to resist. I let the wind suck me over and drop me onto my knees in front of Irene. My hands have found the spot on her stomach, precisely the place of her disease. Abba pours himself through my hands. This one is like a waterfall, gushing and cascading, making Irene's skin ripple and thrum. Then the light comes, growing and growing in intensity. I can't bear it. I bury my face into Irene's side, scrunch my eyes shut, and hold on for the ride. My hands are hot, so hot they must surely melt. I try to pull them away. My skin is melting, and I open my mouth to scream.

When I wake, I'm lying on a blanket on the ground. Someone has piled blankets and coats on top of me. The sun is just beginning to light the sky, and I hear movement nearby. A young woman hovers over me.

"How are you feeling?" She's a pretty woman who keeps her long dark hair in two braids down the back of her head.

No doubt about it, this is Irene. Irene, who should have been dead from diabetes. Only, it didn't happen because Abba's breeze blew me to her and poured healing into her body. I wonder if she knows that she no longer has diabetes.

"Feeling great, except I'm really hungry. Where do you guys go to get food?" I sit up and check my surroundings. The men are just beginning to rouse and to stuff their things back into their backpacks. Glory is nearby, folding her own blanket into a neat bundle. When she sees I'm awake, she comes over and puts her arm around Irene's shoulder and presses her head against her friend's head affectionately.

Then she looks at me in wonder. "I don't know what you did last night, but it was amazing. You looked like an angel, shining all around Irene. We all had to back up because your body gave off so much heat. Are you a saint or something?"

"Yeah," Irene says, "I'm wanting to know that too. And yer name."

They're both looking at me so earnestly, like kids waiting to climb onto Santa's knee, that I have to force myself not to laugh. But still, they keep their distance from me.

"Definitely not a saint," I say, sitting up and stifling a yawn. "Just a flesh-and-blood almost twenty-four-year-old who really needs breakfast."

"What's yer name?" Glory smiles, and it's hard to refuse your name when someone asks in such a friendly way.

"Zara."

Glory smiles even bigger. "That's a pretty name. I like it. Well, there's a mission a couple a blocks away where we usually go for a meal. If you don't mind listening to a religious man who goes holy rollin' from the Bible."

"Careful, Glory," Irene mumbles, still eyeing me cautiously. "If the girl can heal, she might be one of those religious people too."

"Sorry," Glory blurts out. "I didn't mean no disrespect by that. I'm kinda religious too."

Glory is short-ish and apple-shaped and has a cute round face with lots of freckles and a wide, infectious smile. Her yellow-orange hair sprouts from her head in all directions, kind of like rays from the sun. I can't help but return her smile. "No worries." I stand and try to straighten my now wrinkled pants suit. "Do the men know about the mission?"

"Yeah," Irene says. "We usually meet up with them, but because we were all together last night, I 'magine we'll all go on over there together. Nice thing about staying close to RB and Boar is, no one messes with us."

Bernie, RB, and Boar have collected their things, and as they approach, RB and Boar are cautious.

"Miss," Boar says, then pauses to clear his throat, "we sure didn't mean to scare you last night. I'm sorry for being kind of rude. I hope you won't hold it against me." Boar is holding his knit cap in his hands and staring at his shoes.

"I forgive you, Mr. Boar." He's so terribly polite in an old-fashioned way that I'm tempted to curtsey. "Glory says we're going to walk to the mission for breakfast."

"Aye," RB rasps, nodding repeatedly.

"We're kind of regulars there," Bernie says. "Just follow us."

I'm seriously hoping that I can shower at the mission, but I'm afraid to ask my new friends if that's possible. They're all rank, and they might think I'm hinting that they should get cleaned up too.

"Oh, before we go, I would like to ask you all a favor."

"Anything. Ask us anything," Boar says.

"Well, remember when I said that there are two bad guys who want to hurt me? I want you all to promise you won't go talking about what happened last night with Irene.

176

Don't mention my name either. I mean, if it gets out on the street, those bad guys might hear about it, and then they'll know I'm around and who to ask about me."

"You got some bad guys after you?" Irene asks, her face concerned. She edges closer but still doesn't dare touch me.

"They know about my healing. It's why they want to kill me."

"That's just dastardly," Glory exclaims. "They want to kill you fer doin' good? Dastardly." She pumps one fist into the other. "Dastardly."

Boar shakes his head. "We won't say anything about it—you can count on us. Right, RB?"

RB imitates Boar's headshake. "No, no, no, no. No talk."

"Thank you all. I'm very grateful that Abba led me to you and that I can call you friends."

They stop and look down. "No, we're thankful," Boar says.

"I knew you was a good person," Bernie adds.

RB nods and nods.

Irene finally reaches out and touches my arm. "Thank you for putting your hands on me and making me feel better. That was a very nice thing you did." She turns to Glory and whispers, "She's not hot anymore."

I can't hold in the laugh that's been trying to erupt for the last five minutes. And the men and women gape at me like they can't believe a healer could possibly do something so normal as laugh.

It's funny how our lives are so tangled up together. Like last night. I'd been so focused on my own survival I didn't even consider all the people around me who also needed to live. Like Irene. If I hadn't lost my bag and been too afraid to go back to the Field Museum Irene would probably have died. Maybe I was meant to be stuck in Chicago.

As we walk down the sidewalk, I'm close to Irene. In fact, the men, plus Irene and Glory, have surrounded me, like they're my bodyguards. Again, I want to laugh. Not because it's funny but because I'm happy for the first time in three weeks. I don't know how all this will turn out, but Irene made me realize that being a healer is not always a curse.

Irene points at a two-story building. "That's the mission, or at least that's part of it."

It's ugly, but I bet it does a lot of good for a lot of people. There's a brick building with a steeple, which looks like a chapel. Attached to it is a two-story stick-built building. It looks like it's in the process of being painted, with one side a bright white and the other side faded and peeling.

I can smell breakfast, and my mouth waters. "Once we get there, do I have to sign up or be a member or something?"

Boar chuckles. "Nah, you just have to look hungry and dirty, like me."

Everyone laughs, which dispels the knot in my stomach. I'd been worried that the workers would turn me away 'cause I'm not one of the usual crowd. Or that they'd ask me all sorts of questions I can't answer without endangering my folks.

We step inside, and I see a number of people in line. It's a pretty big room with at least ten long tables. It's warm, and they're playing some pop Christian music. We get in line and place our trays on the cafeteria ledge. Irene leans into me and whispers, "Sure hope there's enough of the eggs. I can't eat those pancakes, not without my insulin."

I turn my head away for a second so I can smile without Irene thinking it's at her expense. Then I put my hand on her arm. "Irene, you can eat anything you want today, and the next day and the next, for the rest of your life."

"What d'you mean?" She looks confused and frightened.

"That heat you felt last night. It burned away your diabetes. It's gone. Those pancakes and the syrup won't do anything bad to you. I wouldn't lie to you."

Irene grasps both of my hands. "You're not tellin' me stories?" Tears spring into her eyes and her mouth trembles.

"No. And that ulcer on your foot is gone. And your kidneys are completely normal." I don't know how I know about those other health problems that Irene had, but the words slipped out as sure and convincing as if I were reading a medical chart.

"Pancakes." An expression of pure bliss settles over Irene's face.

"Go ahead and eat one. You'll see."

Irene moves her tray along and accepts a plate with two good-sized pancakes from the guy serving behind the heated trays. She also receives two sausages and two eggs. I accept the same breakfast, and I'm relieved that I don't get suspicious looks that communicate *Who are you? I don't recognize you.*

When I join Irene at a table, I say a quick thank-you to my Abba for giving me food and for my new friends, then stuff a whole sausage into my mouth. Heavenly.

Irene digs into her pancakes and syrup. A tall young man comes around with a pot of coffee. Oh man, I can't wait. I hold up my cup. He pours me some and smiles at my eagerness. He's attractive, his black hair is longish, and his eyes are dark and soulful and slightly Asian. I wonder what journey landed him at this mission. But I don't have time to find out. I need to eat as much as possible because I don't know when I'll get another meal. Second, I need to find a way to get to Titusville without being seen by Clooney and Finn. Then, I need to find out where they stashed my mom and dad.

The coffee guy moves on to another table, and I turn my attention to Glory, who's just joined us.

"Irene, you shouldn't be eating pancakes, not without your meds," Glory says with a scolding tone. "That stuff is just dastardly for people like you."

Irene glances at me, then back at her friend. "Zara said I could have it and it wouldn't hurt me anymore."

Glory's mouth corkscrews to the left. "Really?"

Her round face, round eyes, and screwed-up mouth make me want to laugh again. "No more diabetes," I say.

"Thank you, Miss Zara," Glory says in a loud voice. "You got a gift. We won't ever forget what you done. But I won't tell a soul, not less you say so." She puts her finger to her mouth as if shushing herself, obviously unaware that everyone in the room must have heard her enthusiastic thanks.

"I appreciate that. And now I've got a question for you guys. Is there anyone at the mission I can talk to about getting to Titusville?"

"You can talk to Ron. He runs the place. He might know someone that could help you."

"Ron?" I look around like I could recognize Ron, but all I see are hungry street people snarfing their food.

"When we're done here, you can ask one of the kitchen people to find Ron. He's always around, probably working in the kitchen right now," Irene says.

My stomach zings just thinking about asking for help from someone who doesn't know my story. What if he wants the details of my penniless state? What if he guesses I'm running from bad guys? He might contact the police.

Now, I'm rethinking talking to Ron. Maybe I could ask for a little more food, and then I could hitchhike toward Iowa. That's scary. "You don't know what kind of maniac might offer you a ride," Mom always said. Poor Mom. She lived all her life avoiding danger, and now I've put her in danger because of my "gift." My throat tightens, and I squelch the crying my eyes want to do. I love Mom so much.

When we're done with breakfast, Boar and RB and Bernie walk outside. Irene and Glory say they plan to bum some cash outside the Walmart.

"I'm going to hang out around the mission for a while," I say.

"You gonna talk to Ron?" Glory asks.

"Probably."

We're standing together by our table, and it's clear Irene is still nervous about touching me. Her eyes are saying *Thank you*, but she keeps her arms at her sides. So, I wrap my arms around her, hugging her tight, and whisper goodbye in her ear.

"Bye, Miss Zara."

They go outside, looking over their shoulders at me, as if wondering what will become of the girl who healed Irene.

The servers carry the food trays into the kitchen. This looks like the right time to find Ron. Maybe I can get help without telling him my story.

I make a move toward the kitchen door, but the tall guy who had been serving coffee blocks my way. "Sorry, miss, but only staff can come into the kitchen." He smiles, but he means business.

"I-I, uh, I'm looking for Ron."

"Ron's not in just now. Maybe I can help you."

He doesn't look like he can help me. The guy looks young, maybe twenty-one or two. He looks me up and down, but not in a lusting way. I'm sure he noticed how my clothes are wrinkled and dirty. He's thinking I'm one of those women who ran away from a bad marriage, maybe I'm hooked on drugs, living a dangerous life on the streets.

I feel ashamed. I take a big breath, praying my voice doesn't break. "I need help," I say in a small voice.

"Excuse me? I didn't catch that."

I take another breath. "I need help."

"How old are you?" His voice is mellow and kind. He takes my elbow and steers me through a doorway and down a hall.

"Old enough. I need to get back home."

"And where's home, miss?"

"Iowa. Titusville."

He escorts me into a small room with a table and two chairs.

"Hey, Shirley?"

181

A middle-aged woman plants herself at the door. "How can I help you, Kai?"

"This young lady says she needs to get to Titusville, Iowa. Back home."

Shirley enters the room and pulls out a chair for me. "What's your name, Miss?" She sits across the table from me. Her face is kind and warm.

As soon as he sees I'm being taken care of, Kai leaves.

"Zoe, ma'am." Ick. I hate making up stuff. It makes my mouth quiver.

"Okay, Zoe. Could you give me your last name too?"

My insides feel shaky. Just like I'd thought, the folks at the mission are asking me for all sorts of information, and then they'll know I'm the kidnapped woman, and they'll call the police. And Clooney and Finn will find out that I squealed on them, and they'll order the thugs holding my parents to kill them and dispose of their bodies. "It's Logan." I can't look Shirley in the eyes. She'll know I'm not being straight with her.

"Well, Zoe, we sometimes buy a bus ticket for someone who needs to get back to family."

"No." I start to stand. "No bus ticket. I mean, that's really kind of you to buy a bus ticket, but I can't go there."

Shirley's eyebrows crease. "Can't go home?"

"Not home. The ... the ... the bus station. I can't go there. Not without ID."

Shirley leans toward me, and when she reaches for my hands, I settle back into my seat.

"Did you run into some kind of trouble at the bus station? Because if that's a problem for you, we can escort you there and wait with you until you're safely on the bus."

She waits while I process this. Even if I could get onto the bus safely, if Clooney or Finn are at the station, they'll know where I'm going. Then all they'd have to do is drive to Titusville and wait for me to get off the bus.

Shirley takes a form out of a box sitting on the table. "We'll need some information first. I'm going back to my office for a few minutes. That'll give you time to fill out this form." She stands and gives my hand a little squeeze, then walks out of the room, shutting the door behind her.

They won't help me unless I can provide ID. What a mess. Now they'll know I'm that kidnapped woman. My heart pounds. I have to get out of here.

I peek out the door. No one's there, so I tiptoe back to the dining hall and race outside. This time I run in the opposite direction. Irene said the Walmart was a couple of blocks west. Maybe I can join them and beg for a few dollars too.

CHAPTER NINETEEN

I hang with Irene and Glory. Sometimes, one of them takes a break, and I take over holding a cloth bag for tips, or whatever Glory and Irene call it. Glory's holding a sign that says, *Anything helps. God bless you!* She sings old hymns and taps her feet to the beat. Glory has a pretty good voice. If anyone puts in some coins or bills, she says, "God bless you. You have a great day," and beams like an angel.

It's almost noon, and Irene says we've already made about thirty-one dollars and some change.

We head inside and buy some McDonald's hamburgers and fries and ask for cups of water.

As I munch on my hamburger, I wonder about how to get to the interstate so I can hitchhike west. I hate the idea. A young woman standing out on the highway. It's so dangerous. On the other hand, maybe if I hang out long enough with Irene and Glory, I can earn enough for a ride from someone going west.

We go back outside, and Glory sings a few more songs. She asks me to sing along. I have an okay voice, nothing special, but since I'm an alto, I add some harmony to her hymns. The shoppers must like that 'cause our tips go up. Even while I'm singing, I can't help but keep an eye on the parking lot. What if Clooney or Finn sees me standing here?

After the McDonald's meal, my take at the end of the day is sixteen dollars and change. Not enough for a bus ticket, but it's a start. "Where are we staying tonight?" I ask Glory because she seems to be the leader of our trio.

"We can ask Bernie when we see 'em later today."

"Do you always spend the night near the men?"

"Usually," she says. "It's safer that way. Sometimes, when it's real cold, we spend the night at the mission."

Why don't they spend the night at the mission all the time? If you're homeless, wouldn't it be safer to have a roof over your head and someone to make sure you're safe? But I don't ask 'cause they're the experts about these things, and I'm also making a bit of money. Where else could I do that without filling out an application and being interviewed?

It's after four in the afternoon now. Hungry again, I buy another hamburger and splurge on a chocolate milkshake. But Irene and Glory huddle and discuss their money. Glory hands over some of her cash to Irene, who puts that and some of her own money into a little cloth bag. Then they pocket the rest, which doesn't look like a lot. They kind of smile when I ask them about this, but they don't answer.

When we get settled for the night, I'm sure I can get them to tell me more.

We troop back to the park where I spent the night. I'm not happy about sleeping on the ground again, but I keep my mouth shut. The only alternative, as I see it, is returning to the mission, but Shirley and that young guy will ask why I didn't fill out their form. I can't risk it.

We're halfway back to the park when Irene tells me, "Wait here. We got a little errand to run."

I stand on the sidewalk, feeling exposed and self-conscious. Cars and other vehicles buzz by. It smells like deep city, what with all the exhaust fumes, the delicious aromas of nearby restaurants, the sounds of construction and jackhammering down the street, and some guys having a loud conversation outside a store nearby. Irene and Glory go inside Mickey's Market, and I watch from outside as they empty their little cloth bag into a donation holder, the kind at a checker's station. I get chills when I see them empty at least half of their haul from today's begging session into the see-through bank. There's a photo of someone on the box, but I can't see it clearly from where I'm standing.

When Irene stuffs her now empty cloth bag into her pocket, I turn and pretend to be looking across the street at the park. They come out of the store looking happy.

"I don't get it, Irene," I say once they're both outside again. "You just spent seven hours outside Walmart asking people for money, and now you give half of it away."

"Shh." Glory hunches near my shoulder. "Don't you say anything to anyone about what we do. Someone'll think we're rich."

"But you need money, probably as much as that person you're giving to."

Irene and Glory exchange glances, then turn to me, both looking sad. "There's a baby girl who needs an operation, you see," Irene murmurs. "The family don't have insurance. That little girl will die if she don't get money. We like to do our part."

I get chills again. Irene and Glory have nothing, and yet they think about someone else. My chills send messages to my gut. I feel ashamed. All I'm thinking about is myself. These two women's lives are worse than mine. At least I have family—I hope—and lots of friends who have money and homes and assets. But Irene and Glory have no one but each other. What have I ever sacrificed for anyone? Even when I heal, it's not me. It's Abba. These ladies think I'm some sort of saint 'cause I healed Irene, but it's just the opposite. I'm hanging out with real saints. Or maybe they're angels.

We're a few yards away from a bus stop, and a noisy city bus pulls up, belching diesel fumes, and stops. The bus door opens, and an old lady steps down, followed by two punk-like dudes wearing hoodies. Last of all, a middle-aged man gets out. Usually I don't stare at people, but this guy is so pale, he's almost gray. He holds on to the door as he stumbles off. Then he stands there like he's confused.

The bus pulls away, and the man reaches into his jacket like he's going to pull out his wallet or phone. But then his mouth twists into a grimace of agony. He staggers, his torso bending and twisting, before he collapses onto the pavement.

Irene and Glory rush forward and crouch to check on him. He's breathing, but barely. More like gasping. He looks like ashes. Irene is crying, and Glory shouts over her shoulder for me to do something. I stand there helpless, afraid if I do something, someone will report the miracle and I'll be exposed. Or crowds will take videos.

I'm not a doctor or a nurse. I don't know anything. Abba is not ripping me out of myself and giving me holy energy. Is it because I don't care? Am I afraid of being assaulted again? Standing so close, I feel the man's dying energy, and knowledge of him flows into me.

Another man forces himself in between Irene and Glory's huddle. "I'm a nurse. Move out of the way. Somebody, call 911," he says.

They scramble out of his way and let him do what he's been trained to do. A few feet away, another man shouts into his phone, telling the person on the other end that a man is "having a heart attack or seizure. It's really bad!"

Glory gazes at me, her face registering confusion and disappointment. "Zara, why don't you heal the man?"

I can't act. I really want to help that guy, to be more like Irene and Glory, who are real saints. I turn away. I'm so ashamed because I only care about myself and being normal and safe. *Abba, Abba, help me to care, help me not to be afraid. Abba, Abba! He needs to live. His wife is sick. His employees need him to sign their paychecks. Please!*

"I don't think he's gonna come back," the nurse announces to the other man, the one who's talking to 911. "We need a defibrillator. Where's that damned ambulance?"

Right after he says that I hear a siren, but it's way far away. And in rush-hour traffic, it could take five minutes, maybe more.

More people have arrived, crowding the sidewalk, their phones capturing the dying man's struggle. Drivers are slowing, rubbernecking.

My vision fades. Through the murk, I can barely see the nurse's desperate moves. He's practically bouncing on top of the ashen man's chest. I find Glory's shoulder. She knows exactly what I want and guides me forward. In another second, I'm kneeling by the nurse. He yells at me to get away, but he can't stop my hands from replacing his on the man's chest.

I shake all over, and my body heats up with my tears. So hot I feel like I'm in the path of a giant blowtorch. My fingers pulse red light. Steady heart beats grab the weak and thready ones woven around the man's quivering heart, pulling them away and casting them into the dark place. The white light around my head burns, burns.

Before I open my eyes, I know I'm back in the park. I can feel the hard ground and smell the park scents. I hear soft movements and hushed voices. It's hard to open my eyes, like there are weights on each lid. When I pry them open, Glory is sitting nearby, studying my face with a worried expression. The men's deep voices rumble somewhere behind me.

"How long have I been asleep?"

"A long time, Zara." Irene comes into view, holding a tin mug. "You should have some of this tea while it's hot." She crouches, and between her and Glory, they help me sit up.

My head pounds, and I feel dizzy. But the tea tastes amazing because I'm extremely thirsty. "Thanks," I whisper. "What happened with the guy?"

Glory is smiling her sunflower smile. "It was amazing, Zara. As soon as you put your hands on him, he started to get his color back. That nurse kept tryin' to get you off, but it was like you were glued to him. But then you kinda sighed and slid to the ground. Right after that, the sick man sat up and looked around like 'what happened?'"

"The nurse guy tried to help you, but we stopped him. We told him you had these sleeping fits, and everything would be okay. Bernie and Boar and RB saw the whole thing from across the street. They ran over and helped lift you and get you away before the ambulance showed up."

I sip some more of the tea. "Thanks for getting me away. But I'm worried about all those people with their phones."

Irene's eyebrows draw together. "Those cold people with their phones. They didn't try to help. They only wanted to catch what a death looks like close up. Gives me chills how some people can be so uncaring."

Finn and Clooney like to watch the news. "Glory, Irene, I'm scared somebody might have posted a video of me. If my bad guys see it, they'll figure out really fast where I am. For all I know, they could be coming for me right now. I think they saw a video of me when I was in Manhattan, and it led them here."

I struggle to my feet. Nerves zinging through my body make my feet feel the need to run away. I have no idea what time it is. Is it still early? I hear lots of traffic, so it can't be very late. "I think we have to move."

"Move?" Bernie joins us. "Why do you have to move?"

"Zara's afraid those bad guys might find out where she is 'cause of what happened today outside Mickey's grocery store," Glory says.

Bernie shrugs. "Who would mess with you, Zara? They'd have to get through me and Boar and RB first."

He has no idea the kind of criminals I'm running from. "Bernie, these guys are drug criminals. They've got guns. And money to hire other bad guys. They wouldn't think twice about killing anyone who gets in their way." Now that I see how naive Bernie is, I'm even more ready to escape from the park and hide somewhere else. Except I don't have a clue where to go.

"Mebbe this would be a good night for Zara to spend at the mission," Irene says to Boar.

Boar nods. "We'll take her up there right now. RB, grab yer bat. We're gonna walk Zara to the mission."

I have a strong impulse to hug Boar, but I'm still scared of him, so I don't. I look at Irene and Glory. "See you at breakfast?"

Glory wraps her arms around me and hugs me so hard I can't breathe. "You sleep good and safe tonight, girl." She lets go and nudges me in Boar's direction.

Boar and RB and Bernie surround me as we walk back to the mission. Even if Finn were out here, he'd have a hard time seeing me in this circle of ragged men. When we reach the park border, we look right and left for men with guns. By now the traffic has slowed and it's easier to cross.

We're a long block away from the mission, and I can see its peaked roof sticking out above the other shorter buildings. But now we have to tread along the sidewalk, and it's pretty exposed. I'm paranoid about being watched, almost like I can feel a malevolent presence nearby. The men's shoes are so worn that they hardly make a sound on the pavement, but my right shoe has a squeak that makes me flinch with every step. I don't know why I feel as if I have to sneak up to the mission.

We cross another intersection, and then the mission building looms in front of us. I'm surprised to find no one lingering around the entrance. What if they've locked the doors? What if it's late and they won't let anyone in for the night? My stomach flips. It was scary enough walking all this way. The walk back to the park will be way worse.

Across the street I see dim light inside a parked car. Boar sees it too—I can tell by the way he keeps his eyes trained on the car.

As we approach the mission, the driver's door opens, and a man gets out. Another guy climbs out of the passenger side and follows. They're hurrying right for us. Boar steps into the street and throws his arms out straight. "What d'ya want?"

In my peripheral view, I see RB raise his baseball bat.

The two men slow down. The guy in front reaches into his jacket pocket. Boar and RB and Bernie and I all gasp simultaneously.

But the stranger holds up a badge instead of a gun. "Chicago PD."

CHAPTER TWENTY

How would I know they're the police? I mean, they've got badges, but they could be fake. They're plainclothes men dressed like Clooney when he'd kidnapped me. Just remembering makes me want to hurl. They're carrying flashlights in their left hands. Probably so they can go for their weapons if necessary.

"How do we know you're real policemen?" I edge next to Boar, trying to look tough.

"You wanna call this phone number and give 'em my badge number, miss?" The guy practically pushes the badge into my face and shines a light on it.

"Got any ID on you, miss?"

"She's with us. She's okay," Boar growls.

The officer ignores him and continues to focus on me. "ID?"

"N-no. I lost it." My heart hammers in my chest, and I'm afraid he'll hear it and know something's suspicious.

"You wanna tell me your name?"

The second officer keeps his eyes on my friends. But the first officer is now shining his flashlight full on my face, and even if I were willing to tell him my real name, I can't come up with it. "It's ... it's ..."

"Her name's Zoe, Officer. Zoe Logan."

We whip around at the sound of the stranger's voice. It's the guy from the mission, the tall, dark-haired one with the soulful eyes.

"And she's living at the mission temporarily." He walks down the steps of the mission chapel and approaches the group. "I'm Kai Fujiwara, and I'm on staff at the mission."

Boar relaxes his confrontational posture and rejoins RB and Bernie on the sidewalk.

"Zoe was supposed to be inside by now. Good thing these gentlemen brought her home." Kai gestures toward my protectors. "Thanks, guys."

I move toward Kai, grateful to be free of the officer's interrogation.

"Hold on, miss," the officer says. "Before I release you, can you tell me where you were yesterday afternoon, around four?"

"Around four?" I repeat as if I'm slow. "Uh, yeah, I was with my friends, and we were up at the Walmart, getting a burger inside ... at the McDonald's." Good thing the officer didn't say four thirty, 'cause that's when we were outside Mickey's Market.

"Officer," Kai says, "can you tell me what this is all about? I'm responsible for Zoe's safety. Maybe I can clear up any misinformation you might have."

"Mr. Fujiwara, we're investigating the disappearance of a twenty-three-year-old female. Someone took a video yesterday afternoon, and the woman in it resembled the one who disappeared a few weeks ago."

"Do you have her photo?" Kai asks. "Maybe I can post it on our bulletin board and ask around."

"I don't have the photo with me," the officer says. "We only have a sketch to work with."

"Not even a school photo? Well, can I at least see the sketch?" Kai inches closer, his head tilted like a dog who's hearing something he doesn't recognize.

"Sorry, Mr. Fuji ... uh ..."

"Fujiwara," Kai says.

"Yeah, Mr. Fujiwara. Well, that's official business. Just let us know if you see a young woman, tall, slim, with long dark hair. She might be around these parts. Remember, her name's Zara Nielsen."

"We'll keep an eye out, Officer."

After the two policemen get back in their car, Kai turns to me, his eyes narrowed and his mouth twisted to one side, like he's chewing on his last words. "Come on, Zoe. Let's get you inside before they decide to return and ask harder questions."

I glance at Boar and RB and Bernie. They look so concerned I say, "It'll be okay. I'll go with Kai into the mission ... for tonight."

"We'll be here tomorrow for breakfast," Bernie says. He waves sadly.

I follow Kai up the steps and into the chapel, and Kai locks the doors. For a second, I'm scared. Kai is tall, with a lean strength you'd see in an athlete. Like Finn. What if I can't trust him?

"I thought we could just sit in here for a while." He points to the rows of chairs. "It's quieter and more private than the offices you were in yesterday."

He seats himself a few rows up from the back, and I follow, hoping he won't ask any more questions. I'm glad to be safely indoors, away from those police officers, if they really were officers. After all that's happened in the last three weeks, I'm not sure I can trust anyone.

Kai hasn't turned on any lights, but light filters in from the side where the windows face the street. It's enough to see that Kai is waiting for me to sit next to him. When I do, he just waits. I don't know what he's expecting. Am I supposed to blurt out all the facts of my existence so he can contact the real police or call my relatives and tell them the "missing" girl has been found?

"Thanks for bringing me inside."

He nods but still doesn't say anything.

"My friends were bringing me up here ... to the mission. So I could stay tonight."

"Do you know those men, Boar and the others?" Kai doesn't even look at me. He stares at a spot across the room.

"I just met them a day ago. They're okay, though. I mean, they've been kind of watching out for me."

"Why are they watching out for you?"

"I, um, well, I'm homeless. Duh." I roll my eyes and instantly regret it because it makes me look like the quintessential snarky young woman. "I lost my money and my luggage, and these bad guys were following me. So, Boar and RB and Bernie said they'd keep the bad guys from getting me."

"Bad guys?" Kai looks at me.

My cheeks heat up. I can't tell him too much, but if I give him some truth, maybe he can help me. "Drug dealers."

"What do they want from you?"

He's wondering if I was somehow helping them distribute or sell. "I'm just a farm girl from Iowa. They came after me because they saw me on TV."

"The police or the drug dealers?"

I shake my head. "Those guys"—I gesture toward the street—"I'm not even sure those were real police."

Kai meets my eyes, and his face is deadly serious. "I'm sure they're not."

When I tilt my head at him, he shrugs. "What policeman with an APB wouldn't have a photo of a perp—sorry, I didn't mean to say you're a perp—a victim, to work with? And why wouldn't he at least show me a sketch or a school photo of a missing woman? It's all extremely suspicious. I wonder if I should call the police."

My stomach drops. "No!" I jump to my feet, ready to burst out the chapel doors and run back to the park.

Kai's eyes widen. "Why? Wouldn't you feel safer if we made sure about those men? The police would want to know if there are some guys out there posing as policemen."

I feel like I'm going to blubber, and I can't have Kai see me go all boo-hoo baby. "Please stop asking me questions.

It's too confusing. Too complicated. I just need to get home to Iowa."

Kai reaches for my hand. "Zoe, please sit down. I won't contact them if you don't want me to. But we tried to help you yesterday. Why did you run away?"

"Because you guys are asking questions." I sit down again.

"Well, we have to have at least a little information. How old are you? You said you're from Iowa. What's your address? Do you have family we could contact? That's about it."

I hang my head. "I have to think about this."

"Okay." His voice is all disappointed. "I'll take you to the dorm. You can get cleaned up and get a good's night sleep."

"Thanks."

The aromas of breakfast wake me. Last night I'd taken a shower, and man, was it heavenly. The cot in the women's sleeping room was at least five notches better than the cold, damp ground at the park. And even though I was scared thinking about those fake policemen and whether or not they would come back, and if Kai and the mission staff would pry out my whole story in the morning, I couldn't kept my eyes open more than five minutes.

Now, women of all sorts, sizes, and shapes are getting dressed. Toilets flush. Water from showers and sinks sends steam floating into the dorm room. I guess the women notice me, but they all just mind their own business. I look for my own clothes that I'd folded and laid at the feet of my cot. But they're not there. For a second, I'm about to demand that whoever stole my clothes better give them back. But then I see a note pinned to a pile of unfamiliar clothing sitting next to my pillow.

Hi, I'm Jill, and I took your clothes and washed them. They'll be ready for pick up in the laundry room around nine. Wear these for breakfast.

I sort through the small pile. It's a sweatshirt, sweatpants, and underwear and socks. They'll do. In fact, they're better for travel than the thin jacket and pants Ruby had given me. I dress hurriedly and join the line of women heading downstairs in the direction of the breakfast smells.

Today, it's bacon and scrambled eggs and biscuits and gravy. I don't see any of my park friends in line, but I figure they'll arrive soon enough. I take everything that's offered, because I don't know when I'll eat again. I'm hoping today will be the day I get enough money from panhandling with Irene and Glory to feed myself when I hitchhike along I-80 west.

Kai is pouring coffee again, and when he sees me, he smiles. He moves around the tables, pouring coffee and talking to the people. Does he treat all the men and women with the same focus he gave me last night? A ping of jealousy strikes, because I thought maybe I was a special case for him.

Glory and Irene walk into the dining area and wave at me. When they get their food, they settle their trays next to mine.

"Are we going to go to Walmart again?"

"Not today," Irene says. "It's Sunday. They have chapel after breakfast. You should come with us. It's real cool. They have some great music, and that Ron guy talks about stuff, and sometimes they show some videos too. You'll like it."

My heart sinks, but I don't show my disappointment. At least I mostly feel safe here. But I sure hoped we'd get some more cash today. I'm tempted to go and stand outside Walmart by myself, but I get jittery just thinking about going alone. If those police officers were fake, did they believe me when I said I wasn't the girl they'd viewed on the phone videos? What if they come back and question me again? Suddenly, my food doesn't taste so good. Maybe I should hitchhike today, even if I don't have money. If Abba helps me, perhaps I could catch a ride all the way to western Iowa. My stomach is going all butterflies, knowing the risk I face. Could be a crazy person, or a serial killer, or a rapist out there on the interstate, just looking for a vulnerable young woman. *Zara, you've gotta do it. It's been almost three weeks since you talked to your mom and heard the terror in her voice. What if you get back home and it's too late? What if Clooney murders your mom and dad when they couldn't catch you at the bus station?*

Maybe they think I've gone to the police. No, that couldn't be. Because if I'd told the Chicago police where Finn and Clooney are, they probably would have already caught them.

I picture myself standing at the entrance to the freeway, holding out my thumb, staring into each car that slows, making a quick decision about which ride I'd accept. *Abba, I need a nice family, or maybe a couple, or even a truck driver, one of those huge semis.* I heard they sometimes pick up hitchhikers.

I hear Boar's voice before I even see him. He's telling someone how to take a tray and get their food. A lady blocks my view, but when she moves, Boar and RB are talking to a new guy. For someone who's homeless, he looks well fed. He's walking with slumped posture, though, like he's got a bad back. His greasy dark hair is kind of long and wavy, and he has a big scar crossing one cheek all the way to his mouth. That side of his mouth droops, as if whatever cut him did some nerve damage.

Irene is savoring her biscuit and gravy. She takes a bite, closes her eyes, then opens them and looks at me. "Food just tastes better since you healed me, Zara."

I put my hand on hers. Even her skin feels softer. "I'm so happy for you. But it wasn't me, Irene. It was Abba."

"Oh, I know that. But it was your hands that he poured healing through. I wonder how that man outside Mickey's Market is doing now?"

"Probably enjoying his wife and four kids like he's never done before." I scrunch my paper napkin and toss it onto my plate so I have something to do, because I'm embarrassed to talk about healing. I'm not a good enough person to have this gift. I'm just a woman who wants to study poetry and get a degree and live the way she wants to live. Why would Abba choose someone so ordinary to be a healer? I don't understand it. I would give almost anything not to be a healer. But Abba doesn't listen when I try to bargain with him.

Boar and RB and the new guy join us at our table. Irene stiffens when she notices the man. Glory half smiles, and that's not like Glory.

"This here's Remy. He's new." Boar states the obvious.

We all nod at Remy to acknowledge the new relationship with Boar and RB. But I can tell from Glory and Irene that it doesn't just follow that the relationship with the men guarantees a relationship with the women. He'll have to earn their trust, and by the way he looks, he's going to have to work hard to do that.

Remy smiles at Glory and at Irene, then he turns his eyes to me. He takes in my hair, my face. Strange men have looked at me the same way before, and it's not a nice look. The stare lingers too long. When I blush or look away, they laugh and feel all big and powerful, like somehow, just their awesome manly presence made me blush. I hate that.

When we go into the chapel for the Sunday service, Remy comes with us, and we find chairs in the middle. I'm surprised when Kai walks onto the stage and grabs a guitar set up to the right of the podium. He plays well, and his voice is a nice baritone. I recognize one of the songs. There's also a guy who plays drums and a lady who plays fiddle.

Words appear on a screen. Glory loves to sing, and she seems to know all the songs. Boar doesn't sing. RB, either. Where's Bernie? He never showed up for breakfast, and I'm worried about him. I want to ask Boar about him, but he's three people over. Remy sings, but it's clear he doesn't know the songs. When some people put their hands up in worship, he does too. And he says "Hallelujah, amen" after each song ends. A phony? Maybe I'm wrong, but I'm going to keep watching him.

I love that Kai is smiling. It makes me smile too, even though I've got so much to worry about. Just then, he looks at me, and his dark eyes remind me of Craig. A pang of longing spears my chest. I miss him so much my throat tightens in a prelude to tears. I wonder where he is now. Back on Campus at SUNY?

Ron, the guy I didn't get to meet a couple of days ago, steps onto the stage. He's tall—even taller than Kai—and built like a weightlifter. Not too many men would want to get in his face. He stands at the lectern and talks about making wise choices, how they can affect your life way down the line, maybe for years and years.

When the service concludes, Kai seeks me out. "Zoe, your clothes are ready to be picked up. And also, the clothing donation center is open. I thought maybe you'd like to pick up some items. They have warm coats and shoes and other things you might need."

Glory says, "You go on Miss Zoe. We'll wait for you outside."

I follow him out a side door that leads downstairs to a large, musty-smelling basement room filled with hanging clothes and shelves holding rows of shoes and backpacks and baby items. Like a Goodwill store.

I shrug. "I don't have money."

"Don't worry." He grabs a good-sized backpack off a rack and hands it to me. "Fill it with whatever you think you'll need. It's free."

"Free?" I can't believe he's being straight with me. I bet he feels sorry for me and will probably secretly pay for any items I choose.

This is so embarrassing. I used to collect donations of money and clothing for our Salvation Army store in Titusville. It made me feel good to do something to help people who couldn't afford clothes. Now I'm on the other side, and it feels crappy. Kai is being so sweet and nonchalant, like it's the most natural thing to give out free clothes. I feel like crying, but I stuff it so Kai won't see my humiliation.

He lifts a nice coat from the rack. "This is pretty, and it looks warm. Try it on." He helps me slip it on and turns me toward him, his beautiful dark eyes checking out the fit. "That's nice, don't you think? And the hood will keep your head dry." He pulls the hood up and settles it snug so I can barely see him. His hands linger there, pressed gently against my cheeks, as if he's shielding me.

When I meet his eyes, he drops his hands, and his eyes shift downward. "Well anyway, you can take whatever coat is best." He steps away and turns to check out more clothes.

"I like the coat." I barely mutter, but he hears me.

"And those shoes you've been wearing. They're good for a stroll through the mall. But not good for traveling." He sweeps his arm out to indicate the rows of women's shoes. "I think you could use a good pair of sneakers." Then he walks over to the counter and sits down.

When I'm done, I've got an almost new pair of sneakers, some new underwear and socks, the backpack, and the coat. I walk up to him sheepishly and hope he's not going to have to sort through my underwear items as well as the other stuff.

"Just fold it and stuff it all into the pack," he says. "I don't have to see what you got."

The guy is a mind reader. *Thank you, Abba.*

He takes out a slip of colored paper that looks kind of like Monopoly money. When he sees me staring at it, he chuckles. "This is mission money. You earned it by attending chapel. This'll pay for your backpack and everything in it."

"Wow, thanks." I can't even meet his eyes. I'm not used to charity, but I don't feel so crappy now that I see that I did something to earn it.

"I wish I knew why those fake policemen were looking for that Zara woman. Do you have any idea? Who is she?" He focuses his eyes on entering some dollar amounts in a ledger.

He's so quiet and gentle I almost think I can trust him. I want so much to tell him that I'm Zara Nielsen, the woman who disappeared without a trace, who's being chased by drug-dealing murderers. "I think I heard her whole family disappeared. Why didn't they mention them too?"

"I don't know. I'm sure the real police are working on that."

I haven't been able to see a newspaper or hear anything on TV for weeks. Who knows what the police have figured out by now about my disappearance? I don't even know if Uncle Arne survived his encounter with Finn and Clooney the day they took me. Knowing them, they killed him so there'd be no witness to my kidnapping. Poor guy. He was just trying to help me and my folks.

That thought spurs me. "I'm thinking about hitching a ride to Iowa."

Kai looks up quickly. "Why would you do that? Hitch hiking's dangerous."

"I don't have any choice. I've got to get back home quick."

"Zoe, I'd like to help you, but there's a whole lot you're not telling me."

I turn away because my lip is trembling. "I can't tell you more about my situation."

When he doesn't respond, I interrupt the silence with, "Anyway, thank you for letting me stay here overnight and for the clothes. But I really should be getting back to Irene and Glory. They'll be wondering what's keeping me."

Kai's body language communicates his disappointment as he escorts me to the mission door. "I hope I see you again," he says with a tone of resignation. "Remember, if you need help, we're here for you."

"I know and thank you. I'll be okay."

"Bye," he says mournfully and shuts the door behind me.

I step into the sunshine and find Irene waiting for me. When she sees the backpack, she smiles. "Now you're looking like one of us."

"Where's Glory?"

"She went with the men. I think she wants to check out Remy, to kind of watch him. She doesn't trust him."

"All those 'amens' and 'halleluiahs' during the service." I make a face. "I didn't believe him. Something about him doesn't seem right."

Irene frowns. "That's three of us, then."

We cross the mission's small parking lot and wait at the intersection for the light to turn green. "So, what do you guys do on Sunday after chapel?"

Irene checks out the sky, squinting in the sunshine. "Well, if it's nice weather, we go to Lincoln Park and sing and play. I have a friend who lends out her guitar. And Glory sing songs and plays her tambourine. We put out a jar. Lots of people put money in our jar."

"Can I come along?"

"You gotta sing."

"Okay."

CHAPTER TWENTY-ONE

We buy tacos and savor them on our way back to the park where the men are. Irene counts out our take for singing at Lincoln Park. We each earned twenty-four dollars. That and the nine dollars I already have make thirty-three. It's enough to feed me on the road. I'm ready. With Abba guiding me, I'll find the right driver to take me to Iowa. I haven't figured out what I'll do once I get near Titusville. The problem is, someone might recognize me before I can figure out where Finn and Clooney are holding my parents. That could blow up big. And even if I find out where they're being held, I don't have a gun or any way of getting them free. Maybe that would be the time to reveal that I'm alive and call the police and tell them where my folks are. *Help me, Abba, please.*

I need to tell my friends what I plan to do tomorrow. They'll be sorry to see me go. And to tell the truth, I feel all teary just thinking about leaving them. Irene and Glory are special, and I'm going to miss them so much. And Boar, once I got to know him, turned out to be a loyal friend.

Glory and Irene and I are hanging out with the men. Remy is with us. A bad color rises in my mind whenever he walks by. He says he's an artist, and he wants to sketch me. He pulls out a giant sketchpad from his backpack, but I say, "No, don't sketch me."

"Oh please. You're so pretty," he says with a whiny tone that makes me feel as if there are bugs in my ears.

"The girl said no," Glory growls. Her eyes are narrowed, and her body language is like a cat, all tensed and twitchy, as if she's ready to pounce.

Remy sneers at her and drops the sketchpad with a disgusted flip of the wrist.

Later that night, after everyone's asleep, I wake suddenly to a flash of light. Movement catches my eye. Remy's collecting his belongings and putting what looks suspiciously like a cellphone into his backpack. I pretend to be asleep when he sneaks away into the darkness.

I don't know why Remy would be leaving in the middle of the night, but I have a sudden fear that he took a picture of me. When I sit up, Glory wakes.

"What's the matter?" she rasps.

"Remy just left. Packed up all his things too. I saw him putting a phone away, like maybe he got a photo of me."

Then I remember the fake police the other day and them looking for Zara. Looking for me based on phone videos. Who would send out fake police? Got to be Finn. They have the money to hire all sorts of bad guys to track me down.

"Zara, I haven't told anyone yer name." She sits up and crawls close.

"I know you haven't, Glory." I reach for my own backpack. "I think I need to get out of here. If my bad guys see that photo, they won't waste any time getting here."

"You want us to take you to the mission again?"

It's cold tonight, so I slip into my new coat. "No, not the mission," I say, thinking about Kai's safety, worrying about more bad guys showing up, causing trouble at the mission. "I have to leave Chicago."

Irene wakes up and crawls out of her sleeping bag. "What's going on?"

"Zara needs to get out of Chicago. We're gonna help her."

Now Boar, RB and Bernie are all awake. "Zara in trouble?" Boar asks.

"She thinks that new guy, Remy, was hired to get a photo of her. We gotta get her away from the park, like now."

Boar gathers his things. "RB, you come with me so we can guard Zara. Bernie, you stay here in case any bad guys come here asking where Zara is. You can say she already left, and we don't know where she went."

Bernie nods. "I'll do it. Anything for Zara."

"We're coming too," Irene says with uncharacteristic fierceness.

Boar points in the direction of the street. "Irene, you and Glory should go out toward the street. If you see anyone coming, give a whistle."

"Right," Glory says. She squares her shoulders and dances around like a boxer warming up for a match. "C'mon, Irene."

"Boar." I whisper because I feel too shaky to use my voice. "We've got to stay away from the mission. I don't want any bad guys causing trouble there."

Boar grits his jaw. "Yeah, yeah, we'll keep away from there. We'll head for the I-94 on-ramp. We'll stay with you there until morning. Make sure you got a safe ride. But it's a long walk."

I don't care if it's twenty miles. I have to get out of this dangerous place. Every nerve in me seems like it's on fire. I'm jumpy and my stomach is in knots, and the feeling grows worse as we near the mission. We're still in the park boundaries when I see a dim light approaching from the right.

Boar must have seen it too. "Careful, Zara." He stops and faces the growing light. "Get behind me, girl."

The light is capturing shapes of men, walking fast. Four men, it looks like, and they don't look like they're out for an evening stroll.

RB's got his baseball bat ready, holding it high like he's ready to swing at a pitch. I wish I had some sort of weapon, but if these guys have guns, what good would it do?

"Zara, quick, run for the mission," Boar whispers. "We'll hold 'em off."

I take off running as fast as I can, heading for the end of the park and the sidewalk. I haven't run in weeks, and my legs are stiff from lying on the ground.

Behind me, a man yells, and Boar yells something fierce in answer. Then something goes *pop, pop,* and my heart jumps like it's a wild animal trying to burst free of my ribs. Were those gun shots?

Are Boar and RB okay? Little sobs jerk out of me with each stride. I know I should keep running—Boar told me to run—but what if he was shot? What if he's lying there bleeding to death? Because of me? Tears blur my eyes, streaming down my cheeks. *Oh, Abba, what should I do?*

I have to go back. But when I turn around and start trotting toward Boar and RB, men with flashlights come toward me, blocking my way. They fan out to surround me and hem me in. "Boar! Boar!" I yell. "Are you okay?" All I hear is a muffled human sound, but there's no telling if it's Boar.

"RB, Boar!"

I have one chance, and that's to dodge the man who's almost on me. Get through their dragnet and dash the rest of the way to where Boar and RB are. I feign left, then pivot and dash to the right. I almost make it. But the man hooks my arm, yanks me down to the ground. "Help, help!" They're all on me now, stuffing a cloth into my mouth, taping my arms back. They hold my legs and tape them together too. Two of them lift me and hurry away.

My heart pounds so hard I feel like my head will explode. I can't get enough air through my nostrils, but the gag keeps me from drawing a bigger breath. I wiggle and struggle until one of the men smacks me hard on the side of my head and growls, "Hold still, you stupid girl." I recognize Remy's voice, and my stomach goes sick.

Remy and the other guy still have to get me out of the park. But I can't think of any way to slow them down. I breathe harder and harder, but I can't get enough oxygen. My tongue is worming around, trying to get behind the gag and thrust it forward so I can scream for help.

Now they're trotting, jouncing my head and shoulders with each step. Lights penetrate the darkness. I hear Remy, who's holding my shoulders, panting from carrying me such a distance. We're coming up to the sidewalk and the street. Is a car waiting? Finn's guys? *Oh, Abba, help me!*

Voices carry from somewhere close to the mission. Shoes slap the pavement. My kidnappers stop, hesitate, curse. More voices fill the air. Someone shouts, "Put her down!"

Men and women crowd the area around my kidnappers. I recognize some of the faces. They're from the mission. Close to two dozen people circle me, each one calling for the guys to "let her go."

Glory's voice is closest. "Remy, you hurt her and I'll tear you to pieces."

Irene shouts, "They're calling the police. You better get outta here right now!"

Sure enough, I hear the distant scream of sirens. I struggle to breathe, and my heart slams in my chest.

Remy curses, using words I can't repeat. He pulls some sort of handgun.

Then Kai's face penetrates the crowd. "Hello, gentlemen. Don't even think of using those guns. You can't shoot all of us."

He pushes himself through the crowd of rescuers and is just inches away from my head. "That's right. Just put her down slow and gentle."

The police sirens are getting closer, and I'd laugh if I could. Suddenly, I'm on the ground, and lots of hands touch me, some soothing, others pulling at the tape on my wrists and ankles. Kai bends over me too. He pulls out my gag, and I take my first decent breath in at least five minutes.

There's a scuffle amid the crowd as Remy and the other kidnapper try to muscle their way free.

"Let 'em go," Kai says. "I've already given the police the car's license number."

Irene cuts the tape they'd used to bind me, and she helps me to my feet. "You okay?" She checks me over, dusting off my clothes like a mom would her little kid.

"I'm fine," I rasp, still trying to catch my breath. "But I have to leave. Those guys are going to keep on trying to get me."

"Yeah." She shakes her head. "I'm not gonna ask you what it's all about. I know you got yer reasons."

Glory shouts, "Make sure none of you tell those police people what this was all about. Jes say these bad dudes were throwing their weight around. That's all."

Someone asks, "Why'd they want Zoe?" And someone else says, "'Cause Glory says she's special."

Some of my rescuers trek back to the mission. Others hang around, probably to see what the police will do when they arrive.

I hold on to Glory's arm. "I really don't want to talk to the police. Can't we hang out at the mission till they leave?"

Kai's overhears me. "Good idea, Zoe. You three ladies go on with the others. I'll let you know when they've left."

Glory and Irene and I hurry toward the mission. I look back and see Kai striding toward the two squad cars that have just pulled up with lights flashing.

CHAPTER TWENTY-TWO

It's been almost an hour since we gathered inside the mission. Kai must have let Ron know what was going on, because he made the men and women return to their sleeping quarters, and then he went outside.

I lie on my cot next to Irene and Glory, on edge because I can't imagine what Kai and Ron told the police, and I wonder if the officers will take me to the police station so I can make a statement. Right about the time I decide to try to sneak out of the mission, someone whispers my name. It's Kai, standing at the door, gesturing for me to come with him.

I'd thought Glory and Irene were asleep, but as soon as I rise, they follow me. Kai shrugs helplessly when my two faithful friends crowd around him. He holds his finger to his lips and has us follow him downstairs into the chapel.

"Zoe, are you ready to tell me more about these bad guys? I told the police that they're just some troublemakers who don't like the mission and like to scare our men and women. But I sure don't like telling them things that aren't completely truthful."

I blurt out, "How's Boar and RB? I heard shots just before those guys grabbed me. Are they okay?"

"They're fine," he says. "Boar came out of the park just after you left and asked to speak to the police. He told them what he knew about Remy."

The taut feeling in my stomach relaxes. I'd never forgive myself if Boar or RB were hurt on my account.

"That Remy dude's been watching my friend," Glory mutters, as if she's afraid somebody will hear her. "He tried to take a photo of her tonight, and after he did, he packed up his things and left."

The door opens and closes, and Ron comes in and sits down next to us. "Young lady, why would some dudes be trying to get their hands on you? Have you been involved in a crime or something?"

I shake my head so hard, I see stars. "No, sir. No, sir. I haven't done anything wrong." My chin trembles, and I cover it with my fingers.

Irene puts a soothing hand on my shoulder. "Our girl is good."

"And innocent too," Glory adds. "But she needs to get out of Chicago so the dudes can't find her."

Ron looks exasperated. "But you haven't explained why they want to kidnap Zoe."

Irene looks at me as if asking permission to confess my secret, but I spear her with a "don't tell him" look.

"They ... they wanted to force me to do some bad thing," I say. "But I wouldn't. So now they want to kill me to keep me from squealing on them."

"Well," Ron says, "maybe it's time to go to the police and—"

"No!" I jump up and back away from the group. "They're really terrible men. If I talk, they'll kill me."

Ron and Kai exchange glances. It's clear that Kai has filled Ron in on what little he knows about me. Ron sighs and folds his burly arms across his chest. "So, we won't go to the police. But what *can* we do to help you?"

"I need to get out of Chicago. Secretly. So no one knows where I've gone, or even *if* I've gone."

Glory stands up and puts her arm around my shoulder and squeezes me hard. "Well, we can't just put her on a bus. That's what the dudes expect her to do. She came to us for help. The Bible says, 'Give to everyone who asks.'"

For the first time, Ron smiles. "Glory, one day Jesus is going to wrap his arms around you and say, 'Well done, good and faithful servant.'

"Okay, Zoe, if you don't want to go to the police, I can't force you. But I can help you get out of the city." He gives Kai a look filled with meaning.

Kai turns to me. "Ron's got an errand for me to do in LA, so if you'd like a ride with me partway ..."

"Are you kidding?" I practically dance with joy. "When do we leave?"

I'd said my goodbyes to Irene and Glory right there in the chapel. There were lots of tears, and I said I'd never forget them.

Glory hugged me tight and whispered, "Zara, you jes' keep on touching all the people who need your healing touch."

"I'll do it whenever Abba tells me to," I whispered into her orange hair.

Kai took that time to retrieve my backpack. When he returned with it, we all walked to the back entrance of the mission. Glory and Irene stood at the door and watched us climb into Kai's ancient Plymouth.

We've been driving for a couple of hours. The clock on Kai's dashboard is broken, frozen at 2:36. I'm still wide awake, checking the rearview mirror, scared I'll see a white van following us.

Kai signals to pull into a truck stop. "Here," he says, handing me a twenty-dollar bill. "Get some coffee and snacks. I like a little cream in my coffee."

Inside the truck stop, they're playing some good old country music. It reminds me of my dad, and my throat tightens, wondering where he is. I stuff down thoughts of my parents. Right now, I need to concentrate on getting home safely, not being noticed, and especially avoiding people who need healing.

I head for the women's restroom to wash my face and brush my teeth. It feels amazing to have a clean mouth again. In the store, I buy coffee, breakfast burritos, and chewing gum. When I come out, Kai's parked the car near the store entrance and is standing outside, stretching and running in place.

"Where are we? I know we're on I-80, but are we still in Illinois?"

"We're getting close to Moline. Probably got another hour to the border."

I feel anxious to get over the border, cross the Mississippi, and get into Iowa. Somehow, leaving Illinois feels like a separation, like shutting a door on the awful things that happened in New York City and Chicago.

"So, you want to tell me about those guys who're trying to get you?"

I knew Kai would want my story sooner or later. I suppose he deserves to know just how dangerous Clooney and Finn are, especially since they're still trying to find me. "I've got something they want." I hope a simple explanation will satisfy Kai.

"What? You've got money, jewels, real estate ... a map of buried treasure?"

"No." I ignore his attempt at humor. "It's not something outside of me. It's ... it's inside me."

Kai glances at me, his mouth tightening because I'm not giving him something he can work with.

"Their names are Clooney and Finn. They're brothers. They saw me on the news and—"

"You were on the news?" Kai's dark eyebrows knit in confusion.

"It was about a month ago. There was this little boy I healed."

"Whoa. Back up, Zoe."

"And it's not Zoe. It's Zara. Zara Nielsen. And until a few weeks ago, I lived a perfectly normal life in Titusville, Iowa, on a farm with my mom and dad. I was planning on returning to college next year. Working on my doctorate in English Lit. And afterward, I planned to teach at some college in Southern California. I had my whole life planned. It was going to be so beautiful." My voice breaks.

"Where does the healing thing come in?"

I swallow a couple of times and turn to watch the farmland roll by. "I have this ability. It's not really an ability. More like a kind of, uh, gift."

"The more you talk, the more you're confusing me." Kai is trying to focus on passing a slow-moving truck. "So, you have this ability, only it's not an ability. You ... heal." He doesn't seem surprised. More like disbelief.

I nod, but he doesn't see me, so I say, "That's what I'm trying to tell you."

He shakes his head, his eyes narrowed, and his mouth lifted into a sneer. "People don't do those kinds of things these days. That went out with the apostles. Except for those charlatans who take people's *donations* and then hypnotize them and make them believe they're all better."

He turns to me, and his eyes condemn me, even without a trial. "Is that what you do? Do you take money for your services?"

He's stung me. I can't believe the guy who just a minute ago was trying to help me is now spearing me with cynicism. "No! I'd never do that. It's not like that at all. I don't want this gift, if you can call it a gift. It's brought me nothing but problems. I just ... want to be ... normal." I'm crying hard now, and I turn my whole body away from him and wipe my wet face. Kai doesn't believe me. The one man I thought I could trust.

Finally, I whip around and face him. "If I'm such a charlatan, how come these drug dealers are trying so hard to get me back? They've got a grandfather who's dying of lung cancer. They kidnapped me and transported me to New York City and intended to hold me captive until I healed him. They've got my parents held hostage somewhere, and they've threatened to kill them if I don't do what they want. And don't tell me to go to the police, because they said they'd kill my folks if I do. And I have no one I can tell about this." I huff and snuffle, and I feel my face go all hot and splotchy, just like all the Nielsens when they cry.

Kai pulls out some napkins and hands me a couple. "Here, take this." He watches me while I blow my nose and dry my face. I'm still gasping even though I've quit crying.

"If you don't believe me, get on your phone and google the whole story. I bet it's still on the news."

Kai hands his phone to me. "Bring it up."

I type in my name and the word *disappearance*, and the whole story comes up. Then I shove the phone in his face. "See?"

He's trying to drive and read the news story about me, and it's not working because he keeps weaving. I'm about to tell him to give me the phone and I'll read it to him. But I don't get the chance. A blue truck comes alongside us and veers into our lane. I scream and grip the passenger armrest. Kai jerks to the left to avoid the truck, speeds up, and pulls parallel with a semi. The blue truck comes up behind us like he's all road rage. Kai grips the steering wheel, checking and rechecking the rearview mirror.

He guns it, signals, and moves in front of the semi. I guess he's hoping the blue pickup truck will pass and leave us alone. For a second, it kind of looks like it will. But then it veers over and almost hits us again. Kai yells and slams on his brakes. But the semi blares a warning, and I see its grill in our rearview mirror, about to swallow us whole.

Kai moves over to the left lane and slows so the semi will shield us from the pickup. But that doesn't work because the pickup moves over to the left lane, in front of us, and jams on its brakes.

"Kai, watch out!"

I scream when Kai barely misses rear-ending the pickup. He veers into the right lane again.

"There's an exit up ahead. Please take it." I grip the armrest, bolting upright.

Kai doesn't signal. He jerks onto the exit at the last second, but the pickup follows us. At the top of the exit, our tires squeal when Kai jerks the wheel to turn left onto a two-lane county road. A sign says there's a town two miles ahead. If we can just get to the town before this maniac pickup driver forces us off the road.

"Here he comes again!" I twist so I can maybe get a glimpse of the driver.

"I see him," Kai says through gritted teeth. His face is white.

The truck gets closer and closer. I'm gasping while I grip the armrest. Then in one big burst it accelerates into our bumper with a bang. Kai and I yell in terror.

The truck slams our bumper again, drawing more yells from us. It moves left into the oncoming lane and speeds up. Kai tries to accelerate, but his old car can't compete with the truck. It draws parallel with us, and I get my first look at the driver.

"It's Finn!"

When he sees me so scared, I'm practically slobbering, Finn laughs. Throws back his head and laughs like he's watching a comedy show.

He moves right, edging closer and closer to Kai's car. Kai brakes sharply, and the truck moves back into the oncoming lane again.

I wish there was some traffic, someone to witness this attack.

As if in answer, a car appears, just in time. A big old work vehicle, going slow. And Finn's heading straight for it. He's so intent on trying to force us off the road that he doesn't seem to notice the truck fast approaching. But when he finally sees it, he tries to jam on his brakes and veer into our lane behind Kai's car. But Kai obviously anticipated this move. He slows down, preventing Finn's truck from moving over.

The driver of the work truck blares his horn. Finn tries to speed up and get around Kai's car. But it's too late, and his startled face says he knows it. The guy driving the work truck is not going to be intimidated. He's not moving over, just keeps coming straight for Finn, honking and honking. At the last second, Finn jerks sharply to the left. He loses control on the soft shoulder, and his truck goes over the embankment. The guy in the work truck passes, still laying on the horn. He doesn't even slow to see what happened to the blue truck.

And Kai and me? We keep going too. I wiggle in my seat belt and get one last glimpse of Finn's truck, stuck in the soft dirt at the bottom of the embankment, its tires spinning uselessly.

CHAPTER TWENTY-THREE

Kai's breathing like a bull, his nostrils flared, chest heaving. He accelerates to seventy miles per hour, and I remind him that we're getting into a twenty-five zone, the town coming up fast.

We go the speed limit through the tiny town, both checking the rearview mirror for any sign of the blue truck. Once we pass the town—Kiplinger—Kai floors it again. We turn right, then left and drive onto another county road going west. Eventually we find Interstate 80, go over the Mississippi, and we're finally in my state. I check the map, figuring we should try to get on a less traveled road and go parallel to I-80. We exit and go north toward a county road. I don't recognize the little towns on this route because I usually traveled the interstate whenever I headed to Evanston, Illinois, to school.

The sun has risen. Kai hasn't said anything for about fifty miles. He still seems jumpy from what happened in Illinois an hour ago.

He glances at me and notices I've been watching him. He gives my hand a quick pat. "I think we're okay now."

I'm not sure I agree. Finn seems to have some sort of sixth sense about locating me. How did he know I was in Kai's car? Was someone watching the mission when we left?

I'm hungry, and I want to stop and get something to eat. But I'm also petrified about parking at a gas station or a convenience store and being spotted again.

I jump when Kai asks, "When we get to Titusville, what do you plan on doing?"

He's not looking at me, but I can tell he's pondering about how I'm going to find my parents. "I-I thought I'd look around, sort of scope out the places outside town that have been abandoned. You know, where a criminal might operate from so no one in town would notice anything suspicious going on." I shrug. That's about as far as my detective ability goes.

"You sure you don't want to go to the police? This kind of thing is way beyond what I know about."

I shake my head before he even gets through with his question. "If you'd ever met those two guys, you'd know that they mean business."

"Maybe it's just them. Maybe they're lying about having guys working for them."

"Kai." I practically explode. "I heard my mom's voice. She was terrified. Pleading. Someone was holding her prisoner. And my dad too."

I fold my arms across my chest and think hard about the day Finn and Clooney took me. How Clooney talked on his cell to some nameless associate while driving the van. The two of them whispering about meeting with so and so and arranging to meet a shipment at the harbor. I wonder if they knew I could hear them. And that's another thing. If they knew I could hear them planning their criminal activities, they must have always known they'd kill me after I healed their grandfather. They didn't care that I heard them because I'd be dead in a day or two.

Suddenly, I feel sick. Finn and Clooney are never, ever going to stop hunting me. If I go to the police, maybe they'll catch the brothers, and then I'll be safe. But I'd be sacrificing the lives of Mom and Dad. I can't do that. I love them too much, and besides, they've got as much right to live as I do.

I stare straight ahead, my jaw set. "If the police get anywhere near where they're holding my mom and dad, Finn will order them shot. I know it."

Kai takes a big breath, shaking his head as if he's beyond exasperated. "So, what're you going to do? Check out all the possible places thugs could be holding your parents, then go and surround the place, all by your lonesome? Zara, you don't even have a plan. You don't even have a gun. And you're ..."

He trails off, gritting his teeth.

"And what am I?"

"Well, pardon me for stating the obvious, but you're just a lone woman."

I can't answer. He's right. What's a woman going to do against armed thugs? I guess I'd hoped that, when the time came for action, I'd have developed a plan for extricating my folks. Maybe set up a diversion. A fire or some weird noises outside the place they're holding them. But I know it's stupid. I need help in the worst way. *Oh, Abba! Please help me do the right thing.* I *am* just one lone woman, without help, without a gun or weapon. And I don't want to get Kai involved in my problem, possibly getting him hurt or even killed.

That thought makes me want to tell Kai to just let me off somewhere near Titusville and go on his way to LA. This isn't his fight. It's mine.

As if Kai's guesses my thoughts, he slides his hand over mine and squeezes it. At first the touch of his hand soothes me. But then another sensation takes over, one way more urgent.

"Zara, I'm sorry. I—" Kai starts to say, but then he jerks when a sound comes from him. A kind of *crack, crack, crick.* He lifts his hand from mine and shoves it behind his back. "What was that?"

I try to look like I don't understand his question.

"It ... it was a weird feeling, like my back was being popped and stretched."

I'm too embarrassed to look him in the eyes. "Were you ever injured? Do you have a health condition?"

I glance upward, and my gaze locks on to his reddening cheeks.

"Nothing, really," he says. "Just that I fractured a vertebra in my lower back when I was little, and it's been kind of painful ever since."

He's still rubbing a spot on his back, shaking his head.

"How's it feel now? Is the soreness gone?"

"This is crazy. It doesn't hurt ... at all." He pulls his hand out and reaches over cautiously. With one finger he barely taps my hand, like a cook, testing for heat. Then again, leaving it on my skin longer. "Oh, it didn't happen that time."

I smile. "It only happens when you've got something that needs fixing."

"Really?" he asks, his dark eyes sparkling. "Zara, how do you do it?"

"It isn't me. It's never me."

He's still staring worshipfully, like I'm some sort of goddess, and it really bothers me. "Kai," I say in a forceful voice, "I'm nothing. Get that in your head. There's nothing special about me."

He's still got that absurd look of admiration on his face, and I'm tempted to slap some sense into him. But I'm not a violent woman, and I don't intend to ever become one. Instead, I rotate my body to the right and inspect the farmland and its row upon row of long, long earth furrows racing to keep pace with Kai's car.

It's been ten minutes of silence, and I feel guilty for ignoring Kai. I remember what he said about needing the police because I'm just one lone woman. "I'm sorry for losing my cool," I say. "You were right about getting help. I know you were just helping me to be realistic. Maybe I need to tell the police who I am. They must've been searching for my parents for weeks. Maybe I could help them."

"That's right. They're professionals." Kai reaches over again and absentmindedly strokes the top of my hand with his thumb.

He's not looking at me because he's got to watch the potholes on this bumpy stretch of road, and we're approaching a low-lying bridge that spans boggy land. "They've got those hostage negotiators who know how to talk to the bad guys. You'll see. It'll be all right. By tomorrow—"

"Watch out!"

But it's too late. Kai's right front tire hits a big pothole with a bang. The car veers left, and Kai overcorrects, which sends it toward the guardrail on the right. We hit that too, bumping, then scraping along the rail until he gets the car back under control. But now there's a weird grating sound coming from the front of the car.

"Oh my gosh, is the car okay?"

Kai brakes hard and pulls over. "I'd better check the damage."

Jumping beans bounce inside my stomach, so I hop out of the car too. But it doesn't take an expert to see what that darned pothole did to his tire. There's a slit, and the tire is already deflating.

Kai's usual understated manner slips for a second. He kicks the tire, and by the way he's chewing his lip, I can tell he's biting back some colorful language. On top of that, there's a painful-looking scrape along the side of the car, and the bumper above the right front tire is bent wickedly inward.

"It's okay. We'll just put the spare on," I say with as much optimism as I can muster. "I change tires all the time on the farm."

"Except I don't have a spare." His voice is so soft, I doubt what I've heard.

"What? You don't have a spare?"

He shakes his head slowly.

"Who doesn't carry a spare?" I shouldn't have said it, but it just popped out of my mouth. I mean, what kind of moron would go on a cross-country trip without a spare in the trunk?

"Most of the time I carry a spare." He says it with a look of surrender, and I feel like a jerk.

"The last one went kaput after I used it. I didn't have time to get another spare. You were in trouble, and my only thought was getting you out of Chicago as quick as possible, okay?"

"We'll call your insurance." I put a lot of understanding in my voice. "They'll come out and fix it."

"They're gonna have a hard time fixing this." He's crouches and pulls gingerly on the bumper with the wicked bend. "We try to put another tire on, and we still won't be able to drive until this is fixed. See how it's scraping the tire?"

"Okay, so we get towed into town, wherever that is, and get it fixed."

Kai drops his head in defeat. "All right," he murmurs. He walks around to the driver's side and picks up his phone, makes the call, then plops down onto the soft dirt next to me under the warming rays of the early morning sun. "It's going to be a wait. The nearest good-sized town is about twenty miles away."

CHAPTER TWENTY-FOUR

Tow-truck driver Joe, unloads the car in front of a run-down garage in a town that couldn't have more than a population of a thousand. I didn't even catch the name of the town. Andy's Body Shop is just off the main drag. On our way in, I noticed a café, a gas station, a supermarket—not too super, by the looks of it—and a motel. I'm sure there are more businesses, but my eyes glossed over them 'cause they're all run down, just like the fix-it business we're sitting in front of.

"Andy—that's the owner—is real good at fixin' your kind of crunched-in bumper," Joe says as he climbs out of his truck and heads to the back to unload Kai's car.

Kai steps out and politely holds the door so I can scramble down. While he goes into Andy's Body to take care of business, I wander toward the sidewalk. Weeds and grass sprout in the cracks. That always bothers me. I like a smooth, well-tended sidewalk. It says something about the people who live there. It says, "We care about our town. We're proud of the place we live." Maybe it's Finn slamming his truck into us a couple of hours ago, but I don't like this place. Wind kicks little bundles of dried plant debris and dust in little swirls, and I feel as shiftless and nervous as those bundles. I want to get out of this place in the worst way.

When I turn around and enter the shop where Kai is talking to Jeff, the clerk or mechanic or something, I feel even worse. Maybe it's the odors of chemicals and solvents and the banging and screeching of tools and machines. The guy who's helping Kai goes into the workroom. They're playing loud rock and working on some Harleys. A couple of rough-looking tattooed guys are hanging around, half talking with and half assisting the mechanics. The quintessential biker types.

When Jeff comes back, he's accompanied by a tattooed boulder of a man. He's part bald, and the other part is grizzled long hair pulled into a ponytail. His face is tanned and lined, and his mouth is shaped like it's used to swear words coming out of it. It isn't just his size or his tats. It's the attitude in his swagger. It shouts, "I'm the biggest bad actor you'll ever meet."

I'm properly impressed by his size and attitude, but I try not to show it. The name *Andy* is stitched on the pocket of his dirty blue work shirt, which is hardly the name I would've expected. He looks like he should be called Bull or Moose. He's slit his sleeves vertically, probably so his big muscles underneath his grisly tattoos can glisten and ripple and contract unhampered. His beefy hands are black from working on engines.

He's got a deep, angry voice, and when he talks, it's laced with blankety-blank words, so I wander to the window and try to tune it out. But I hear the part when Andy says it'll take two or three days to get the bumper fixed, which makes me want to march over to the desk and pound my fist on the countertop and insist he fix it tomorrow. I bite my tongue, seeing that beggars can't be choosers. After all, Andy could just say, "Take your blankety-blank car and tow it to the next town if you don't like it."

"You sure you don't want to fix the back bumper, too?" Andy asks, and I hear Kai reply, "I'll wait on that."

Kai shoots me an apologetic look and shrugs. He turns back to Andy and nods, then bends over to sign some paperwork.

Andy points outside to the left. "There's a motel down two blocks. You and your lady can get a queen for about sixty bucks."

I'm about to protest. What kind of woman does he think I am? Kai and I are obviously not married, and Andy just assumes we're shacking up. But Kai's left hand, below the counter, signals *chill*. So, I keep my mouth shut.

We go outside and grab our backpacks out of Kai's car, then head in the direction of the motel.

"Look," Kai says, "I don't have much money for this trip, so I hope you don't mind just sharing a room. I'll sleep on the couch. It's not like we have to tell anybody about being in the same room overnight, you know."

I trust Kai to keep his hands to himself, so I nod, though I avoid meeting his gaze.

After we drop our stuff off at the motel, Kai, says, "I'm starved. Is there any place to eat around here?"

"I didn't see any fast food, but we passed a little café. I think it's down the road a block, maybe two. There's a big tiger on the marquee."

"Great. Let's go."

In ten minutes, we're settled in a booth in Fat Cat's Café and perusing the menu. There are no other diners, and the waitress comes right over. She's tall and solid and tough looking too, like a female version of Andy. She's got tattoos all over her neck and down her arms. Her face is weather-beaten, and her voice is husky, probably from smoking, and I wonder what her life outside of the café looks like.

We order the cheapest item on the menu—grilled cheese and fries—and water. The waitress examines my face while we order, like she's trying to memorize my features. I try to look nonchalant, but her eyes make me nervous. Maybe she recognizes me from the news or a newspaper. I avoid looking at her as I hand her the menus, but my fingers carelessly come into contact with hers. And I hear it, the barely audible gasp and the slight startle of the hand that happens sometimes when I touch someone.

I blurt out, "Sorry, ma'am. Guess I'm all static electricity today."

"No worries, hon," she says with a phlegmy laugh. "I'll get that order right up." But her eyes say she's mighty curious about that snap of electricity. Especially since it's warm and muggy inside and outside and there's no dry air to make things all staticky.

"What was that all about?" Kai's studying my hands like they're a pair of strange zoo animals. "Is that something you do a lot?"

"What? I just zinged her with static electricity, that's all."

He doesn't look convinced. "Did she need healing too?"

"No, not her. Someone else. She smiles, but she's very, very sad." Then to distract him from thinking about what I said, I ask, "How many more miles do we have before Titusville?"

Kai swipes his phone and checks his maps app. "It's about one hundred miles away." And with hardly a pause, he asks, "Have you thought up a plan for your rescue operation?"

My stomach tightens. The way he says "rescue operation" sounds like he's mocking me. I still don't have a plan, and I can tell he thinks my quest to find my parents and help them escape is totally hopeless. "I have some ideas about where they might be held. Three of them, in fact." I square my jaw and stare him down. "They're all outside town. My friends and I used to ride our bikes along the unpaved roads near our farm. Inside some of those buildings we could tell some druggies had been there. Needles and stuff. One was an old, abandoned plant. It had a basement and storage rooms. It made me think of some of those horror movies where the maniac imprisons his victims." I shudder when I think of how creepy that place was, then imagine my mom and dad being held there.

"Just one thing, though," Kai says. "Why wouldn't the police have already checked out these places?"

I've wondered about that too. I shake my head and look at him with eyes that tell him I don't have an answer.

The waitress shows up just then, and we wait while she settles two waters on the table. Her name tag says *Roz*.

"You two just passing through, or do you live round here?" She's making polite talk while she places two napkin bundles on our place settings.

Then I see her glance at Kai's phone, still opened to the map with *Iowa, Titusville* clearly marked as the end destination and a little blue line showing the best route there.

"We're headed west ... to see ... family." Kai sweeps his phone off the table and into his jacket pocket in one swift motion.

Roz seamlessly turns her attention back to my face, studying. "That's nice. I don't get out to see my folks enough 'cause they're in Phoenix, but I'm going down there for Christmas."

We both duplicate her nod and make approving noises, and then she leaves.

"Face it, Zara," Kai says when Roz is out of earshot. "You're gonna have to get the police involved when we get to Titusville."

I'm about to vehemently protest, but he puts his hand up to stop me. "If we show up anywhere around your town, someone's bound to recognize you. Then the media will pounce on your miraculous return, and the police will jump on it too. But I bet you and the police working together will figure out where your parents are. If you go to them first, the media won't know and then your bad guys won't know you've squawked. The police have got swat teams and negotiators and snipers that can take down those drug thugs before—"

We're so busy talking, we've gone all deaf and dumb to what's around us, and we don't hear Roz return with our grilled cheese orders. "Here ya go." She puts our plates down. "And you've got ketchup and Tabasco sauce in the caddy there. Is there anything else you need?"

I try to look innocent. "No, thanks. This looks great."

Roz smiles her professional smile, but there's something added in the mix of muscle contractions on her face. Maybe a muscle that doesn't usually get drafted for smiling. It alters the expression just enough to make me stiffen.

When she leaves, Kai says, "Crap, Zara, do you think she heard our conversation?"

My lips barely move. "I think she did, at least part of it." I dart a glance at the entrance to the kitchen, but I don't see Roz or anyone else. "Let's finish up quick and get out of here. The way she looks at me, I keep thinking she recognizes me."

Kai says a quick grace, and then we dig into our food. I haven't heard grace since being home. Kai's voice is a mellow baritone, and his words comfort me.

After we leave Fat Cat's, we buy some snacks at a convenience store on our way to the motel so we don't have to return to the café again for dinner.

As soon as we step into our room at the Shady Oaks Motel, Kai turns on the news on the TV. There's nothing on about my case, just a heartbreaking story about a bombing at a church in Africa and then a clip about some government investigation.

Kai shuts off the TV and sits down on the office chair. He types some words into his phone. He's quiet while he reads, but whatever he's reading seems to upset him. He looks up, his brows knit.

"Tell me about your healing gift, Zara."

He takes me by surprise. I thought he didn't believe me or that maybe he thought I was just some loony woman who's spent too much time reading up on mind games or hypnosis. I stand in the middle of the motel room, fiddling with a thread that's come loose on the cuff of my sweatshirt, and all I can picture is Aunt Evelyn sitting on my bedroom floor, weeping.

"My aunt had the gift. But she died a while ago. It showed up in me when I was still little. I touched a kid who had asthma, and it went away right in the middle of an attack. My parents knew then they had to keep me away from school so no one would find out I was like my aunt."

"Away?" Kai tilts his head, his brows scrunched together. "Why wouldn't your folks have been happy about you having such an unusual ability?"

I sigh deeply, and suddenly, overwhelming fatigue makes my legs tremble. I settle onto the sofa before my legs give out. "Think about it, Kai. Remember that story in the Bible about Jesus? He's going around preaching and healing, and what did the local people do? They followed him everywhere. He went into a house, and there were so many people wanting to touch him or have him heal their child or wife or father. Remember what the friends of the paralytic had to do? They couldn't get inside. So, they climbed up on the house and took the roof apart and lowered their friend down into the room where Jesus was. It got so Jesus had to put out to sea in a fishing boat so the crowds couldn't overwhelm him."

Kai's nods like he gets it. "And your parents were afraid that would happen to you?"

"It's what happened to my aunt. She could never stay in one place for long. Compassion compelled her to touch people who needed healing, and as soon as she did that, word would get out. And then she'd be mobbed. If she couldn't be found, then people would break into the last place they'd seen her and they'd go and loot whatever objects she might have touched. Like they thought her shirt or cup or whatever had power too. It was a wonderful gift, but also a horrible gift. My mom and dad wanted to spare me that kind of life."

"And then word spread about you and how you could heal," Kai said, looking out the window with worried eyes, as if imagining crowds of people mobbing our motel room.

"Yes."

He turns and meets my eyes, and I catch the understanding, the compassion, the wonder of it.

He lifts his phone. "The report says here that the police found your uncle's abandoned truck, burned, but no one inside. Then when they went to notify his next of kin, your mom and dad and you were all gone, and even your sister and brother-in-law didn't know where you were. So now there's a giant investigation, and the police are hooking up with the FBI to try to solve the mystery of the Nielsens' disappearance. I wonder if they've figured out yet that your disappearance was separate from your parents.'" He puts the phone down and hunkers over to rub his forehead. "What a mess."

"You see what a challenge it is to have the gift of healing?"

"I want to say I'm sorry, but I can't really argue with God," Kai says softly. "I mean, if he's the one who gave you the gift, he must have some really big purpose, one we humans can't comprehend."

I drop my eyes to the errant thread on my sleeve and tug at it again. "So far, healing has brought me only tragedy. But lately I've been thinking about the people I've touched. The little boy, his body all smashed by a car. I met his soul hovering above his body at the hospital, straddling two worlds. Tommy—that's his name—will live to grow up and become a father. He'll tell his children how Abba called me to his bedside one scary day when he was only six.

"Then there was Pete and Irene and the businessman, and the people in New York City. They're all physically whole now. Is my desire to live my own life worth more than their lives? I keep trying to protect myself, to stay anonymous, but I'm beginning to wonder if life is not about self-protection. Maybe it's more like being a firefighter."

Kai's still rubbing his forehead, but he looks through his fingers, urging me to explain.

"Everyone else runs from a fire, but a firefighter runs toward it so he can save lives."

Kai sits up. His eyes are wet, and his mouth is twitching.

"Aunt Evelyn had the same kind of struggle. Sometimes she stayed and faced the crowds of desperate people. Other times it got to be too much and she ran. But eventually the gift killed her. I guess I'm more selfish than she was. I want to live."

Kai leans forward in his chair. "Why is it selfish to want to live?"

I shrug. "I ... don't ... want to do what Abba wants me to do." And then my anger boils over. "I want what I want." I pound my fist down on my thigh. "I want to go to school, and then I'll be a teacher and I'll have the normal, safe life I've always wanted. That's all I want. Couldn't Abba just let me have that one wish—to be normal?"

"Why would you want to be normal?" Kai stands and sits next to me on the sofa, sliding a comforting arm around my shoulders. "Normal is average. Normal is getting a C in English. It's undistinguished. It's easy. No one remembers normal. It's the Napoleons and the Caesars and the Isaac Newtons and the Sojourner Truths that people remember. Zara, you've been chosen."

He's quiet, and I sense his own emotions swirling around in his gut. In a quiet voice he says, "I wish I could be chosen."

CHAPTER TWENTY-FIVE

I wake early, enjoying the feel of the clean sheets with that motel scent and the wideness of the mattress. I've hardly ever slept in a queen, and I stretch my arms and legs out to feel its expanse. With my eyes still shut, I feel Abba hovering over me. *I'm with you, Zara.*

I sit up and glance over at the couch. Kai's there, his back to me, and a tangle of dark hair peeks out between rumpled layers of sheets and blankets. I hear him breathe slow and steady.

I slip out of bed, tiptoe to retrieve my backpack on the luggage rack, and head for the bath. After my shower, I slip into the only other pair of jeans and T-shirt and socks I own. My other clothes are hanging up on a hook, still damp from being washed in the bathtub last night.

I recall what Kai said yesterday at the restaurant, about how maybe we should get the help of the police. But even if I could find out where Finn is holding Mom and Dad, how would I manage to rescue them? I've been so naïve, thinking just like an idiot. This hostage stuff is way beyond my understanding, and I really do need help. And I wonder if I should contact Abby and Rolf when I get back to Titusville. Let them know I'm all right. But not yet. I don't want anyone there to be waiting for me. I don't want this rescue operation ripped from me, even if by the police. After all, I know Finn and Clooney way better than the law.

When I come out of the bath, Kai's up and dressed, and I put on my most optimistic expression so he won't worry about me still intending to do foolish things when we get to Titusville. I'm about to tell him what I've been thinking, when he interrupts my thoughts.

"You hungry? I thought we could go back to Fat Cat Café. They've got waffles."

It's so unexpected and innocent that I have to laugh. The earnest way he says "waffles" and how his eyes go big and little-boy-like. I guess waffles are Kai's standard of excellence for breakfast dishes. I get it. My dad loves waffles, and Saturday mornings aren't complete for him until he has his eggs and bacon, topping off the meal with strong coffee and a Belgian waffle.

My heart clutches at the memory of my dad snarfing his Saturday morning waffles. I wonder what his captors are feeding him … and mom too. My eyes sting, and I turn away so Kai won't see the tears.

He shrugs into his jacket. "And afterward I wanna go over to Andy's and see how they're coming along with the fender repair."

At the Fat Cat Café, we're seated in a smaller booth, one for two people. There are other diners in the room. Lots of trucker types and groups that look like the regular crowd. Sixties pop music plays in the background, and two waitresses take orders. I'm relieved that I don't see Roz.

The aromas of coffee and hash browns and pancakes and bacon tease my nostrils, making me hungrier each passing minute. We both order waffles and eggs and bacon, and Kai orders coffee and a side of hash browns too.

"Where'd you learn to love waffles?"

Kai watches me over the rim of his coffee cup. "My grandpa. No one could make waffles like him. He'd whip the egg whites and put whipped cream in the batter too. And a bit of vanilla extract. Sometimes he'd put some mashed banana in too. They were amazing. I had 'em all summer. Then I'd go home in September and eat nothing but Cheerios because that's all there was in the house."

"Nothing? Didn't anyone cook for you, Kai?"

He shrugs. "Every once in a while, my mom would come home sober and make hamburgers or fried chicken or spaghetti. She'd play ball with me in the apartment parking lot." Kai's lips screw up. "But then she'd disappear. I never knew when she'd return. Most times when she came back, she'd be all drunk and would sleep it off on the living room couch. When she sobered up, I tried to tell her she should quit drinking because she was so much fun when she wasn't drinking. She'd say, 'You're right, Kai. I'm gonna quit real soon.' But she never did."

Kai shakes his head, like he's picturing that ancient conversation with his mom. "Mostly I was a lonely kid. I used to get picked on by a group of bullies. Until I took some jujitsu." He grins. "But after I put 'em on the ground a couple of times, they left me alone."

My heart hurts to picture kind, soft-spoken Kai having that kind of upbringing. Every kid needs loving parents.

"At jujitsu, I found an older man who took me under his wing. He became my Big Brother, and I think that's why I didn't go off the deep end, being neglected by my drunk mom and not having a father. My father left when I was a baby. But between my jujitsu Big Brother and my grandfather, I think I did all right. As soon as I got out of high school, I took off for Colorado, where my grandpa lived. We spent the summer fly fishing and selling lures and being guides for out-of-state fly fishers."

"So, you're in Colorado hanging with your grandpa, and suddenly you're in Chicago, Illinois, working at a mission?" I can't believe Kai's had this kind of life. I'd thought he had a more traditional childhood.

"That was my grandpa's idea. He said I had to do something for other kids who had the same kind of life I'd had back in LA with my alcoholic mom. He kept saying, 'Son, you've got to give back.' And I'd say, 'What did I ever get that was so great that I'm supposed to give it to someone else?' And he'd say, 'Pain. No one understands pain more than one who's felt it all his life. Kai, you go and help those other kids make their lives better.'

"The next thing I know, I'm being interviewed at the mission for an internship. Six months later, my grandpa died of a heart attack. I think he knew his end was coming and wanted to make sure I didn't just hole up in Colorado feeling hurt and useless. Every summer I'd visited, he'd say, 'The best way to heal from your hurts is to turn around and help someone else.'"

"So, Ron hired you?"

Kai nods. "He and my grandpa were friends from years back, and I'm sure Grandpa told him all about me."

Our waitress brings the food, ending our conversation. As I polish off my waffle, I remember how he said, "I wish I'd been chosen." Funny how that works. "Chosen" doesn't seem to settle on the most noble or deserving people. Kai's suffered way more than I have, and he has a pure and self-sacrificing heart. But it's me, a selfish farm woman from middle America, who's never had to sacrifice anything more than an afternoon of hard farm work while surrounded by kind and loving people, who gets chosen to be a conduit for Abba's healing energy. Why me?

Aren't chosen people the ones who have endured terrible suffering and deprivation? It seems it's always those who end up doing spectacular services for humanity. I've always had plenty to eat. I have loving parents, a loving sister, a healthy environment, and a library up the road where I can read all the poetry and short stories that were ever written. And I've been blessed to have studied and earned two college degrees already. But here's Kai, unselfishly pouring his energy into making sure I'm safely returned to Titusville, even if it means he gets hurt or killed in the crossfire. And he has no idea what a truly wonderful guy he is. I think of Craig and realize how similar Kai is to him. My Abba is at work in both of them.

After breakfast, we step outside Fat Cat Café and almost knock into Roz, in a hurry to get inside.

"Hi, guys," she says with enthusiasm, like she's greeting a close friend she hasn't seen in twenty years. "You're still here? I thought you'd be on your way by now."

"No," Kai mumbles, not making eye contact. "We're still waiting on our car repair."

"Oh, yes, I thought you mentioned that. Well, Andy's the best. He'll get you fixed up as quick as a snap."

I wave goodbye, and we go down the steps. But I can't resist looking back, and when I do, I see Roz, still outside the restaurant, watching us as she talks on her phone.

"Weird. Kai, don't look back, but Roz is still watching us," I say through clenched teeth. "What is it with this lady?"

"She's just nosy," he answers. "They probably don't get too much excitement in this little town."

"I'm trying to remember what we said to her yesterday. But I can't remember mentioning that we were getting your car fixed."

Kai's eyebrows cinch together. "Yeah, me too."

"How'd she know that?"

"Dunno. Let's hurry."

He quickens his pace, and I have to hoof it to keep up. When we get to Andy's Body Shop, there's another client finishing up with the clerk, so we take seats and wait. I see Andy through the window to the work area. He sees us and waves like we're old friends.

When the customer ahead of us leaves, Jeff, the clerk, calls us up to the desk. "Andy wants to talk to you guys about your car. I'll go tell him you're here."

Jeff leaves, and we stand there for at least ten minutes wondering what the delay is. I can see Jeff and Andy through the window, talking, looking pretty serious, and I sure hope there isn't anything else wrong with the car that's going to delay us further.

Finally, Andy comes out and gestures for us to follow him through the door into the work area. It's noisy in here, but he points to another door on the opposite side of the shop. We follow him through this door and wind up in an office. Andy closes the door and asks us to take seats.

I'm nervous. If we're meeting in a private office, the cost of Kai's repairs must be way over what we estimated.

Andy takes a seat at the desk and leans his giant elbows on the table. "Mr. Fujiwara, it looks like your repair is going to be a little more than we originally thought."

Kai's brows contract, and his jaw clenches. "How could a bumper and a new tire cost more than the two thousand estimate you gave me?"

Andy's wearing a little smug smile. "More like ten thousand."

"What?" Kai sits up straight and his nostrils flare. "That's outrageous. My insurance is never going to pay ten thousand for this kind of repair."

"Hold on, son."

"And don't call me son."

Andy nods, but he's still got that one eyebrow raised, like he's got all the power in this confrontation. "I know ten thousand is a mite high, but there is a way you could cover the cost and not even have to use your insurance."

"Yeah?" Kai's eyes narrow, like he's preparing to hear something even more outrageous.

"We have lots of customers that can't pay all their bill, so we're prepared to barter."

"What could we possibly barter? I don't own anything but my car." He takes his wallet out and waves it. "I've got maybe twenty-five dollars in cash."

Andy takes his arms off the table and leans back in his chair. "It's not something you've got. It's what that pretty gal next to you has," he says and settles his gaze on me.

Kai and I jump up simultaneously. "C'mon, Zara, let's go. We'll catch a bus home."

We open the office door and gasp. There's a guy bigger than a grand piano blocking the doorway, staring us down, and it's clear we're not getting out of Andy's Body Shop anytime soon.

CHAPTER TWENTY-SIX

"Better sit down and hear my proposition." Andy hasn't even left his chair. His dark eyes are calm, even expressionless. He's used to making deals. He's confident it will go his way.

I stare at Kai, waiting to see what he'll do. He's tall and lean and athletic, but he's no match for Andy or that giant muscle man blocking the door behind us. Kai reaches for my hand and pulls me close. He slides his arm around my shoulder as if to protect me. "What do you want with Zara?"

I can feel him trembling. But his voice stays calm, even. "Zara's a special girl. It would be dangerous to try to traffic her. She's—"

"We know all about her," Andy says. "In fact, we've been following her story on the news. I always thought it was a case of sex trafficking when she disappeared. We wondered where she'd end up. Nice to see she's alive and well."

Andy points to the chairs we'd been sitting on, indicating that we should sit down again.

The muscle man comes inside and shuts the door, stationing himself behind us with brawny arms folded at his chest.

"It's a really simple proposition. Zara is a healer. We have a sick boy that needs her touch. She heals the boy, we forget the fee for fixing your car. We make sure you make it to wherever you need to go safely."

I stare at him and wonder how he knows we're in danger.

As if he guesses my thoughts, Andy says, "Yes, we know there are some dudes looking for you. Why? I don't know, and I don't care. We just want you to do this little favor and then you can go on your merry way."

I take a breath. "It isn't like that. I can't just lay my hands on someone and heal them."

For a second he looks confused, then his face clouds, and I see the coiled-up viper hiding behind the calm mask.

"His name's Robbie. Only twelve years old. He's a good kid. Before he got sick, he was in little league, basketball, soccer. He's real talented in sports. Just lives to throw a ball. The doctors say he's got maybe ten percent chance of living. That's not good enough for me. With you here, it'll be hundred percent."

"I'll do what I can, but the healing doesn't come from me. It comes from—"

Andy stops me with a quick chop of the air, like he's swatting at a fly. "Don't tell me who it's from," he says angrily. "I don't want to hear it."

"Where is the boy?" I ask like I'm suddenly in charge, even though my mouth is dry and my stomach is so tight I feel like I'm going to hurl.

"He's home," Andy says. "I'll take you to him."

I look over at Kai, and I can tell he's as scared as I am. What if Abba doesn't choose to heal the boy? What will they do to us? It could be bad. Anyone who'd kidnap a couple of people wouldn't think twice about killing them either.

I stand, and Kai follows me. "We go together or not at all."

"Naturally," Andy says. He gestures to the giant behind us. "Hoss, get the vehicle."

Hoss exits and shuts the door behind him. We wait silently, watching Andy, who says nothing. He's good at the poker face. His phone beeps, and he pulls it out and checks the message. "Let's go," he says without any emotion or urgency. He opens the office door and gestures to a delivery truck backed into the shop, with open cargo doors. Once we're inside, Hoss jumps in and puts blindfolds on us. The truck lurches, and I quickly sit and feel for Kai. He's close, and he grabs my hand.

Someone slams the doors shut. The truck starts up, and we brace ourselves as best we can so we don't roll around when the truck moves.

I hate closed spaces, and I hope we're not going far. The thought of being trapped in this windowless space makes me hyperventilate. But then I remember Abba's presence this morning, how he'd said, *I'm with you, Zara.* It will be okay. Kai will be okay too.

Kai squeezes my hand, then pulls me to him, and we cling to each other. My head rests against his chest, and I hear his heart beating hard and strong in his perfect body. *Oh, Abba, please keep Kai safe.*

The truck takes several hard rights, then steadies for a long stretch, then a hard turn onto a bumpy road. It's been about twenty minutes since we left, and we must be out of town. Probably out in the farmlands. Now on a bumpy road, the truck crawls for a few seconds before finally coming to a halt.

Feet crunch on gravel, and the latch is unfastened. Hands lift us, separate me from Kai, guide me to the cargo doors. Someone lifts me down to the ground and leads me down a paved walk, then steps. A screen door creaks, and when I take a step, I'm walking on carpet. We go straight, then a turn. My elbow scrapes against what feels like another doorway. Then I'm guided to a chair and pushed down onto it.

Only then do they remove my blindfold, and I blink to adjust to the light. I'm in a boy's bedroom, with famous athletes tacked up on the blue walls. On shelves and the dresser are trophies and other sports memorabilia. A boy lies silent in his bed. There's a couch nearby, probably for the boy's mom or dad to sleep on so they can be nearby. Kai is sitting there, his eyes large, like he's overwhelmed.

Movement behind me alerts me to the presence of others. Andy is standing at the foot of the bed. So is Roz. I should be surprised, but somehow, I suspected that this man and woman were linked. They're watching me, waiting to see what I will do. Roz is clasping her hands to her chest in a silent plea for her son's life. Andy, though poker faced, communicates the deepest pain a parent can experience.

Breathing sounds remind me of the boy, Robbie, whom I'm supposed to heal. He's buried under mounds of blankets. He moves, and one emaciated hand and then his skeletal forearm appear. I stand and bend over his bed and gently pull back the covers.

He might have been a handsome boy before illness ravaged him. His large brown eyes, gazing up at me, are glassy and blank. The skin—translucent. He's completely bald. A photo nearby shows a healthy youngster in a little league baseball uniform with buzzed, brown hair and a broad smile and adorable dimples. Andy and Roz's pride and joy.

My heart squeezes. This should not be. No one should have to watch their child waste away and die. Even an evil man like Andy doesn't deserve this. *Why, Abba, why?* Robbie should grow to be a man. He should bring his family joy, not sorrow. I slide my fingers over Robbie's bony shoulder and rest them on his chest. His heart is weak. Chemo has sickened him, and it's not destroying the cancer cells. There are renegade cells sneaking into other organs, setting up sleeper training camps, preparing to launch surprise attacks on his kidneys, his liver. The doctors don't even know yet the extent of the enemy's plans to extinguish Robbie's life.

I tremble, my gut overwhelmed with grief for this lovely boy who won't see thirteen. My God, it's not fair. I think of all the children who die each year, and I hear mothers and fathers weeping, thousands upon thousands of them. *Abba!*

I'm sobbing now, hot tears splashing onto Robbie's blankets. My back burns with the awful pain of cancer, and my stomach is sick, sick from the chemo poison. We're burning with fever, Robbie and I, and I'm too weak to hold my head up anymore. I fall forward onto Robbie's body, and the world turns bright, searing white.

There's a sound banging against my head. I'm driving Kai's car, and it still has a flat, and as it goes down the highway, the tire goes *bonk, bonk, bonk*. When I wake from my dream, Kai is leaning over me, stroking my forehead. He breathes a relieved sigh when my eyes focus on him, and I give him half a smile.

I'm lying on a couch, still in Robbie's room. "How's Robbie?" I rasp because my throat is sore and dry.

"He's fine. Zara, you should have seen him. After you fell asleep, he sat up and asked for food. Said he was so hungry he could eat all the chickens in their chicken coop. And all the eggs too. Then he got up just like a normal kid, his cheeks all pink and his eyes sparkling, and Roz grabbed him and held him like she'd never let go. She was crying, and Andy's tears were flowing down his cheeks. Then Andy swooped his son up in his arms and carried him out of the room. That was hours ago."

The *bonk, bonk, bonk* sound from my dream goes on. It's coming from outside. "What is that?"

Kai grins. "That's Andy and Robbie playing basketball in the driveway."

Now I'm fully awake, and I jump up to look out the window. Sure enough, Robbie, still dressed in his pj's, is running circles around his big dad, shooting hoops, dodging and faking his way to the basket. Roz is sitting on a lawn chair on the sidelines, smiling.

Kai puts his hand on my shoulder. "I think that big guy, Hoss, is guarding this room to make sure we don't leave."

"I figured that. Do you think they'll let us go?"

"Don't know."

"Could we sneak out?"

Kai tiptoes over to the door and opens it a crack, then shuts it quietly. "No," he whispers. "Hoss is still standing in the hallway."

I hold my hands out in a gesture of helplessness. "I'm so sorry for putting you in this situation."

Kai hurries to me and pulls me into a protective embrace. "Shh, it's not your fault. None of this is your fault. People are selfish. And when they're desperate, they'll do things they shouldn't."

If we weren't kidnapped and scared, and if I hadn't already met Craig, knowing our futures will meld one day, I might have been tempted to let him hold me. But Kai and I have different roads ahead of us. And we need to come up with a plan of escape. I look into his eyes, and I can tell he wants to kiss me.

But then he shakes himself, pulls me over to the couch, and makes me sit. "I've been thinking about these guys who took us, and I've got a hunch they're more than just tough auto workers. I noticed this tattoo on Andy's arms. I recognized it, because I helped this guy once back in Chicago. He was running from a biker gang and wanted to get out of the life. He had the same tattoo on the same place on his arm. He never told me the name of the gang, but he said it controls a big section of the country. Hoss has the same tattoo, and I'm willing to bet those biker guys in the shop the other day have the same mark."

"So? How does that help us?"

Kai joins me on the couch and hunches close. "See, they control a lot of drug action and other illegal stuff around the state. If they found out that the guys who kidnapped you were part of a drug cartel operating in their territory, they might get riled. I'm wondering how we could use this to our advantage."

"Kai, you're a genius. So, you're saying we somehow convince these bad guys here to fight *my* bad guys in Titusville."

"Right. They don't care about our business, but they sure as heck care about their own business."

At last, a glimmer of hope for my parents' safety shines into my heart. But I'll have to do a really good job painting Clooney and Finn and their thugs as challengers to Andy's biker operations.

The sounds of the bouncing basketball have ceased. Kai peeks out the window. "They're not out there anymore."

Footsteps in the hall outside our door make us both sit up straight. The door opens, and Roz and her healthy son step inside.

Roz rushes over and throws her arms around me and holds me so tight I can hardly breathe. "Thank you. Oh, thank you for healing my son. I'll never be able to repay you." She sobs, her whole torso quivering.

I hug her back and make little sympathy sounds so she knows I'm happy for her and Robbie.

When she finally lifts her body, she turns and gestures to Robbie, who's standing at the doorway, looking shy and uncertain. He approaches with awkward movements. "Um, thank you, ma'am. For making the cancer go away. I feel good now, and I know it was you, so thank you."

I hold my hand out, and he takes it, and I can feel the warmth, the strength in his grip, his pulse coming regular. I sense strong, healthy tissues where once freakishly hard and hateful masses had pillaged his systems. His face is growing more handsome with each passing minute, and I see the man he will become. He won't be a criminal biker, like his father. He'll be the founder of a new legacy within the family.

"It wasn't me, Robbie. It's Abba. It's always Abba who gives life."

Andy's shadow darkens the doorway. Roz and Robbie see it and immediately move aside. Andy lets them go out, and then he shuts the door.

Kai and I go stiff. What will Andy do? Order our executions? Keep us prisoners?

"I'm a man of my word. I said I'd get you safely to wherever you need to go."

"Mr. Andy, sir." I stand and plant myself right in front of him. "Will you listen to me? I need to tell you a quick little story."

Andy looks surprised. I guess not many people talk to him so forthrightly.

He nods, looking serious. "You gave my boy back to me, so I'll listen."

He stays where he is, not moving but waiting for me to speak, so I take a breath. "Mr. Andy, I've had this gift, or whatever you call it, all my life, and my parents managed to keep it a secret because they knew it would complicate my life if word got out that I could heal. But about a month ago, we had two life and death situations in Titusville."

He nods again. "Yes, that little boy."

"Yes, and one of my dad's farmworkers. Well, it got out on the national news, and some very, very bad guys—drug dealers and expediters ... I'm not sure what the correct name for them is—but anyway, they needed me to heal their grandfather, who is the head of their cartel. I heard them talking—Finn and Clooney, that is—and they have deals going on all over the country, probably Iowa too."

My heart lurches when I say "Iowa," as Andy's face reacts with surprise, and his eyes harden.

"So, they set up an ambush, and they kidnapped me and murdered my uncle. They drugged me and took me to New York City and held me prisoner, saying they'd let me go when I healed their grandfather. But it doesn't work like that, and I knew I'd never get out of there alive. I escaped, and they've been trying to recapture me ever since. Mr.

Andy, they're holding my parents as hostages somewhere near Titusville. Jim and Astrid Nielsen. Finn told me they would kill my folks if I went to the police, so I haven't told anyone that I'm alive and ... well ... and trying to get back home."

"Finn and ..."

"Clooney. Finn and Clooney Finnegan. They've got men all over the country who take orders from them. Who knows? They might have already ordered my parents killed. I don't know. But I have to get back there and find them. I have to rescue them somehow."

"Titusville," Andy says with a kind of steel in his tone, like he knows something. "Nobody operates in my territory without me knowin' about it."

I sense the anger in him. His body fills with adrenaline, like a wrestler on the mat.

"I have to work tonight, but Roz is gonna fix you dinner. When I get back home tomorrow, I'll tell you what I can do to help you."

He turns without another word and strides out, leaving the door open for the first time in two hours.

CHAPTER TWENTY-SEVEN

Kai was given the foldout couch in Robbie's room. But they offered me the guest room. Roz must have put a lot of energy and heart into this room. She decorated it with a pretty wallpaper border and white beadboard, frilly eyelet curtains, and watercolor paintings of hummingbirds. I'm in a brass bed with a handmade quilt and crisp gingham sheets. I'm guessing Roz and Andy don't intend to kill me.

I smell bacon and coffee downstairs, and I'm not sure I can eat another big meal. Last night, Roz served roast chicken and garlic mashed potatoes and all the fixings. Then she set a slice of apple pie à la mode in front of me, and I could hardly find a spot in my full stomach for the dessert. Kai ate it all and happily accepted another helping of everything.

I climb out of bed and find my clothes freshly laundered and folded, sitting on the chair next to the door. I dress hurriedly and go in search of Kai. Now that we're not facing imminent death, I enjoy a memory of Craig and me, talking and singing as we traveled through Pennsylvania.

I find Kai in the kitchen, helping Roz. He's tied a big kitchen towel around his waist and is flipping pancakes while Roz scrambles the eggs. Robbie is setting coffee cups on the dining table.

Kai meets my eyes with a "How are you feeling?" question on his face. My answer is a big smile. It's such a lovely domestic scene, I almost convince myself this is normal and we're not wondering what Roz's biker husband and his gang are planning to do about Finn and Clooney. I want to forget about all these criminals for a half hour or so, just long enough to enjoy watching a healthy Robbie enjoy his breakfast.

This may be the last day of normal—uh, that's completely inaccurate. Nothing about this last month has been remotely normal. I guess I mean this may be the last day before I find out if my mom and dad are still alive. How will Andy and his men find my folks? Will there be a violent showdown? Will the police get involved too?

Roz greets me with, "How's the healer this morning?"

And I respond appropriately with, "Just fine, thank you." I wish I could tell her not to call me by that name. I'm not the healer. And I'd prefer people know me as just plain Zara, the woman who's planning to return to school in a few months, the farm woman who can heft hay bales and drive tractors, who loves poetry and writes sonnets about the larks' heart-stopping songs out in the rolling fields of alfalfa.

A *beep, beep, beep* comes from a little box on the counter. Roz glances at it, then announces, "The guys are here."

She turns to her son. "Robbie, go on outside till I call you."

Robbie leaves immediately.

Seconds later, the front door opens and Andy walks in, dressed in some biker getup with patches and other insignias on his vest. He's followed by four other guys—including Hoss—wearing the same kind of vest. The guys I haven't met stare at me as they file in and head for the dining room table. Obviously, Andy has told them something during their all-night meeting.

"Zara, Kai, please sit here next to Andy." Roz points to the two chairs to the left of him.

We do as we're told, and neither of us says anything. If Andy and his gang are going to help me, I plan to stay out of their way and let them do whatever it is they do. That sounds awful, coming from me, a healer, but I hope when Finn couldn't take us down the other day, that he drove to Titusville. I hope he's waiting there, waiting to murder us when we show up. Won't he be surprised when Andy's gang shows up instead? I'm hoping to see Finn get what's coming to him.

We eat breakfast together, and my heart is beating like a drum, thinking that any minute these dangerous dudes are going to start talking about their plans. I'm dying to ask, but I don't dare. My gaze moves from face to face. Maybe when they've finished breakfast, they'll start talking. But no. Roz keeps replenishing their plates, pouring more coffee, and still no one says anything. It's like they've taken a vow of silence. It's driving me crazy.

Kai has long since finished his breakfast, and I can read his body language. He's waiting too. He looks up and meets my eyes. They seem to say, "What the heck is going on here?"

Finally, Andy puts down his fork. "Zara, Kai, these are some of my associates who live round here. You already seen Hoss. This here is Racer. And Pug is next to him. Then we have Hammer and Zeke. We'll have more guys showing up soon, and more when we head west."

I wonder about these men. They probably have families and jobs. The air in the room buzzes with a malicious warlike energy, and I hope I don't have to shake any of their hands. Their faces show years of hard living, like Uncle Arne's face. He'd been a heavy drinker and womanizer till he decided to reform, and afterward his face was all lined and puffy and droopy.

"We have guys checking areas around Titusville right now. If Finn's gang is still out there, we'll find out quick. Kai, your car is ready. You and Zara will drive it, and Hoss will lead on his Harley. The rest of us are gonna split up so the police don't get suspicious."

That's it. Everybody stands as if by some secret cue and heads for the front door. Kai and I barely have time to grab our stuff and hurry outside. Kai's car, pulled up close to the front walk, is already running, and Hoss is astride his giant Harley, watching us. We throw our backpacks in the backseat of the car and jump in.

Andy and the other guys are riding big, muscle-type motorcycles. They take off, and in seconds, dust forms a trail, marking the westward direction of the biker convoy. Hoss waits another couple of minutes before signaling for us to follow. We take another route, turning onto several county roads before we meet the big highway. My stomach jolts when we merge into westbound traffic. I recognize this section. It's where we'd stop for breakfast whenever Dad and Mom and Abby and I went to Chicago. In happier times, there was this cute little rustic café called the Tin Horn, decorated with western stuff on the walls. It was just off the highway, and Dad said it had the best waffles in the state. It became a tradition that we'd have waffles at the Tin Horn every time we went on a road trip going east. But I don't see it, and I wonder if the old building was torn down. Somehow, that feels like a bad sign—like this rescue trip won't go well.

I look over at Kai. His hands grip the steering wheel. "Kai, this isn't your fight. It might get seriously dangerous."

"Uh-huh," he says, keeping his eyes on the road. "I'm not leaving you until I see you're gonna be safe."

"You don't even have a gun. What do you think you're going to do?"

He shrugs. "I don't know. Maybe just stay close to you so you don't try to rush into something dangerous, like a gun battle."

I roll my eyes. "Kai, I'm not an idiot."

He takes a giant breath and releases it, and his shoulders relax. He reaches for my hand and warms it in his. "Zara, I don't think I could stand it if something bad happened to you. You ... you're ... someone special, and I know we have different pasts, and we're—"

I gently take my hand away. "And you're going to LA, and I'm going to college next year, so we shouldn't be thinking of such things just now."

Kai's about to reply, but then Hoss signals that he's going to exit at the next off-ramp, and Kai huffs as if he's super exasperated. "We'll talk later."

I hope we'll be able to talk when this whole thing is over. But right now, we're following Hoss onto a county road that I've been on many times. We're only a few miles from Titusville, and my gut sickens with nerves.

"I wish Andy, or someone, would tell us just where we're going or what their plans are," Kai mutters. Sweat beads his upper lip, and he dries his hands on his thighs.

"Yeah, me too." I try to sound calm.

We're going west, judging by where the sun is still behind us. After a few more miles, Hoss leads us onto a gravel road. I feel like someone watching a movie with the sound off, trying to guess what the characters are saying.

Hoss slows, then turns into a lane bordered by poplars, and our vehicles stir up dust again. There's a farmhouse up ahead, and I spy more motorcycles parked in front. The guys waiting along their bikes are not the ones Kai and I met back at Andy's house. These guys are wearing the now familiar vests, and they're all sketchy types with long beards and dirty hair ... and the attitude. A bunch of bad actors, just as bad-actorish as the ones with Andy.

When we get out of Kai's car, one of them says, "Better git in the house quick."

I don't argue, and neither does Kai. Two of them flank us as we walk up the steps. Another sketchy guy is already inside, and he opens the door as we approach. "C'mon in." This one smiles revealing missing teeth.

The place is a mess with broken-down furniture and posters on the walls that I wouldn't want my mom to see. It smells like booze and other stuff, and I briefly see a woman through the kitchen door. But she ducks when we meet eyes, and that's the last I'll likely see of her.

We stand in the front room, not knowing if we're just waiting for Andy or if we're supposed to make ourselves comfortable. But there's no place I want to sit, and I can tell Kai is thinking the same thing.

When more bikes arrive, we look through the front screened door. I recognize Andy right away with his thinning salt-and-pepper hair and the fact that besides Hoss, he's the tallest in the group. He talks on his phone, then to the men standing around him, then listens to his cell.

We back away from the door when he starts up the porch steps. He looks pretty grim when he sees me, and I'm afraid he's going to say he's found my parents and they're dead.

"Zara, we've found the place where your drug gang is hanging out. It's an old, foreclosed farm on County Road 16."

"Did you see my folks? Are they okay?" I blurt.

Andy raises one eyebrow as if he's considering ignoring me. After seconds of silence, he says, "Not yet. We haven't gotten inside."

Kai moves toward me and slides his arm around my shoulder. "Shouldn't we just call the police at this point?"

Andy snorts. "We don't mix with those dudes. We're way more effective than them." He glances at his watch. "Soon as the sun goes down, we'll surround 'em."

CHAPTER TWENTY-EIGHT

Andy has made Kai and me wait in the basement. Above us, numerous voices yell and sing along with loud rock music. Footsteps pound the wood floors. Men's and women's voices. They're obviously having a great time. The odors of beer and marijuana float down through the main floors. I've heard about bikers and their counterculture lifestyle, but this is the first time I've ever been so close to it.

Through the egress windows, the sun's arc has made shadows advance across the basement floor. We have no way of telling the exact time because they've confiscated Kai's phone. It's May, and the sun doesn't go down until about eight thirty. I wish I could run up the basement stairs and bang on the door. *It's time to go. C'mon! I'm tired of waiting.*

Upstairs, the music ceases, and I don't hear voices or footsteps. Finally, the basement door opens, and a man's voice calls for us to come upstairs. The main floor stinks of booze, and marijuana smoke hangs in the air.

Hammer is waiting for us. "Time to go," he says.

That's all. *Time to go.* No details, no final instructions. No "good luck" or "be careful out there."

Hammer walks us outside, and Andy waves at me. "Yer ridin' with me," he says. Hammer gestures for Kai to come with him. He and the rest of the guys have been smoking and drinking, but they don't seem impaired.

I've never ridden a motorcycle, let alone a Harley that's made for a humongous man like Andy. But I hop on without a thought about safety. The only thought on my mind is rescuing Mom and Dad. The men start their bikes, and the roar is deafening. We take off, and I cling to Andy so I don't bounce off on the rough gravel drive. I try not to think about what Andy's gang will do when we get to our destination. Do they have guns? They must be carrying. How else could they face down a rival gang? Do they have other weapons? I can hardly believe I'm riding a Harley with a bunch of bikers intent on murder. But nothing matters except Mom and Dad. I sure hope Finn and Clooney and their men don't have superior firepower. But at least we have the element of surprise on our side.

It's so loud in the midst of this biker convoy. How are we going to sneak up on anybody? They're going to hear us coming from a mile away.

I estimate we've gone about three miles when we slow to a crawl and finally stop. Andy dismounts and gestures for me to follow.

"We're gonna hike up this hill. The farmhouse is over the ridge. We got some trees and stuff we can hide in."

The bikers obviously know the drill, because none of them makes a sound. Some carry rifles and shotguns, others carry assault-type guns, and my heart beats so hard I feel like I'm going to faint. Kai is behind me, but Andy won't let me go back to be with him. He's got my wrist firmly in his grip. It's a pretty dark night, and we all step carefully because the grasses are tall and they snag our ankles and boots. Thunder rumbles and lightning flickers occasionally, and I can't believe I might actually be only a few hundred yards away from my folks.

We tread down a dip, and the boggy ground sucks at our boots. Now we're climbing up the hill. I can see the trees Andy was talking about a hundred yards farther up. I'm breathing hard from the climb, and my hands are clammy, anticipating the coming battle with Finn's guys.

We get to the top and take shelter behind all the shrubs under the trees. I can see the farmhouse, and I'm surprised no lights are on. I guess that was dumb to think they'd have lights on since it's supposed to be an empty house. Andy makes us lie down on our stomachs and gestures for us to be quiet. He crawls over to Hammer and whispers something to him. Then Hammer and those other guys, Racer and Pug, head toward the right, staying slightly below the ridge. I remain where I am and keep my eyes peeled on the house, still hoping I'll see some movement there.

There's a barn that looks to be about a hundred feet away from the house. Would my parents be in there, or would they be in the house? It would probably make more sense for criminals to keep them in the house, close to a bathroom and a kitchen. Maybe in the basement where they couldn't be heard if they shouted for help. Poor Mom. What has she been going through being a hostage of these awful men? I want to cry for her and Dad, but I'm angry. So angry I want to do something violent.

The shapes of three men attract my attention. Moving from the field and toward the barn. It must be Hammer and Racer and Pug. Are they going to sneak inside the barn? Wouldn't it be locked? No, they don't even try the doors. They creep around the side away from view of the house. About a minute later, fire lights up the area. It ignites the side of the barn, climbs up the wall. The three men dash away and throw themselves behind a grassy berm behind a pile of old tractor parts.

A light flicks on in the house, but no one opens a door to investigate. What if my parents are in the barn? I start hyperventilating. I need to run down there. I start to rise, but Andy slams my body down. "Stay down, woman. You wanna git shot?"

The garage door opens, and a chubby man lumbers out to investigate. I recognize him right away. "It's Clooney." I almost yell but stifle it.

"You sure?" Andy mutters.

"Yeah, it's him. Fat, clumsy, curly brown hair. That's him. And if he's here, then you can be sure his brother is here too."

Clooney trots back inside and returns with a fire extinguisher. As he unleashes the spray, something catches my eye. It's Hammer and Racer and Pug coming from the other side of the barn, dashing into the garage. Clooney, concentrating on the extinguisher, doesn't see them. He empties the whole canister, and still the fire isn't all the way out. He hurries back to the garage, and I expect him to come out with a bucket of water or a long hose. But he doesn't.

"You and Kai stay up here until we call all clear," Andy growls.

He and Hoss and everyone else—seven or eight more guys—crawl down the hills, mostly hidden in the grasses. Halfway down, some go left and some go right. Andy heads straight toward the front door. There's a hedge between the driveway and the overgrown lawn, but the men still have to get over or under the barbed-wire fence separating the field from the farmhouse lawn.

I almost can't stand watching them while doing nothing. Kai scrambles over to me. "You okay?"

"Yeah. But I want to get down there."

"Are you crazy?" In the dark, Kai's eyes are black holes in his light skin, but I know he's staring at me. "Those guys all have guns and—"

The blast of a gunshot makes us both jump. The lights in the house go off again. More shots are fired. They seem to be coming from all directions, and all I can think about is Mom and Dad right in the middle of it all.

Before Kai can stop me, I jump up and race down the hill.

"Zara, Zara!"

I don't stop. Andy and most of the others have made it under the barbed wire and are hiding behind the hedge.

They've shot out most of the windows. Yelling comes from the house and from the hedge, but I can't tell what anyone's saying. Then the front door opens, and two shapes appear in the darkened doorway. *It's my dad!* He's standing in front of another man who's holding a gun to Dad's head.

I flop to the ground and peek over the grass. *Oh, Abba, that's Finn holding my dad.* He's taller than Dad, and his dark hair is peeking out behind my dad's mostly bald head. *Abba, I hate that guy.* Finn walks Dad in the direction of the barn. The side of the barn is still smoldering, but the fire didn't damage the rest of it.

While Finn hides behind his hostage's body, Dad uses a key to unlock the padlock on the barn door. One of Andy's guys comes around the unburned side of the barn, his rifle aimed right at Finn's head. But another shot rings out from the house, and Andy's guy buckles. Finn shoves my dad into the barn. Seconds later, I hear the roar of a diesel truck. The barn doors burst open, and the truck barrels out amid shotgun and rifle blasts from all sides. The truck swerves and heads straight for the house.

"Dad, Dad!" I don't care about the guns and who's still inside the house. I dash straight for the truck, which has crashed into the front porch, taking down half of the porch roof. I throw open the passenger door. Finn's body is riddled with bullet holes, and he's slumped over the wheel. But my dad is not in the truck. "Dad!"

A bullet whizzes past my head, and I drop to the ground and scramble under the window just to the right of the damaged porch. Someone from Andy's side is shooting at the house, and Andy is using that cover to rush toward the porch. He makes it safely. But what happened to Clooney? And how many of Finn's guys are still left in the house?

I hunker down in the bushes right underneath the window. I don't dare move. I know that whoever's still in the house is waiting to get off another shot. I can just see Andy, crouched down below the porch and watching the front door. He makes a gesture, and one of his guys skulks toward the back of the house.

A shot rings out inside the house, and then it's dead quiet. Hammer creeps out of the garage, his handgun held on someone I don't recognize. It must be one of Finn's guys. The two line up against the wall, clearly visible to any of Andy's men.

Then a voice from inside calls to Andy, "Clear in the front room." Racer's face appears in the broken window.

Andy crashes through the front door. I don't know where all the other guys have gone. Maybe they're all keeping their guns on the house in case someone escapes. And where's Pug? Did he go after Clooney?

Where's my mom and my dad? That's when I remember the barn. Dad must be still in there. I jump up and race toward it. Inside, it's totally dark except for the gleam of the grill on another vehicle. "Dad? Dad, where are you?"

Moans come from the back right corner, and I rush toward the sound. "Dad?" I trip on something and fall flat. But a hand reaches out and grabs my leg.

"Zara? Zara, is that you?"

I roll over and reach for him. He's sitting up, and he reaches for me and pulls me into his arms. "Zara, baby."

I've never heard my dad cry before, and I cry too. I hug him tight.

"You're okay!" he says through his sobs. "We prayed and prayed for you to be rescued."

But I can't stay here with my dad, not when I don't know about Mom. "Dad, where is she? Where's Mom?"

"She's in the basement. They're guarding her." Dad's voice sounds weak.

"Are you okay? Did Finn hurt you?"

Dad gives me a reassuring squeeze. "He hit me on the head, and I've sprained my ankle, but I'll be okay."

I reach up and feel his head, and he jumps when electricity zaps him. "Sorry, Dad." Sure enough, there's a big bump on the back of his head.

I cry again, but I pull myself together because I need to find Mom. I wrestle out of his arms. "I'll be back, Dad. You stay here and stay safe."

"Zara, don't leave. They'll hurt you," he calls, but I can't stay.

Outside, it's still quiet. The inside of the house is dimly lit, and I see a shape crossing one of the windows. I don't know who it is, so I dash to the front porch and listen at the door.

Someone whispers my name fiercely, and I drop onto my stomach. But when I look where the voice came from, it's Kai. He's hiding around the corner of the house. "Zara, stay out of the house. Let Andy take care of it."

But I shake my head. I don't hear any movement or voices inside, so I enter and cross the room and make for the kitchen, and that's when I see the body. It's not one of Andy's guys. I shudder at the bloody sight, but I keep going. The bedrooms are empty too. Did they all go into the basement? I take the first stair going down, then another. Then I hear it. Andy's voice. "You're not going anywhere, man."

I hear my mom crying softly, and that makes me sneak down the rest of the stairs. Another man's voice—this one sounds desperate—says, "Make another move and she's a dead woman."

"You kill her, we kill you," Andy says.

The desperate voice says, "I'll let you have her, but not till we get upstairs. So back off, you—" He uses some bad language.

Footsteps come closer, so I hurry back upstairs and hide in the nearest bedroom. Now I hear someone moving slowly. I peek through the space between the door and the doorjamb, and the first person I see is Andy, then Racer. Then my mom. I have to hold my hand over my mouth and nose so they don't hear me breathing. The guy holding a gun on my mom is a little skanky guy with stringy hair and pale skin streaked with grime. He's breathing loudly from the effort of climbing stairs, holding on to Mom, and trying to control his panic. I'm so close I could touch Mom, but I control myself.

Andy says, "Okay, yer upstairs. You let us have the woman, and you can walk out the door."

The skanky guy makes a snorty, chuckling noise. "Sure, sure." He drags Mom with him to the door. I come out and follow Andy and Racer, and together we watch the man force Mom toward the barn. I figure he's heading for the vehicle that was parked next to the truck. Andy and Racer follow him, keeping their distance, and I follow them. Out of the corner of my eye, Hammer forces his prisoner toward the barn too.

Mom's kidnapper pulls her into the darkness of the barn. We can't see them, so we move to the side of the barn door, which is hanging off its hinges. I expect the vehicle to roar to life, but instead I hear a crunching sound.

My mom starts crying again, and my dad shouts, "Don't shoot. Don't shoot. It's Jim Nielsen, and I just took out a bad guy."

Racer pulls the broken barn door all the way open, and my mom and dad are standing there, holding each other, both crying. On the ground next to my parents is the man.

"Mom!"

Andy and Racer startle. They must not have known I was behind them. I dash through the doorway and throw myself on Mom and Dad, hugging them with all my strength. We're all crying, and Mom is sobbing. "My baby! My baby's safe."

"Such a touching scene."

We whirl around, and Andy goes for his gun.

"Drop it!" Clooney shouts. He's breathing hard, his face is mottled with rage, and the way he's holding his handgun looks like it wouldn't take much to make him fire. "Zara, get over here." He points to a spot next to him. "Can't risk shooting my precious healer."

My whole body trembles, and my voice is hardly more than a whisper when I say, "If you hurt my friends, I'll never help your papa."

"Move over there, away from the car," Clooney says to Racer and Andy and Hammer, pointing with the barrel of the gun. "Bilagi, put Zara in the car."

"What about Lenny?" Bilagi says, indicating with a thrust of his chin toward the unconscious man.

"Forget about him," Clooney growls.

Bilagi, Hammer's ex-prisoner, grabs my elbow and shoves me to the passenger door of the minivan.

"And now," Clooney says in a gloating voice, "I'm gonna enjoy putting as many bullets in you dumb jerks as you put in my brother's—"

Out of nowhere, Kai throws himself on Clooney's back, taking him down. The two wrestle on the ground, each trying to seize control of the gun. Andy, Hammer, and Racer retrieve their guns. But there's no way to shoot and not hit Kai. They watch helplessly. I try to jerk my arm out of Bilagi's grasp so I can help Kai, but Bilagi grinds me into the side of the van.

A shot explodes, and Kai slumps onto the floor. I scream and shove Bilagi away. Andy brings down Clooney with one shot. He falls prone onto the concrete and doesn't move.

Bilagi is coming toward me, probably intending to grab me and use me as a shield, but someone puts a bullet in him, and he drops.

I only know I have to get to Kai. He's lying on his side, gasping for air. Blood pours from his side, puddling all around him.

"Kai! Kai," I call as I run to him.

His eyes are open, but he doesn't seem to hear or see. "No, no, no, no." I'm almost to him, when something rockets through my shoulder like a burning spear. It knocks me flat, and when I look up, Clooney has raised his body and is aiming his gun for another shot.

"You witch," he groans. "You'll never heal again."

But before he can take his shot, Andy takes him down with a bullet right through the forehead.

The pain in my left shoulder is awful, but I have to get to Kai, to put my hands on him. I crawl forward with only one good arm and touch Kai. His heart is beating, barely, but his breaths are tiny puffs of air, and I know he won't last long. I pull myself to his head with one last burst of strength, whispering, "Abba, Abba, I need you. I need you so much. Please touch Kai."

Nothing happens, and I can't help wailing, "Abba!"

Mom and Dad rush over and try to pull me away, but my one working hand clings to Kai's lifeless body.

Suddenly, we hear the distant scream of sirens. I look up at Andy and Hammer and Racer. "You guys have to go." When I turn back to Kai, I'm only vaguely aware of the rush of men's bodies as they run back to the hill where we had come.

Andy leans over me. "I'll stay if you need me."

"No," I whisper, as breathing is difficult. "You have to go. Mr. Andy, thank you for helping me."

I feel a big hand on my back, and then he's gone.

"Kai," I gasp, pressing my head against his. "Come back. You can't die. Please, Abba." I put my hand on his belly and try to stop the blood. He's still alive, barely.

The sirens shrill louder. "Oh, Kai." I manage to crawl onto Kai and rest my chest on his, my belly staunching his burst abdomen. Kai's blood soaks my shirt and jeans. The iron of it is so hot, I feel my flesh burning. I'm a current of blood, flowing to shore, and Kai is riding the crest of my wave. We rise higher and higher until I hear Kai screaming. Then I fold and send him rocketing downward. Somewhere during that ride, I meld with Kai. My belly is a lake of fire, burning eternally. It consumes me, and still it burns. The pain is unendurable, and I shut my eyes and scream for death.

CHAPTER TWENTY-NINE

"Zara? Open your eyes, honey."

The sound is beautiful. It's my mother's voice, calling me out of bad dreams and dark skies. I try hard to wake. My eyelids feel as if they're taped to my cheekbones, but I fight the weight of them. Finally, I open my eyes and see Mom's face, weary and wet with tears, but smiling.

"Zara, baby." My dad's face appears next to Mom's. He struggles to say something, anything, but the words don't come.

My left arm won't move, so I reach for Dad's hand with my right hand. He takes it in both of his. Then I notice that Mom and Dad are wrapped in bathrobes, and Mom isn't even wearing her makeup and pink lipstick.

"Are we home?" I'm groggy, and it hasn't even occurred to me to look around the room.

"No, honey," my dad says tenderly. "We've all been patients in the hospital for the past twelve hours. Your mom and I are going to be released later this morning. You're going to have to stay for a while longer."

I make my eyes turn to look around the room—which hurts. A printed artwork decorates the wall to my left. An IV-line pumps liquid into my wrist. And on the nightstand are three bouquets of flowers. A *Get well soon!* balloon floats above one of the bouquets. Opposite my bed is a mounted TV, and below on the little dresser are more bouquets. On my left is a couch and a window. A shaft of bright light coming from outside heats the lower half of my hospital bed.

I'm foggy about my recent past. I know it was unpleasant, but I can't remember faces or names or events. Except for Kai. All of a sudden, I'm fully awake and worrying about him.

"Kai, where's Kai? Is he okay? I need to see him. Please let me see Kai." I slip my legs over the side of the bed, but Mom stops me.

"Honey, he's fine. He's been here all night. Slept right there on the couch. We sent him to our house to get cleaned up. He should be back here shortly. You'll see. Abby was here for a while, but you never woke up. She had to go home, but she'll be back tomorrow."

"Abby." My throat is tight picturing my sweet sister, whom I tried to shield by leaving her ignorant of my whereabouts. I hope I did the right thing. "What happened? Why are we here?"

Mom and Dad exchange glances, and I can tell they're concerned. "Honey, don't you remember last night?" Dad asks.

"It's … it's all a blur, except for Kai getting shot. I remember men's voices, all angry and mean, and gunshots."

Mom leans over and kisses me on the forehead. "It will all come back once you're feeling better. But Kai is fine." She pulls back and inspects my hurt shoulder but doesn't touch it.

"I wish that doctor would get up here and take a look at Zara," Dad says. He walks over to the door and peeks down the hallway.

"How're you feeling, Zara?" Mom is trying to read my face. "Do you need some more pain meds?"

"My shoulder hurts. Mom, what happened?" I reach over and try to touch it, but Mom takes my hand.

"That awful man, that one that was going to murder us all—Clooney—he shot you."

There's a look of horror in Mom's eyes. "Such a terrible man, that Clooney. He and his brother, they said they were waiting for you to show up so they could kill me and Dad ... right in front of you." Tears well in her eyes, and she turns away.

Dad stands in the middle of the room, looking at Mom as if remembering, and I read in them how helpless he felt.

There's a knock on the door, and when Dad says, "Come in," Dr. Wellsley enters. "Well," he says with his best cheery bedside voice, "Miss Nielsen, it seems as if you've been very busy this month, making a lot of bad people mad at you." His eyes take me in, and I can feel his relief to see me awake and alert.

"Let me take a look at that itty-bitty war wound." He looks at my chart and reads through it quickly, then comes to the head of the bed and puts on gloves so he can check under my bandages. "Hmm, looks good. No sign of infection. No fever." He stares at my face, looks into my eyes. "How do you feel?"

"Sore. Hungry."

He smiles. "I'll make sure the nurses give you something. Breakfast too. Mostly jello and broth."

I make a face, and he laughs. "Probably by tomorrow you'll be able to eat something more solid. By the way, just a suggestion ... stay away from the emergency department, at least until your shoulder is healed. Concentrate on taking care of your own health, okay?"

After he leaves, Mom and Dad surround my bed again. "Zara, we're going to go back to our room so we can get ready to go home," Dad says. "But we'll be back as soon as we can. You get some more rest."

He kisses my cheek, then stands and looks at me like he can't believe I'm here safe and that this awful ordeal is over.

"It's good to be home, Dad," I say, putting words into his silent lips.

I wake to movement and soft voices. It's more than Mom and Dad. Another man's voice, deep and gentle, and I sit up in bed suddenly, startling all three of them. "Kai!"

He rushes over and bends to embrace me. "It's so good to see you alive and kicking. I guess nothing can keep you down, not even a gun fight between two rival criminal gangs."

"You're looking pretty healthy yourself." I gaze at Kai's face, trying to dispel my most recent memory of him lying in a puddle of his own blood. What if I'd passed out last night before I could touch him?

I pull him closer with my one good arm. The scent and warmth of him have brought all the memories back. "Kai, you didn't tell the police about Andy and his gang, did you?"

"Nothing that they won't eventually dig up themselves. They found Pug's body in the garage—aka John Askew—along with the dead Finnegan thugs. The police say that they've been following Finn and Clooney for months, way before you were kidnapped. As I see it, Andy and his guys just did the FBI a big favor by taking care of Finn's thugs."

"Yeah, well I hope the FBI sees it that way too. Mom and Dad would be dead if it weren't for Andy."

"And if there's a trial ..." Dad says.

"If?" Mom says, expelling an exasperated breath. "Jim, you know this is going to be national news." She moves next to Kai. "But we'll tell them just how terrible Finn's guys were. How they liked to scare us by telling us how they were going to torture us and then bury us alive out in the field. And they kept telling us all the bad things that were happening to you, how Finn loves pretty girls and hinting that he was molesting you. And that Bilagi thug? He admitted it was Finn and Clooney who'd killed Uncle Arne. I think that biker guy—"

"Andy," I say.

"Yes, Andy," Mom says, "and his friends helped rescue all of us, so he's not going to see prison time."

What Mom and Kai said helps me relax. I'd hate for Andy to go to prison. *Abba, please help Andy ... and all his guys.* But if he does go to trial, I'll tell everyone what he did. How he and his men put their lives on the line for me and my folks.

This thought makes me peaceful, and sleepiness weaves around my brain again. I'm only vaguely aware of Kai and Mom slipping away from my bedside.

I've been home for two weeks now, and my shoulder is slowly improving. My regular doctor, Dr. Schein, has ordered some physical therapy. "Don't wait too long to do therapy, or your shoulder will get stiff, and it'll be harder to work with," she says.

Kai has stayed here on the farm, helping Dad. My mom and dad like Kai, and even though he'll soon be leaving for LA, I can tell they hope we'll keep communicating on a steady basis. Dad has been paying Kai for his work, and that will help fund the rest of his car trip to California.

I hate to see Kai go, but he has some important relationship-healing work to do with his mom. And I have to start applying to colleges. I think of Craig and wonder if I should research some of the schools around New York City.

"I called my mom last night. She's still living in the same apartment," Kai says. "Can't wait to see me."

"How long do you think it will take for you two to square things?" I ask Kai as he washes Dad's truck. I'm sitting in the shade of the equipment barn, and Kai's standing out in the June sunshine, turning the hose on his torso when the sun heats him up too much.

"There's no telling, Zara. Ron told me not to think about coming back until I've done everything I can to show Mom

I love her and I've forgiven her. I left her with some pretty harsh words, and I feel awful about it. I'm determined to make it better."

He turns off the hose and grabs a bucket filled with rags. I rise to help, picking up one of the rags.

"You shouldn't be doing this," Kai says.

He's about to take the rag from my hand, but I whip it away. "I'm only using my right hand."

He shrugs, and we both start wiping down the truck. After it's gleaming and streak-free, we take lawn chairs and sit under the shade of the maple in the front yard. I'd made some lemonade, and I pour us each a glass.

"I've been meaning to ask you. It's weird, this healing thing, Zara. How come you could put your hands on me and heal me, but then you were shot, and you couldn't do anything for yourself?"

I purse my lips, half because the lemonade is a bit tart and half because I don't know how to answer his question. "The gift isn't for me. It's like that hose you used to wash my dad's truck. Abba turns on the spigot, and something goes through me and ends up where Abba wants it. I'm just the delivery system."

"Yeah, but I can turn on the hose and water myself." He's grinning because he thinks he's got me with his superior reasoning.

"Okay, so the hose analogy is lacking." I take another sip of lemonade.

"And another thing, if you're just the delivery system, why do you feel things about certain people, and why do you know what's going to happen to them?"

I shrug. "The only thing I can figure is when Abba is pouring through me, I get a glimpse of his knowledge."

Kai's almond eyes are marveling. "Do your parents even know the half of what you're telling me?"

I shake my head.

"Why not?"

"I think it would terrify them. They saw my Aunt Evelyn and her gift and how it destroyed her."

"But did the gift destroy her, or was it something else?" Kai looks like he's figuring out something that only a really smart person would think. "You said she was sad all the time. Maybe that was something else in her, not connected with the gift. I mean, you're so positive. You've gone through something traumatic, but you've stayed optimistic about your future.

"Your parents are afraid of your gift, but how could something that comes from your Abba ever destroy? It's people that do that, not God."

I put down my lemonade and study Kai's face. "I've had the same thoughts. Growing up, all I ever heard from Mom and Dad was the awful effects of being a healer. But I've been wondering lately if my emotional response to the urge to heal is the one thing I can control. And if that's true, I can choose to welcome it and not try to resist. If Abba is calling me to heal, then why am I so afraid of the outcome?" I smile because I'm recognizing the last few weeks have taught me more than ten or twelve years of hiding my lamp under a bushel.

"Ruby, Pam and Emma Joy, Craig, Frank and his daughter Lynette, 'Farmer' Herb and his supernatural Thanksgiving meal. Ian, the angel on the bus and his assurance of God's protection, Glory and Irene and the rest of those street people in Chicago. You, Kai."

Then, I have to chuckle. "Even the provision of Andy's biker gang."

Kai is smiling broadly even though I can tell that he finds most of these names I've recounted mystifying.

"Someday I'll tell you what happened before I arrived in Chicago. It's almost unbelievable.

"I felt as if Abba had given me a job to do but then he threw me under the bus, so to speak. But Ian told me to open my eyes, that I was surrounded by God's helpers.

And he was right, I really didn't have my eyes open nearly enough. Perhaps I can be forgiven for not seeing the real world. Abba's world. I was so focused on two wicked men, and their guns, and their fists, that I forgot the constant care of my Abba. If he could be so loving as to bring me to each of those people who needed my hands on them, then surely, he was also aware of my needs, too. Just as Ian said, 'It's good to have memories. They remind us to be thankful.'

"I'm thankful that when I tried to reject Abba's plan for me, he didn't let me succeed."

"What will you do after you get your doctorate?" Kai asks. It sounds like he's changing the subject, but I have a feeling that he's gauging whether or not I've placed my entire future into Abba's hands.

"Look for a teaching position, naturally." *Well, maybe.*

EPILOGUE

AUGUST, THREE MONTHS LATER

I managed to pack all my stuff in my little car. It's all new stuff because my old stuff was burned up when Finn and Clooney killed Uncle Arne and set his truck on fire. The police never found his body. Poor Uncle. At least he had set his feet on a better track before his end came.

I'm on a road trip to my new school. It's in Colorado, at the foot of the Flatirons. Great program for English Lit. And they have a program at Oxford, England, where I can do research for my dissertation. I know, you're probably thinking, how in the world did I get into a doctoral program so fast? I can only say, "My Abba is amazing." I just hope I'll be able to move around campus there relatively unnoticed. But again, that depends on Abba.

Craig and I have been talking and texting. He's just about to start a new semester of teaching, but he asked if I could fly out for fall break for a visit. His parents said they'd love to host me. I'm beyond excited about seeing him again. We've exchanged photos, and I put his in a frame that I keep on my nightstand.

I'll keep studying until I reach my goal or until Abba says it's time to do something else. Even if I never live in a stucco house in southern California, I know better things are on the horizon. Lately, a new vision is taking shape in my mind and my heart. It's kind of blurry right now, like an unfinished watercolor.

I can either fight this thing Abba has for me, and be miserable and fearful all my life, or I can get on board with it and stay the old spunky, joyful Zara. The Zara who's bested two drug dealers, survived on the streets of New York City and Chicago and persuaded bad-actor bikers to help me fight my enemies.

I'm driving over the crest of a hill in western Nebraska, just shy of Ogallala. The setting sun is blinding me, and I'm tired of driving. So, I think I'll take the next exit and hole up for the night. Tomorrow night, I'll make it to Boulder, Colorado, and the University.

And after that, who knows? The next couple of years could get really interesting. Only Abba knows.

The End

ABOUT THE AUTHOR

Dena Netherton grew up in the San Francisco bay area. As a teen she wrestled with whether to be a writer or musician. But her relatives counseled her to "do life first, then later, write about it." She took that advice and trained at Oberlin College Conservatory, the University of Michigan, and the University or Northern Colorado to become a professional singer/musician/actress and later, a teacher.

But when she was ready to retire from teaching and devote her days to writing, all that musical and dramatic training helped her grab characters off the stage in her mind and plunge them into adventurous or suspenseful circumstances.

Now, with seven novels under her belt and more in the works, plus numerous short stories and articles, Dena is forever searching for her next fascinating concept in which to plop her characters.

Ms. Netherton is a member of American Christian Fiction Writers, and President of Northwest Christian Writers Association, a group of five hundred plus Christian souls who desire to grow as writers, encourage other writers, and spin stories that draw readers to God's truths.

Dena's biggest prayer as a writer is that God speaks a word of comfort or encouragement through her stories. And her goal is that her stories are compelling enough to keep you 'up all night.'

Find Dena on her website: https://denanetherton.me

Made in the USA
Columbia, SC
17 November 2021

49008946R00159